Isabel Costello's lifelong connections with France started through her mother, a languages teacher, and developed into a passion for books, languages and travel. A degree in French and German led to a career in marketing and communications and on to writing fiction and founding the Literary Sofa blog. She lives in London with her husband and sons but is often to be found on the other side of the Channel.

❧

'A story of lust, love and loss with a beautifully described Paris as its backdrop. I galloped through it in a couple of days' *Claire Fuller*

'One of the best novels I've read this year. I recommend it if you're open to a bold female protagonist' *Literary Lightbox*

'This is the stuff of good book group discussions!' *Reader review*

'The relationships within this heart-breaking story are well drawn and believable. I felt deeply involved with every character and was moved to tears by the end' *Pamreader*

'A candid and seductive debut. Emotional but ultimately uplifting' *My Chestnut Reading Tree*

'Sultry, dark and very readable' *Trip Fiction*

'Isabel Costello writes with authority about Paris and the French, love, desire and marriage. I can't recommend it highly enough' *Goodreads review*

'A grown-up look at adultery. The author does an excellent job of describing how torn and guilty people can feel, yet continue to do the things they feel bad about' *Finding Time to Write*

'This is not tourist Paris. Costello captures something ineffable about the city, its habits and attitudes, its interiors, its inscrutable layers' *Reader review*

'A compassionate, sophisticated look at love in all its forms. There are no good guys or bad, just an absorbing bunch of humans – confused, dishonest, jealous and often scared' *Goodreads review*

'Paris sparkles in all its sexy glory' *The Booktrail*

'Alexandra shares her reflections in a way which shows enormous courage and insight. Costello handles the sexual scenes extremely well' *Vicky Newham*

'A remarkably assured début' *The Fiction Fox*

'There are so many things to savour here – from the page-turning plot to the intoxicating intensity of the affair, from the seductive aura of Paris to the superbly drawn characters' *Reader review*

'Passion written into the heart of the story. Totally addictive' *The Last Word Book Review*

'Paris, the city of love and sexuality, is almost a character itself. Classy and subtly erotic' *Reader review*

'Told with honesty and insight, Alexandra's story reflects Paris as it really is: beautiful and romantic, troubled and dark' *Peter Nichols*

'Thoughtful, beautifully written and compelling' *Charles Lambert*

PARIS MON AMOUR

Isabel Costello

Literary Sofa

First published in the United Kingdom in 2016 by Canelo
This print edition published in the United Kingdom
in 2017 by Literary Sofa www.literarysofa.com

A CIP catalogue record for this book
is available from the British Library.

ISBN (ebook) 9781910859353
ISBN (print) 9780995724204

Printed and bound in Great Britain by Clays Ltd, St Ives plc

Cover photography © Anna Thomas
Cover design by Dan Mogford
Typeset in Bembo MT Pro by Simon Collinson

For JC, my love

As a child, I felt in my heart two contradictory
feelings, the horror of life and the ecstasy of life.

*Tout enfant, j'ai senti dans mon cœur deux sentiments
contradictoires, l'horreur de la vie et l'extase de la vie.*

Charles Baudelaire

After and Before

The first time I caused terrible harm to those I love it was an accident. The second is the reason I'm here.

Not just here in this place with the paint box aquamarine sky, the gulls wheeling overhead, the warm salt air on my skin. I mean *here*, right now, on my way to our first session. I say 'first', but it's hard to imagine lasting one, let alone many. It's good that you're up on the hill, near the fine art museum with these dusty exotic gardens. I can come here afterward to pull myself together.

And before. This is going to hurt.

I pause in the gardens to reapply my lipstick, checking in my compact mirror, not that I need to. I learned the outline of my mouth from his finger mapping it, just like every other inch of me. Eyes closed, I can trick myself into believing he is still with me, up against me; I see his smile, the way he used to look at me. I remember the heat of my hands on his body, him in mine. What began as everything would be almost the least of it, in the end. And when I reach the end, as I always will, it's to find he's left me all over again.

I smooth my hair and my dress in one sweep, fingertips skimming my breasts as the heels of my hands trace my new shape. A man catches my eye and smiles. Younger than me. Handsome. I turn away.

Continuing up the street, I look for the building you described with the mosaic over the entrance. You sounded kind when I called, as if you understood when I said I needed to talk to someone and really didn't want to at all. I'm not exactly at my best right now but I guess you're used to that. For now it's this or nothing. And nothing really isn't working.

You said that your room has a view of the bay and on warm days you leave the balcony door open. The ocean has always been part of this story even when it was miles away. There is no shutting it out, not ever.

1

Both parts of my story involve my mother and things she should never have said. Thirty years ago, she told me never to call her *Mom* again. But I can't go there yet. Since you said it was up to me, I'm going to begin with last summer, when she'd just arrived in Paris.

You do realise he has another woman?

That's how it all started, with those few words, not telling me anything that wasn't already known to me in the place we hide what we can't bear to look at. Or speak of. Yet here I am.

It was the first night of Mom's visit (of course I never stopped calling her that in my head) and I was holding off dinner, trying to judge the point at which it would no longer be worth eating. As I fixed her another drink, she lit a slim French cigarette, pausing to stare at the lighter flame before taking a deep drag as if her survival depended on it. When she went home to California, it would be back to Marlboro Lights and business as usual.

Philippe hadn't called. I checked again for a text message I knew wouldn't be there; the alert was too irritating to miss and I'd never worked out how to change

3

it. Maybe his phone was out of charge. Or maybe he'd forgotten my mother was arriving. Lately there had been a lot of *maybes*. Our last long walk by the river was months ago, before my surgery. Nothing had been in kilter since.

I handed the cocktail to Mom, who always called it a martini although she liked it heavier on vodka. At the rate she knocked them back I was tempted to switch to a bigger glass. I gravitated toward the open window, which was one of three. On a corner, our living-room looked both across and down the street and those views still affected me after five years. It divided further along, leading to the Théâtre de l'Odéon on the left, the Sénat on the right and beyond that the Jardin du Luxembourg, where I now ran almost every morning, trying to get back in shape after a stint of ill-health and inactivity. Before last summer French food was my greatest temptation.

Opposite there were elegant buildings, close relatives of ours, with iron balconies and double windows that gave way to mansards higher up with rotting frames no painter could reach. In summer the glazed squares and rectangles held their secrets for longer with the light evenings. After dark, less imagination was required. Not that I'm a voyeur, you understand; I did more wondering than watching. And I had to wonder what anyone would make of me standing there as I often did, unsure what to make of myself.

I turned back to my mother who was bristling with boredom. Without Philippe the part of me that believed the evening could be a success had gone missing. His kindness and solicitude toward my mother compensated for my deficiencies; he made her feel good and sadly I couldn't say the same, but it never stopped me trying. Forty years old and still I craved her approval. We all want things that are never going to happen.

'Would you be more comfortable on the sofa?' I asked.

If she were to act on my suggestion, either I would end up on one of the upright, thinly upholstered chairs that looked straight out of Versailles or we'd find ourselves awkwardly close together on the squashy blue sofa where Philippe and I sat to watch TV. A memory caught me between the ribs, of a tiny me with Mom on the swing seat on the porch. Just us – maybe my little brother Christopher was sleeping. We're reading *The Velveteen Rabbit* and she is hugging me. We can hear the Pacific Ocean, the soundtrack of my early childhood, a half block away. What's hardest is knowing that we were happy. I couldn't share this with her now because it didn't last. Over time the two of us had been reduced to a single memory, the chapters that came before torn out and borne away on the wind.

Mom said she was fine where she was with her cocktail and cigarette: blood and oxygen, life's essentials. As our habitual loaded silence descended she looked around the room, following its progress into every corner. I took another sip of the excellent flinty Chablis, which I'd brought up from Philippe's cellar in the basement the day before, the effect fortifying and agreeably numbing. I was overcome with weariness trying to come up with

5

a safe topic of conversation. We had a tendency to fall into the same old grooves; I guess it must be like that for everyone. In any case, she spoke next.

'I'm disappointed you can't take time off, Alexandra, when I've travelled five and a half thousand miles to be with you.'

Five *and a half* thousand? She must have looked it up. Ocean plus continent.

If I'm going to be frank – and there really isn't any point doing this otherwise – that was the distance which worked best for us. Her visit was shorter than usual, only four days, and having spent two weeks on a painting trip in the south of France for once she wasn't jet lagged. She was primed, with red-painted claws, always making an effort when in Paris. Same with the Sobranie cigarettes in their candied pastel colours, too pretty to burn. Whether this was a treat or a coping mechanism, something to sweeten the ordeal, I couldn't be sure. It was a miracle that Mom and I had a relationship of any kind. We both have a good side the other rarely gets to see.

'Sorry, it's just the timing,' I said. 'Things are always frantic when we have a new book coming out. It's too bad you won't be here for the launch.'

'I suppose Philippe will at least turn up for that?'

I breathed in through my nose. As I felt my mouth tighten, my mother's did the opposite, relaxing with amusement. She liked to see if she could push me into lashing back. I doubt that she intended to hurt me and, in any case, I was complicit by never telling her she did.

Once you're assigned a role, be it victim, fall guy or guilty party, it's hard to imagine things any other way.

The launch was to be held at Philippe's gallery in rue Mazarine in two weeks' time. When the day came I would be grateful for every one of those five and a half thousand miles between Mom and me. And yes, I had the decency to feel bad about that. It went with the territory.

'We're hoping this volume will attract a lot of attention,' I said, although the situation was considerably more urgent than I let on. 'It's about some rare Romanian icons very few people have ever seen. It took the author years to persuade the monastery to allow a photographer in, but the pictures are absolutely stunning.'

Although my mother had heard me mention it before, I didn't expect her to remember. 'Who on earth is interested in Romanian icons?' Mom ground her cigarette butt into the ashtray as if defacing one then and there.

I went to defend them then thought better of it. The icons weren't in the same league as the Turin Shroud or the Terracotta Warriors but they had something special. It was unlikely, but if there were to be huge interest the monastery might relent and allow an exhibition. Editions Gallici, the small fine art publisher I worked for, would have been there first.

My mother painted seascapes, selling to tourists through a gallery in Mendocino County which gouged her on commission. I was the one with the degrees in art history, an acute eye for colour ever since I was a child, fascinated not only by new shades but the exotic words that went with them: cerulean, magenta, burnt sienna. But Mom was the one with the actual talent, the ability to create. She conveyed things which defied capture: the immensity of the Pacific, the wild beauty of the shore in all weathers, its mutable skies. I had to hang her canvas of Cannon Beach, Oregon, in the guest room because I couldn't pass it without stopping, as if I could entreat the ocean to give back what it had stolen from us.

For an artist, my mom could be quite the philistine. She gave a polite show of respect toward Philippe's gallery but my career was granted no such favours. 'Coffee table books,' she called them. 'Nobody wants them anymore.'

Needless to say, it was about other things than that. After sending me to boarding school in England at the age of twelve, she'd acted surprised when I decided to settle in Europe. She never understood why I had decided to pursue my career here when I could have done so in San Francisco or New York.

Unfortunately she wasn't wrong about our books. The way people looked at (or to use that awful word, *consumed*) art had changed. Even faced with the original in a museum or gallery, many preferred to take photos they'd never look at on their phones. It was easy to kid yourself you were cultured: here, buy a Monet mouse mat, a Hockneyesque silk scarf. Where sophisticated tourists and business travellers once leafed through glossy pages in luxury hotel lobbies and corporate reception areas, now all they cared about was getting a wifi connection.

The bells of Saint-Sulpice struck nine, the room still pulsing with summer light. There was a timelessness to much of European life that I found immensely comforting. I'm only half American, after all, half British. That might account for my strong sense of having two distinct sides to my nature.

I bet you hate it when people turn up with their own half-baked theories.

'What a racket!' Mom said, and not for the first time.

I took a skewer and prodded the chicken breasts wrapped in Parma ham, now mummified. 'We should go ahead and eat,' I said, sliding them onto plates with a serving of green beans that no longer had any bite. Mom had joined me in the small kitchen and was wrestling with a bottle of red wine and a counterintuitive corkscrew which even endangered the misplaced fingers of the stone-cold sober, which she was most emphatically not.

'Give me that.' I pointed her toward yet another uncomfortable seat, at the dining table. For a contemporary art dealer Philippe had a curious fondness for antique furniture; I don't think he can have spent much time at home before he met me. The velvet sofa was my idea, although in hindsight French navy wasn't the best choice. It really shows the dirt.

I made no further mention of Philippe but for a second my mother and I both stared at the empty place setting, which a tactful waiter would have removed in a restaurant. She unwrapped the Parma ham from the chicken, reached over and dumped it on my plate. Funny how a simple gesture can make a person feel large *and* small. So what if I'd gained weight since I married and started cooking a good dinner every night? It gave me joy and if I've learned anything, it's to take that wherever you can find it.

Paris was always an excellent source of small moments of joy. I could have lived there the rest of my days and not taken those things for granted: to me the city was one big gallery, one big theatre. I used to think I'd never leave but I was wrong about a lot of things. One was believing the worst experience of my life was behind me.

I found myself staring past my mom's shoulder at a canvas of the Bay of Antibes which hung over the mantelpiece, an original by a minor Impressionist that had been loaned to us by another gallery in Saint-Germain-des-Prés when I admired it just for something to say. They'd forgotten to ask for it back and in all that time I had barely appreciated the artist's reproduction of the vivid turquoise and transporting luminosity of a place that held sway over painters, writers, all kinds of dreamers.

I don't know how long my daydream lasted but when I zoned back to the dinner table I got the feeling Mom had been scrutinising me. The ticking of the clock seemed abnormally loud; I almost expected her to object to that too. Instead she looked pensive and it was making me nervous. She was not normally quiet at mealtimes, nor when she was the worse for drink.

'You do realise he has another woman? *Philippe,*' she added, as if I could have thought she meant anyone else. There was a blank interval, probably only seconds, in which my body suspended all functions – my lungs failing to inflate, my blood not pumping, my eyes blurring – before I could gather myself to respond.

'How can you say that? You haven't laid eyes on him in a year. You don't know anything of the sort.'

And nor did I know, not for certain. But something changed the moment her words made it out into the open. As long as I was alone with my suspicions that Philippe was cheating and in ignorance of the details I could just about deal with it, suppress the thoughts I'd been having for a while now. And of course there was the possibility that I was wrong, although suddenly that seemed unlikely. The discomfort of denial was nothing to the hair-pull hurt of being yanked out of it without warning.

'Still, I suppose you must have known what you were signing up for,' Mom went on, heedless. 'After leaving it so long. And staying in France.'

For *so long*, I heard *so late*. I heard *not coming home*. It was safer to keep quiet than to say something I'd really regret, a decision vindicated by the next absurdity she came out with. 'It's like your father and me all over again.'

Behind my hand, my top and bottom teeth clashed together. Even if she was right about Philippe, the situation bore no resemblance to what made my father go. It's true, there was someone else at one point, but did she seriously think that was why he left us?

My mother has never understood that you can't pull someone to you by pushing them away. Even as a child of ten I knew she blamed me for my brother's death. She'd never found a home for the love that once belonged to Christopher and I had brought no one into the world on whom she could bestow it. Through no lack of longing on my part.

And now I had something new to add to my collection of losses.

2

I've come back for more and I really didn't think I would. Last time was so strange, listening to my voice revisiting times I don't even want to think about. I can tell you want to help me but it's down to me whether this is going to work. Whether I'll be brave enough, honest enough, to get anything out of it.

This is a gorgeous view – I've always loved the Mediterranean. But I miss Paris and everything it was to me. I miss the beauty and the ugliness, the exquisite morning light and the mournful greys. Despite the reason I left, I'll always think of it as the place I was the happiest, the most alive, the most loved – all in more ways than one. Remembering the good times is the worst part.

The night it all began I lay awake with my mother's words on repeat in my head. I was not so much thinking about Philippe *having another woman* as the time I was the woman he wanted. We met at a very chic party hosted by a wealthy art dealer in his huge house near the Bois de Vincennes. I rarely attended such fancy events and once I'd become separated from my companions I felt more uncomfortable than ever in my one posh dress, a fitted black shift with a daring neckline and transparent half-sleeves, falling away at the elbow. Together with my highest heels it was the kind of dress that says *I feel good about myself. Sexy, even. I want men to look at me.* But I didn't. I really didn't. Five years after the broken engagement that brought me to Paris I had lowered my expectations of love. I couldn't seem to let it happen, sabotaging occasional forays into dating even if it was going well. Especially then. I hurt men's feelings trying to protect my own. On a slow descent into loneliness, I'd started to think it was probably for the best. I was only thirty-five.

I was about to leave the party when Philippe struck up a conversation with me next to the chocolate fountain, which had an accompanying mountain of the most sublime profiteroles. 'It's the exact colour of your eyes,' he said, of the chocolate, a lighter, much warmer shade than the sauce served in restaurants. The aroma it gave off was so delicious I could practically taste it. I was searching for a response to this terrible chat-up line when the young woman replenishing the fountain with cocoa nibs looked at me and said, 'He's absolutely right, you know.'

So I looked again at this tall, rather attractive older man who knew all about colour, and shape, line and texture, as I would soon discover.

'I've been looking at you all evening,' he said. 'I couldn't help it.'

I felt myself smile. It could have sounded very different, as if he'd been mentally undressing me, only after one thing. But it was never like that with me and

Philippe. I could see he was nervous. He hadn't only waited to see if I was with anyone but to work up the courage. 'You shouldn't have waited so long,' I said, 'it's not been the best night.' But now it was as if the brightness had been adjusted in the magnificent room full of glamorous people and flowers and paintings. He invited me to go for a drink elsewhere and before we'd even left it felt like the start of something.

We drank champagne in a hotel bar and talked into the early hours. Philippe knew Editions Gallici and he liked what we did. He told me about his gallery. We traded tales of London and New York, where I'd done my masters, both of them cities he knew well. He was captivated by my foreignness, telling me he'd guessed before we spoke that I wasn't French. Like me he was a fan of Jeffrey Eugenides, though he said his English wasn't up to reading the original.

We'd both been through bad times, which for some inexplicable reason we didn't hesitate to share. Affected by his openness about a bitter divorce, by the time he saw me home in a cab I'd told him things I'd only ever confided in my friend Emily; things I'll have to tell you, although God knows how. In the bar, he had laid his hand on mine a couple of times, no more, and now he asked if he could kiss me, no more, when I was aching to be held. I found that sweet and old-fashioned – as well as disappointing – but it gave my body the chance to wake up, to reacclimatise to the possibility of being wanted. Of wanting.

He made up for it with the kiss.

The next day, waiting for a call I knew he'd make, I panicked, purchasing a weightless pile of matching lingerie and slinky nightgowns I couldn't afford, my sexual allure in serious need of a revamp. Within days I had a lover, within months, a husband; but the loss I felt most keenly in the sleepless hours following my mother's observation was that of my closest friend, even after he came home and lay down next to me.

It's okay. I'll be all right in a minute. I don't understand; I was fine last time. I haven't cried like that since all this happened. Haven't dared. Now my face will be all pillowed-up. Some tears can't be wiped away; they soak in and for a while the pain you're schlepping is on the outside for all to see. I saw this so often in my mother's face that it became normal, but it's not me at all.

Everybody knows life's not all plain sailing. It has its downs and ups: it's like there's a league table of adversity. Some of it is just part of the deal: the inevitable bad patches with love, work and money. Health problems. Losing your parents and shifting up a notch on the ladder of mortality. Family has a lot to answer for. Sooner or later friends begin to disappear.

In the second column are the cruel and exceptional losses, the *tragedies* most people will never experience first-hand. But for those who do, surviving one offers no protection against the others, as I am proof. Both 'my' tragedies have had the shape people are programmed to seek in the search for sense where there is none: a before/after, identifiable victims, an obvious person to blame. But whereas my brother's accident decimated my family in seconds, sad to say, our marital crisis in its early stages was nothing out of the ordinary: cheating husband, aggrieved wife. It was impossible to pinpoint when it all started to go wrong between Philippe and me.

But I had the most vivid memory of the last time things were right. It was late September, just eight months earlier. We took a walk to see the new floating gardens that had just opened on the banks of the Seine and witnessed a sunset that was the last-minute reward for a grey day: the sky mottled with scraps of cloud, backlit with a blaze of violet and grenadine that poured down onto the river. It was before they started raising the gangways at dusk. We lay on one of the two-person wooden loungers, the pampas grass in the planters behind us swaying and rustling on the breeze. When night fell, the temperature did too. I shivered and, without a word, Philippe held me tight, my head resting in the dip of his collarbone, and we stayed there like that a long time. Certain moments of heightened emotion are seared into me, and this was one, if you can say that of something so overwhelmingly tender.

Enough tears for one day.

3

The next evening Philippe, my mother and I had dinner plans with the Malavoines, who had assumed such a significant role in her imagination over the years that she had asked to meet them. It was a wish which they and Philippe seemed happy to accommodate.

I'd known Geneviève and Henri almost exactly the same time as I'd known my husband, but it felt far longer than five years. When Philippe and I married just four months after we met, it was as if I got this other couple thrown in for free. But there was a cost. Since my husband's relationship with the Malavoines was personal and professional, our circles overlapped to an extraordinary degree. Even when it wasn't planned, we would bump into them most everywhere we went.

Philippe and Henri were both from Nice and their families were close. Ten years older and a successful fine art auctioneer by the time Philippe arrived in Paris, Henri assumed the role of mentor, father figure and older brother and Philippe couldn't have established the gallery without his backing. In the early days of our marriage, I thought the Malavoines' money came from Henri but it didn't take long to realise my mistake. And in fact it was Geneviève my mother really wanted to meet. I mentioned her and Henri often, as you would anyone you see all the time.

'I can't think why you've never introduced us,' Mom said. They would have met at our wedding but I wasn't about to rake that up. I should have tried to explain what it would mean for her to be part of something good that was happening to me. She was leaning awkwardly over the mantelpiece to apply a new deep red lipstick, the poor light and speckled antique mirror offering less than ideal conditions to attend to one's *maquillage*. When I heard that the girl at the Chanel counter had helped her match it to the dress she'd bought that afternoon I felt a twinge. I *was* busy but I could have found time to take her shopping, even if only to the BHV department store minutes from the office. Not everyone had my familiarity with the Pantone chart but the lipstick was two, possibly three, shades off for the dress and too bright for a woman of my mother's age and complexion. And yet she had the kind of beauty that was more touching faded than it ever was in bloom. She used to be a life model in her art student days in San Francisco.

Anyone who saw us together would instantly know we were mother and daughter but I've never been beautiful in that way that is almost a burden. Christopher was the pretty one. I am *striking*, with the kind of face which constantly makes people ask what I'm thinking, as if I'd tell them. On the plus side, it's a face that suits me better than when I was younger – you might say I've finally grown into my looks. The source of my most prominent physical imperfection is also the means of registering it: my eyes are too close together. But being good with a brush, I soon figured out a way to minimise it using dark colour and heavier mascara on the outer edge of my eyelids. I pluck my eyebrows as wide apart as I can get away with.

Mom's new red dress was absolutely perfect and I'd told her so.

'It honestly never occurred to me to get you together,' I said, referring to Geneviève. I'd come to Paris to draw a line between my current and former lives, with varying results. It's always the things we want to forget that have the most tenacious grip: the grief, the rejection, the accumulation of humiliations. It was ten times harder when my mother was in town, stirring up a maelstrom which took weeks to still.

'Geneviève is charming,' I said, hoping Mom would understand that this was what was required of her in return. It was years since I'd witnessed her in the company of others and I was trying not to dwell on the worst possible scenario. Evidently there had been a few flare-ups during her painting trip, when she'd accused another woman of deliberately blocking her light on the first day, making herself unpopular for the duration, and complained that the resident artist paid more attention to the other painters. 'Geneviève is actually from Paris,' I added. 'So please be diplomatic.'

My mother's criticisms of the city were not entirely unfounded. Every city has its problems – there are destitute and unhappy people in Paris just like anywhere – but by acting as a magnet to me, it had made itself a target for her.

But it was still Paris, for God's sake, famously lovely in spring but for me never more enchanting than now, in early summer when promise and delivery are in perfect balance. I made excuses for it the way I would for a person I loved. The way I privately did for my mother: she's lonely. She's getting older. She's never recovered.

I'd said as much as I could with a gentle warning. It wasn't for me to lay down conditions. When you're responsible for something terrible as a child, your whole life ends up as an attempt at redemption. More than once I've felt vindicated when things went wrong for me – it must be obvious already that there's no simple answer to 'why I don't think I deserve to be happy'.

My mother looked at me with the appraising eye she turns on a scene or figure she wants to paint. 'You have good genes, Alexandra. You don't look your age and some of that extra weight has ended up in the right places. But in your situation it's important to make the best of yourself.'

My situation. It wasn't just the oblique reference to Philippe that made me look away. Not once on the assault course of adolescence did Mom tell me I was smart or pretty or any of the things a girl needs to hear to believe. We were tiny figures in each other's landscape, spoiling the picture. There's no guarantee of closeness between a mother and daughter but we might have stood a chance if I'd grown up by her side. Whatever I'd become, I'd had to get there on my own.

In the privacy of the bedroom I wept off my mascara, starting over with a bolder touch and zero interest in the result. I swapped my chic Comptoir des Cotonniers outfit for a figure-hugging emerald dress I hadn't worn in over a year. As I walked out to face the verdict I couldn't have been less in the mood for the dress, for the evening, for any of it. The thought of eating made me as nauseous as the prospect of Philippe acting like nothing was up.

Mom brought her hands together in triumph. '*That's what I'm talking about!*' she said. I could easily have missed the tremble in her voice.

4

'*Après vous, mesdames.*' Philippe held the door of the restaurant for us, anxious to make amends, if not to offer explanations, for his absence the night before. We had muttered only a few words in the interim – I was not inclined to interrogate him. At least we were not going to be finding ourselves alone anytime soon. He'd turned up for dinner and for now that was all I asked.

Mom gasped on entering the restaurant Geneviève had chosen. Some of the tables had a spectacular three-tier centrepiece of *fruits de mer,* and seeing a woman drizzle shallot vinegar onto a plump, glossy oyster made me impatient to dispense with the niceties of introduction – I *was* hungry after all. This was *une bonne adresse,* off the tourist circuit and popular with the well-heeled residents of the elegant and conservative 7th arrondissement, which was home to the Malavoines. The only jeans were designer and baseball caps didn't stand a chance. Mirrors and soft lighting made a large proportion of the diners look ludicrously attractive and I was certain the staff had been chosen on precisely those grounds.

Henri and Geneviève stood and beamed as we approached the table. They declared themselves *enchantés* to meet Mom, who blushed as Geneviève kissed her on both cheeks, a habit I'd adopted on moving to France and practised with just about everyone. Henri was so quick to compliment me on my appearance that it was hard to know if Philippe's unspontaneous agreement meant anything at all.

'I've heard so much about you,' Mom told the Malavoines, which was received with polite smiles. A Parisian would not have to hope it was *all good*. They would assume that was the case.

For Mom's benefit we were all speaking English, which made everything feel strange. 'I can hear that you've spent time in England,' my mother said to Geneviève.

'That's right,' she replied, pausing as the waiter dipped between them to pour champagne. 'I studied at the Courtauld Institute. A long time ago, of course.'

'I expect you know that Alexandra's father was British.'

Which Geneviève did, but would have been too tactful to mention. Discretion was of the essence. My father rarely visited Europe and I had never been to Brazil, where he currently lived with wife number three. She was around my age, if I remembered correctly. Of the three of us, my dad had made the best job of getting on with his life, albeit on a trial-and-error basis. He had this endearing belief that things would eventually come right. It's too bad the Amazon was no place for a single man to

24

raise a daughter – it would have done me good to spend more time with him.

'*Is* British,' I pointed out. 'He's not dead.'

My mother waved her hand as if to say, *details!* 'I was young when I met him,' she said, to have married a British person a lapse of judgement requiring explanation. 'It was the summer of love, in San Francisco...'

I cringed. The actual Summer of Love was a good six years before they met.

'What a delightful story, Carolyn!' said Henri, catching only the tail end and unaware of the minefield (or more accurately, desert) that was my mother's love life. He proposed a toast. 'To love.'

We all clinked glasses around the table. Philippe was misty-eyed when he turned to me, oblivious to my urge to kick him. He could be embarrassingly sentimental some-times. In my admittedly limited experience it wasn't the physical side of love French men were particularly good at, it was saying what women like to hear.

'Yes indeed,' said Mom, for once without any hint of bitterness. 'To love. It's a wonderful thing, if you can find it.'

There were many definitions of love. In Paris it was the acceptable term for all kinds of goings-on. But often it just meant sex, which didn't appear to be *that* hard to find.

Somehow the evening brought out the best in all of us. Philippe and Henri made an attentive double act, oozing the charm that foreign women love, especially when they reach the age when they feel invisible at home. In France men don't stop admiring a woman who has passed the flush of youth, or any other flushes and flashes for that matter, as long as she still makes an effort. Letting yourself go was a greater crime than not being beautiful to begin with. There was only so much you could do about that.

Geneviève was surpassing herself with my mother, with a warmth she had never extended to me. It was a strange experience to see the two significant older women in my life together, their vastly different circumstances no barrier to conversation. Geneviève had been married for as long as my mom had been alone. They were both in their early sixties but mom had me and Christopher young, whereas Geneviève had come to motherhood late, her adored only child still only twenty-three years old.

Savouring a delectable raspberry tart, I found myself momentarily outside the two conversations at the table when Henri's phone rang. Geneviève's face betrayed a hint of displeasure when he went to answer it with a broad smile. 'It *is* our son,' he said, pointing the screen at her. '*Allô*, Jean-Luc! You're here already?' He listened for a moment. 'Oh, sorry, we forgot to tell you the locks have been changed. I'll be right there...'

Henri was halfway out of his seat when Geneviève intervened. 'No, Henri, we're not finished. Get him to come here. I really want to see him!'

'*Maman veut que tu viennes ici*,' Henri said. The restaurant was very close to their apartment but he would not have made that request.

Geneviève was telling my mother about the theft of keys from the concièrge. 'We haven't seen Jean-Luc since Christmas,' she said, her eyes gleaming. 'He wasn't due back until later tonight.' It was the third time she'd mentioned this.

'He got an earlier connection from Heathrow,' Henri explained. As the chatter resumed, I found my attention straying. One glamorous couple nearby had spent the whole meal on their iPhones, barely speaking – the woman gave her boyfriend a porn star pout for the camera, unaware of what I could see over his shoulder: the Facebook upload was of himself.

When I looked back to see another young man approaching us, if it weren't for his parents' reaction I would never have guessed he was Jean-Luc Malavoine. We had only met once before, when he was about to leave for college in Marseille shortly after Philippe and I married. There had been heated whispers from the hallway of their apartment as Geneviève insisted he come to say hello, a rare instance of her losing her cool. When he finally appeared it was over in seconds.

He'd looked nothing like *this* back then. It was dark by now, the restaurant animated by soft light, shadows and reflections. I registered stubble, messy hair falling into searing eyes it could not obscure: enough for me to feel a physical bolt, effervescence in my blood. No sooner had he reached us than he was being passed round the table like some kind of trophy, from his parents to Philippe. Every time Jean-Luc went to embrace one of them his

27

gaze headed so resolutely in my direction that I looked over my shoulder, thinking he must be checking out a cute waitress. There was no one there.

'You remember Philippe's wife, Alexandra?' his mother said, when it was my turn. Clearly he didn't, but there was no reason he should; I had barely paid him any attention either that day. As he moved toward me, I noticed a pulse at his temple and had to fight an urge to reach for it. And we ended up touching anyway, although to my relief not in an exchange of kisses. Like anything that's over in an instant it was hard to say quite how it happened, but there was something unsteady about him that made me grab his upper arm.

'Are you okay? I think you need to sit down.'

He did, and someone poured a glass of water, which I handed over, adjusting my position so his knee wasn't touching my leg. He was in no state to notice. 'I'm so sorry,' he said faintly, just to me. *Je suis mort de fatigue.* And anyone could see he was *dead tired*: drawn, crumpled, touchingly wrecked.

Philippe offered to get the check so the Malavoines could get him home. As Jean-Luc's mother fussed to his visible annoyance, I could relate to that primeval impulse to take care of him. It was the least troubling of my instincts.

5

Philippe groaned and reached for his alarm clock as I got out of bed much earlier than usual to take my mother to the airport. Quarter to six and the bright orange light announcing another hot day was filtering through the gaps in the shutters. There was already a sheen on his brow; he preferred summer by the Med to Paris with its pollution and sinister iridescent air. July and August were still a way off.

I could feel his eyes on me as I dressed, pretending not to notice he was awake. All the tiny signs I'd been trying to block out kept making a picture I didn't want to see. Like the seascape on the wall, it had been there for quite some time.

When Philippe looked at my body he must compare me to the other woman. Someone younger, I assumed. Which was to say, *even* younger than me. There was no doubt that he was still capable of attracting women who went for the older man – he was physically imposing and his looks were holding up, more rugged than ravaged, like Vincent Cassel in a good suit. And that charm, of course. They all have that.

Two days had passed and still I couldn't stop Jean-Luc intruding on my consciousness. The truth is that I didn't try very hard. The intensity in the way he'd looked at me had triggered a pressing physical need that was proving difficult to ignore. I knew that in my distress I was reading too much into what had passed between us but I was getting off on the feeling of excitement and unease.

My guess was that Philippe had gone for someone petite and svelte again. Over the last decade here I'd had fun unravelling some of the clichés about Paris – though each of them had a molecule of truth as all clichés do – but Parisiennes who push lettuce leaves around a plate to work off calories did exist. Philippe claimed to find such women tiresome but the requirements for a fling must be different from those of marriage. If not, what would be the point?

I was engaged to a man named Jonathan for three years before he decided I wasn't marriage material after all. When I failed to meet his criteria he thought better of it. Endometriosis had dogged me since my late teens, proving to be severe and accompanied by salpingitis – inflamed and damaged Fallopian tubes. I had to admit there was a brutal kind of logic to Jonathan's decision: why stick with me and my terrible odds of giving him children when there were so many lovely fertile women out there? *Time to move on*, which he certainly did, getting a new girlfriend pregnant in a matter of months.

I left London for Paris and it took me five whole years to move on. I had a job I enjoyed in a city I had always loved but was looking at through a veil, its beauty somehow dimmed. And as is so often the case, it was only when I'd abandoned all hope of finding love that I found Philippe, whose situation mirrored mine to an uncanny degree, or rather, he found me. I stopped thinking I'd never find happiness. It isn't allocated by who deserves it most. Same with luck or success.

And I made him happy too.

Five years after his divorce, Philippe wanted someone to look after him, someone to come home to. We were both sick of having no one care about our day, nobody to tell those silly little stories you wouldn't call a friend for, like the funny incident in the boulangerie or someone being a pain at work. I suppose I'm talking about the small intimacies of the everyday, so easily taken for granted when you have someone to share your life and so painfully missing when you don't. Not everyone wants that, but we did.

Sexually there was definitely a spark between us but it was never just about that. We loved each other's company and we both loved art and books. With him there was no deal breaker: Philippe's experience of parenting had been anything but joyful and at forty-seven he wasn't looking to start over. I was enough for him, whereas Jonathan hadn't loved me enough to sacrifice becoming a father. Strangely, that was the one thing I didn't hold against him – I'd wanted kids just as badly. You can't help how you feel.

31

Philippe proposed before we really knew each other but if I'd turned him down saying it was too soon that would have been the end of us. In a city full of stunning women, I still wasn't entirely sure why he'd picked me.

But so much of who we are is an infinite mystery. I was unusual for a woman in that there was nothing on the outside I was desperate to change. Not because my body was perfect or my proportions corresponded to any ideal, far from it. Maybe when some parts of your anatomy rebel and inflict physical torture, it makes you more accepting of the rest. According to my mom, I had my Irish grand-mother to thank for my dark wavy hair, which I wore long. I had real hips, a round bottom, breasts large and shapely enough to make for an impressive *décolleté* and still roughly on the same latitude.

Small wonder that everyone had sex on the brain when even the language sounds so erotic. *Décolleter*, to bare the neck, to be uncollared; unbridled, like passion, another concept so deeply engrained in the national psyche it could get you off murder. At this point I couldn't see Philippe or myself committing a *crime passionnel*.

Clearly I still had some effect on him. He threw back the sheet to let me see he was hard and patted the mattress either side by way of an invitation. He liked me on top, my knees indenting the bed as he lay there waiting for it to happen – for him, primarily. Since I'd fully recovered from my surgery and gotten my libido back he'd turned into a lazy lover, not surprisingly if he was saving his best for someone else. Who'd be interested in an affair if the sex wasn't good?

'Are you insane?' I said. 'My mother's here!'

I was glad of the excuse, for all that it was about to expire. We could hear her moving around in the spare room next door.

'You think your mother would be shocked to hear us making love? She is a grown woman, not a nun.'

His smile disgusted me. Philippe was precisely halfway between my mother's age and mine, twelve years either side. *Making love!* If what he and I had was love, he'd have no desire to do it with anyone else. Sex wasn't the most important thing to me but it was what distinguished a relationship from every other bond. Obviously that only held true if it was exclusive, so the idea of him screwing me and someone else interchangeably was revolting. Things are pretty messed up when you hope your husband uses a condom when he's having sex with another woman. She'd chosen that, assuming she knew he was married. I had not, and I wasn't sure I could live with it.

I breathed deeply, waiting for a monstrous desire to smash something to subside. This anger that kept surging through me was unfamiliar, more proactive and risky than the sadness that makes a person settle for little, expect nothing, not feel worth very much. It shocked me, but it permitted me some self-respect, making me realise I was worth more than this. Seeing that he wasn't getting anywhere, Philippe reached inside his shorts, which was the best idea he'd had so far. The way I felt right then he really could go fuck himself.

₰

When Mom gave me a big hug at the airport security barrier it felt weird. We didn't do hugs. She was as fragile in my arms as I was in hers. 'I hope you had a good visit.' She hadn't stopped talking about the dinner and the day she'd spent with Geneviève, who took her to an exhibition at the Petit Palais followed by lunch at the Hotel Vendôme and a stroll around the Seventh with her bichon puppy, Gigi. All *très agréable*.

'You know what? I really had fun this time.' Mom made no secret of how amazing this was. 'I'm starting to appreciate the appeal of Paris. And you seem to be in a better place somehow.'

I looked at her and blinked – did she actually just say that? I guess everything's relative; I've been in some bad places. As she fussed over her documents and her travel-size toiletries I watched her in an attempt to capture this unprecedented *entente cordiale* for posterity. She looked back to wave one last time before disappearing round the corner to line up for the X-ray machines.

As I crossed the crowded terminal toward the RER station I witnessed all kinds of interactions: a college athletics team in high spirits and red hoodies; couples clinging to each other weeping; a woman crouching down, her face transformed as a small child barrelled into her arms, a feeling unknown to me.

My mom and I have more in common than I like to admit. It's hard to be good at the here and now when you can only think about what's lost, or what you want and can't have.

6

I could no longer trust myself to be alone in the apartment which looked so bare without my mother's belongings strewn all over the place, the surplus bags, books and purchases now at 30,000 feet along with their owner. I was certain the evidence would be there if I stooped to going through Philippe's pockets or sniffing his clothes for perfume I didn't wear. In any case, actions speak the loudest, like the winter's afternoon he came home in the full flow of a phone call in Italian, drying up the second he found me in bed doubled up in pain. Sometimes you don't need to understand the words.

But no amount of corroboration would help me know what to do. My absolute ignorance of the rules of infidelity felt like a failure to get beneath the surface of this country where the prevailing morals of mine – America and England – were often mocked as puritanical. The moment I confided my troubles to someone in the know I'd be officially falling apart instead of doing it quietly on my own time. I had always been private by nature – to an unhealthy degree back then – and shrank at the thought of having to provide ongoing marital status updates. The humiliation was mine but to discuss it with anyone who knew Philippe would still feel like a violation, almost a betrayal. Whatever their view, they would never see either of us the same way again.

The friend who'd be least fazed was the last person I could ask: Suzanne was an expert in sleeping around and loved to regale me with her exploits, some of which she'd had to explain to me (I was lost once there were more than two people). She was also Philippe's gallery assistant. In the end my only attempt to reach out was a bigger mistake than I realised at the time. I called my former neighbour Christine purely because she didn't know my husband or anyone else who knew us. We met briefly in a café near my office. Her shrug and her attitude had a similar effect to the bitter espresso, leaving a worse taste than I'd started out with. According to Christine, there was no reason to get so worked up unless falling in love was involved. *Wonderful.* By local standards, there simply was no case to answer. Seeing my expression as I got up to leave, Christine added that nothing was stopping me from indulging in an *aventure* of my own. She had the cheek to say it might do me good.

There seemed little option but to turn a blind eye and hope for the best. I can't believe I ever thought there was a knack to this, some way to gain immunity. Everybody hurts, just like the song says. The heart has no nationality.

Unable to settle at home, I set off down the rue de Babylone without changing out of my work clothes or checking my make-up. My route to the Malavoines' apartment took me past the Invalides with the resplendent gold dome that usually gave me a boost whenever I saw it. Being able to walk most places I needed to go was one of the greatest pleasures of Paris but in my current frame of mind a mission was better than an aimless wander. Once I'd crossed this particular job off my list I could concentrate on the launch of *Icons*.

Due to the relentless heat I delayed buying the flowers until I got to the 7th arrondissement. When she heard my accent, I could practically see the florist planning to overcharge me. We English-speaking expats get lumped together under the Anglo-Saxon banner, regardless of our actual origins. In my case it's not wildly off with a father from Kent and a Californian mother of Irish and German descent, but the assumptions that go with it make me want to say (quietly, because not all Americans shout): *I live here! I do speak the language!* although to my great regret, I did not speak it beautifully. I had the professional competence demanded by a job in publishing but I would never pass for a native, unable to roll my *Rs* no matter how I tried.

But I knew what passed for Parisian good taste: a single variety of flower, all one colour. I watched the florist clip the stems of the white lilies, stripping off most of the leaves and substituting a different type of foliage. A good-looking man being served next to me had his phone between his ear and shoulder, accepting a huge bouquet of red roses in one hand as he held out fifty euros in the other. 'I know, *chérie*, but this is a crisis – I'm going to be here for hours.'

I gaped at him as he gave me a *you know how it is* grin. I grabbed the lilies and left without waiting for my change.

Yes, I thought. I know exactly how it is.

If I hadn't texted to tell Geneviève I was coming I would have turned around and gone home. My skirt was deeply creased over the hips and my underwear was chafing at my skin. In the confined space of the elevator the mirror confirmed I looked a total mess and I could detect a trace of my body odour in the air. A long strand of hair had escaped from my ponytail and was clinging damply to my neck, but short of putting the flowers down, I couldn't do anything about it.

When I reached the sixth floor, I had a vision of Geneviève which proved accurate in every respect when the door opened: light brown bob so meticulously maintained that the roots were never visible for more than a day or two, discreet but perfect sweep of make-up. Her white linen shirt would have to be fresh on to look the way it did.

Although Geneviève exclaimed dutifully on seeing my offering, we were both just going through the motions. Being of another class and country I was unclear what could give pleasure to someone this privileged. I'd barely stepped into the entry hall before the cloying scent of a near-identical vase of lilies reached me from the living room.

'Don't worry!' she said. 'Those are yesterday's. They will make the perfect duo.'

She ferried various receptacles to and fro, placing the matching bouquets at either end of a polished console table between the huge windows. The Malavoines lived in a grand neoclassical corner building closely overlooking the Eiffel Tower. To the left was the Champ de Mars with its quaintly named 'streets' frequented by lovers walking hand in hand and citizens of the entire world in search of a photo opp. The view from our apartment was something, but this was something else. After the spirit-flattening fifth-floor walk-up near République where I lived before meeting Philippe, the Malavoine residence would always bring out my inner American tourist.

Geneviève had been left this apartment *de grand standing* (it amuses me that a stilted form of English is used to express snobbery the way English speakers use French) by an unmarried aunt. She was from that kind of family, I was not.

'These are to thank you for being so lovely with my mother,' I said.

Geneviève waved my gratitude away. 'It was my pleasure, I assure you. Carolyn is delightful. Quite different to how I expected her to be.'

Like so much of what Geneviève said, this was open to various unnerving interpretations. It was a *faux pas* to have predisposed her to think badly of my mother. Speaking ill of a parent sounds awful in any language or country although I'd never done so in so many words. But apparently it didn't take words – I guess sometimes it's what you don't say that makes an impression.

'It's a shame we didn't get to know her when Jean-Luc was still in California,' Geneviève continued. I didn't follow – wasn't he just home for a visit? Despite my wish to discuss absolutely anything but him, I prepared myself for another gush about the only subject which raised any real emotion in Geneviève and, since the dinner, the cause of increasingly troubling thoughts of my own. Jean-Luc may never have been far from the conversation with his brilliant academic record and myriad achievements but it seemed to me that he'd given his parents a wide berth since going to college, staying put and leaving them to visit him.

But Geneviève was heading somewhere far less predictable. 'Your *maman* was kind enough to invite us to visit. San Francisco is beautiful – maybe Henri and I will go back one day.'

She must not know that Del Norte County was a six-hour drive from San Francisco, my home town only ten minutes from the Oregon state line. Hiking in the redwood forests swatting at bugs or walking on foggy beaches were hardly Geneviève's idea of fun. The closest posh restaurants were a hundred miles away. It was beyond me to picture her in the clapboard house where I'd grown up, so exposed to the elements that it should have been painted every two years. Now my mother left it to peel until the job cost twice as much.

'You don't go back very often, do you?' Geneviève said.

I didn't, for the same reasons my mother could never bring herself to leave. There were precisely two other people in my life who knew why and Geneviève wasn't one of them.

None of this mattered because I'd have put money on this visit never happening. She fanned herself with a copy of *Figaro Madame* and her hair barely moved. 'This heat is unbearable,' she said. 'Shall we have tea?'

It was my job to offer to make it, being half British, not that I could recall my dad ever drinking tea. But since the stuff Geneviève favoured had more in common with the latest Parisian tearoom craze than anything they'd drink in England, I figured I stood as good a chance as anyone. I spooned loose-leaf raspberry-scented Assam from *Mariage Frères* into a porcelain teapot so delicate I could see my hand through it even after adding the boiling water, orange and indistinct.

'Mom had a great time,' I said, bringing the tea into the living room. 'It was so thoughtful of you to give up your day.'

'It was nothing,' Geneviève replied, and in fact it wasn't far from what she normally did, a gentle circuit of cultural hobnobbing with stylish refreshments. But I was genuinely grateful to her for making this year's visit so much easier for me. I hoped my astonishment was not too obvious when Geneviève said at dinner that she regarded me as a kind of daughter, nor when my mom appeared to accept this as a compliment to herself – one she had not earned. And since I'm being mean already, I may as well say that even if I'd been looking for another mother I wouldn't have chosen Geneviève.

I find that the French excel in the art of conversation, of debate. Of course they talk about which is the best dry cleaner's or complain about the damp in the cellar, but the to and fro of intellectual discussion is seen as normal, not pretentious. In California people would be curious to know how much you earned or what car you drove; here they'd rather get your take on the meaning of life.

But that's not how it was with Geneviève and me. There was a coolness about her that seemed contagious when we were together, making me shut down instead of opening up. I could never relax and enjoy her company the way I do when I click with someone, and in five years we had never progressed much beyond chit-chat imposed by our husbands' friendship. Neutral subjects, enjoyable when we got onto art or literature, I'll give her that.

We knew very little of each others' real lives and yet she continually sought me out, sought us out as a couple, troubling herself to make the kind of arrangements men rarely bother with. Making an issue of it with Philippe would have hurt him. There was a lot about me that he accepted unconditionally and it couldn't all be in one direction. I understood when he first introduced us that Geneviève's opinion mattered to him. He wanted us to be friends and I tried to like her. I really did.

The conversation stalled and I couldn't be the one to resurrect it. By now the situation with Philippe had sunk in, saturating my heart and body with an unbearable heaviness. I was an idiot for being shocked, though I wasn't the first to think that talk of widespread affairs in Paris was an exaggeration. *Is* an exaggeration, but it makes no difference that not everybody's doing it if your spouse is one of the ones who is.

I'd come to visit Geneviève out of goodwill but my predicament made a giant, pointless pretence of everything: my marriage, my hopes of reviving a dying business, this forced acquaintance masquerading as something we both knew it wasn't.

Lifting the cup to my lips too soon, the tea scalded the lining of my throat and it served me right. I was being unfair because of what was happening to me. Geneviève and I had been brought together by the friendship between people we loved and we made the best of it. Philippe and I were in a situation of his making and I'd have to make the best of that too, hoping it really was just a fling. That must be what people do when they find out what they're not supposed to know. Plenty of cheats must be women. Mothers, even. Except that here they aren't called cheats. They are *amants*. Lovers. That sounds much more romantic.

The unfamiliar compassion in Geneviève's expression worried me. I actually wouldn't put it past my mother to discuss my private life with someone she'd only just met. Geneviève leaned across to lay a tiny cool hand on my forearm. 'Is everything all right, Alexandra?'

'Not really.'

As I waited for her to ask what was wrong, every muscle tensed to keep me from heading for the door. This was not the place to turn for comfort. At best Geneviève would trot out the same platitudes as Christine. *C'est comme ça.* That's the way it is. It wouldn't surprise me if she took the old-fashioned view that men are poor creatures driven by uncontrollable urges and really can't help it. Her loyalty would not be to me.

And then I had the strangest sensation. It was as if I were standing on the opposite side of the room, watching myself go berserk, nerves snapping as I span around, shattering the carefully positioned vases, trampling the perfect lilies; slashing silk cushions to send the down of dead ducks billowing everywhere.

The fantasy version of me was losing control. It felt so amazing I wanted it to be real.

But when Geneviève spoke it was in her usual measured tones. 'I know how you feel,' she said. 'Having houseguests really takes its toll.'

I seized the excuse, and with apologies for my sudden departure, just about made it to the elevator before I was convulsed with sobs. Philippe was the only person I could bear to see me cry, but that wasn't much good to me now.

7

Avoiding the person you're married to isn't easy but for three days I saw as little of Philippe as possible. I was sleeping so badly it was a relief to get up at six and run in the Luxembourg many times the usual distance. Pushing myself so hard that I could barely breathe caused a horrible burning in my chest and throat but since it also cut off my ability to think, it was worth it. The more athletic runners I'd been seeing for years began to give me a nod of respect as we lapped each other for the third or fourth time. If they'd ever noticed me before they probably thought I'd started training for a marathon with a *lot* of work to do. One of them went further. He was probably a little younger than Philippe, with sandy hair – attractive in the same kind of way. Too similar all round.

I thought he was being friendly striking up a conversation as we happened to exit the park gates onto rue de Vaugirard at the same time. Then out of nowhere, he invited me for coffee, though I don't know why he even bothered to call it that. Not even in a café and there were two within sight.

'My place is just five minutes away – less if we keep running,' he said, like that would seal the deal. This truly is another world to me. I suppose logistics must play a big part. Living one life is complicated enough, how on earth did anyone cope with a second, hidden one?

My admirer seemed amused when I shook my head at his nerve. 'Can't blame me for trying,' he called over his shoulder as he sprinted off, not caring who heard. It got me thinking about how these 'just sex' liaisons begin. Was it as arbitrary and banal as propositioning a sweaty stranger in a park? We'd been acquainted for less than five minutes and this guy thought he was in with a chance! Maybe the sight of a woman exercising suggested strong physical appetites, in a similar way to Philippe finding my love of food sexy. Clearly some men cast the net wide to improve their hit rate, not being too choosy. You only have to watch a few movies and TV shows to know that for some it's as primitive as *whether they would*. Like they were grading goods. It was different for women: what we wanted, whether we would. Now I was thinking about Jean-Luc, *again*.

I crossed the Place de l'Odéon and as I turned into our street I looked up out of habit at the fourth floor to see Philippe standing on our tiny balcony, still in his robe, smoking and frowning. It was too late to pretend I hadn't seen him and anyway, I needed to get to the office.

'I have to talk to you,' he said as soon as I let myself into the apartment.

'Wait a second,' I said, heading him off. I made straight for the bathroom and peeled off my running kit. I wanted to lock the door but if Philippe realised he would have found that odd. He often came in when I was showering to brush his teeth after finishing his coffee, or to tell me something or other. It was vital for things to appear normal.

I'd never minded him sitting on the lid of the toilet shouting at me about some outlandish artefact over the sound of the water. Some of his habits had jarred at first but I had even gotten used to him peeing in front of me, though I wouldn't have dreamed of doing the same. A French maxim I adopted without question was that a woman needs to preserve a sense of mystery. But it's a short hop from mystery to secrets and an even shorter one from there to betrayal.

I didn't want my husband looking at me now, naked or clothed. I didn't want to talk because of what one or both of us might say. I wasn't completely naïve – you can't help but pick up a few things about adultery living in this city for ten years, but it was hard to square what I knew with *us*. Men are said to do it to ward off boredom and fear of mortality, to feel like a man. I think the theory was that it didn't impact on the love and respect they felt for their wife, the mother of their children in this country where an overwhelming majority of women do marry and reproduce. That straying is a midlife phenomenon is the same the world over but here's the part I didn't get: Philippe had divorced ten years ago and been a free agent for half that time before meeting me. He could have stayed single and fucked whomsoever he pleased without being accountable to anyone. But he didn't. He married me, so in the circumstances I really *didn't* think I was signing up for this.

None of which makes it right, but I did sort of get why men had affairs. When it came to women, I really had no idea. Not then.

8

My noble resolution not to snoop on Philippe was short-lived. The facts could not be worse than the torment of my imaginings and I needed to know where I stood. After my shower I slipped back into the bedroom and dressed as quickly as possible, as if it were me about to be caught in an illicit act. And so it was, of a kind. I heard Philippe's electric razor start up, which told me I had several minutes. There was no sign of his phone in our bedroom. I went through to the kitchen: not there either. And then, as if it knew I was looking, it buzzed from under his creased cloth napkin on the table, next to the auction catalogue.

It could have been anyone: Henri, Suzanne from the gallery, France Telecom with a monthly minutes update. I snatched the napkin away just in time to see the message ID flash up and fade away – NICO. Usually a man's name. The only Nico I knew was the muscular Italian behind the counter at our local butcher's. It was a step too far to think that Philippe was secretly into men.

For too long I stood with his phone glued to my palm until I heard the whine of the razor finish. I breathed again on hearing the sound of running water. He still had to brush his teeth. Two minutes should be enough. Unless he'd changed it, I knew Philippe's unlock code from when he'd been driving and asked me to find an address. 6274. For his year of birth and mine.

It worked! There it was, the text from Nico: *After auction but quick.* There was a string of older messages in bubbles I barely glanced at, most of them rather businesslike in tone. But one stood out, from the night Philippe hadn't shown up for dinner with my mom: *Studio plus tard. Envie de toi.* Studio, later. (What studio?) *I want you.*

I had just put the phone down and was sweeping crumbs off of the table into my hand when Philippe appeared in the doorway, freshly cologned. I grasped the back of the dining chair next to me, my nails digging into the soft antique wood. Does everyone have a kind of emotional homepage they revert to in a crisis? I do, and I was back there like I'd never left. Mine is feeling abandoned.

Compartmentalising is supposed to be a male habit but against the odds I managed to lose myself in everything I had to do that day. With rising production costs and sales that had been falling steadily for years, time was running out for Editions Gallici and it certainly wasn't the moment to be looking for a new job in fine art publishing. My boss Alain had founded the business but he was almost sixty and lately he had visibly tired of it, effectively leaving me to run the place. He would take the opportunity to duck out and play more golf if it went under; the others were younger than me and would migrate to other things. None of them cared about it the way I did.

So I didn't spend the whole day thinking about the auction (it helped that I hadn't noticed what time it was taking place) and what Philippe was doing afterwards and with whom. As long as I was at work I could contain my anxiety but that changed when I stepped into the courtyard and through the huge wooden doors separating the calm of the office from the crowded narrow streets of the Marais. On a rational level I knew it was nothing to do with the man from the butcher's but that didn't stop me calling in for two steaks on the way home. I waited in line behind a statuesque blonde in black linen, admiring first her impeccably highlighted up-do and then, as she pointed to some *paupiettes de veau*, the butcher's skill in making raw flesh look so appealing with carefully knotted string and sprigs of rosemary. As she turned to leave, I was forced to confront the possibility that Philippe's lover might not be younger at all. This woman – natural, graceful, trying hard but not too hard – was at least fifty and still *canon*. Knockout. *Une bombe*. All these terms linking beauty with destruction. I needed to think this through. Making a scene about the affair could backfire, bringing everything crashing down.

When it was my turn, the butcher named Nico persuaded me to take a little tub of his homemade béarnaise sauce to accompany the steaks. Like many French men, he wore a thick wedding band. Philippe wore one too, the perfect circle, a symbol of eternity. Or a zero, something that counted for nothing. I just didn't know any more.

Though my feet were throbbing after all that extra running and the long, hot walk dodging tourists on the Ile de la Cité, I plodded up the four flights of steps to our apartment, not bothering with the tiny claustrophobic elevator.

It's not that I thought cheating was confined to the legendary *cinq à sept* timeslot – a kind of sexual happy hour – but nonetheless I wasn't expecting Philippe to be home already. He was sitting in the upright chair where I could still picture my mother on the evening she lit a fuse under the dry powder of our marriage.

The discovery of the text from Nico had come as a perverse relief after the agony of not knowing: my mother wasn't wrong and I wasn't paranoid or allowing her to mess with my peace of mind for no reason. Philippe *was* definitely having an affair. But in the forty minutes it had taken me to get home the tension had wound up tighter than ever. I was desperate to have it out with him, find out who this woman was and what she could give him that I couldn't, or didn't. Where the studio was, how long it had been going on. Whether there had been others.

When Philippe heard me come in he looked up from his iPad with a cloudy and preoccupied expression and I recalled with a jolt that whatever it was he wanted to say to me that morning, he hadn't said it. Convinced he was about to confess, my instinct was to tell him to shut up when he hadn't said a word. I'd changed my mind yet again. The less I knew, the better. I couldn't decide what I thought or felt from one second to the next, lurching from one position to its opposite pole: I wanted the truth/I didn't. I was justified/I was overreacting. It would have helped to make a list of pros and cons, but that called for distance and objectivity I couldn't possibly muster by myself. Confrontation and resignation were equally unappealing; since meeting Philippe I'd never been happier, until all this.

There had to be some way to come to terms with what was happening to us. If infidelity really was so common maybe I could find other women in the same boat and get some tips on how to live with it. Or maybe it *was* just a short-term thing and would soon fizzle out – I could only hope. The issue of fidelity had never come up, although from what he knew of me, it wouldn't have been hard for Philippe to guess at my take on it. I could try to engineer a conversation, rent a movie about an affair, somehow make my feelings known without confronting him… so he'd be overcome with guilt? Because that was *really* going to work. This was the stuff of desperation.

Even when Philippe was hurting me, I was still bending to accommodate, just as I always did with my mother. The difference was that I hadn't hurt him first. I had reason to believe he'd bedded some other woman that afternoon and still I was going to serve him steak and ask about his day.

9

'How'd it go at the auction?'

Philippe shook his head. 'Outbid on all but one. Real waste of time.'

I didn't make the usual effort to commiserate and went to wash the grime of the city off my hands and face, wishing I could return to the ignorance of that morning. Where suspicion nibbles, truth bites hard.

'Sit down,' he said, when I went back into the living room, pouring me a glass of the Chablis I liked. 'Brigitte called today when you were out running.'

Stupidly, I looked at him as if I wasn't sure who he meant.

'I was as surprised as you are.'

Brigitte was almost as taboo as infidelity. Philippe hardly ever said her name. He'd given me the condensed version when we first met on the unspoken understanding that it was a topic off limits from there on out. Following a vicious custody battle over their daughter, then only seven years old, Brigitte had poisoned Vanessa against Philippe so successfully that he had given up all attempts to see her by the time we got together. He told me it was doing more harm than good.

From the beginning I was moved by Philippe's inability to conceal how much he minded this, by his sense of having failed as a father. It made me feel close to him. He couldn't see his child; I couldn't have one. Maybe he felt the same about me. As bonds between couples go, it's rather unusual but I felt it even now and it surprised me how strongly. I didn't have it in me to hate him – God knows, it would have been much easier that way.

I waited for him to continue, figuring it couldn't be that important if he'd left it all day to tell me. 'So what did she say?'

His Adam's apple twitched and he breathed out noisily. Why didn't he just come out with it?

'I guess it's to do with Vanessa...' I couldn't imagine what else it could be.

'That's right,' he said. It was a sign of his agitation that he offered me a cigarette when I rarely smoke and a sign of mine that I took it, bending toward the lighter. I puffed out instead of inhaling, and it took a few tries to catch. I began to cough and when Philippe finished his cigarette I handed him mine, wishing I'd stuck with my Chablis. The taste would be ruined.

'Brigitte and Vanessa have fallen out,' he said. I nodded despite having no context for this. Neither of them was part of our lives and for all we knew they fought every day. Brigitte was that kind of woman, from what I'd managed to gather. 'A really serious fight,' he said, and then I got it. This *was* something to do with us after all. 'Vanessa's coming over.'

It's funny how the mind takes refuge in the smallest details. 'Gosh,' I said. 'She's coming here? Tonight? You could have told me earlier – I only bought two steaks.' It seemed that Nico the butcher and I were destined to meet again.

Philippe reached for my hand, with an imploring look. 'She needs a place to stay, Alexandra.'

'*What?*'

'I wanted to discuss it with you but Brigitte put me on the spot. I couldn't refuse. Vanessa's my daughter.'

At least he didn't pretend that Vanessa was my step-daughter, not in any meaningful sense. I had seen her just once, at a large wedding outside Paris, but we'd never actually met. It was more a case of Philippe pointing her out across the room, a young girl on the cusp of adolescence. Even at such a distance I could see Vanessa had his intense dark brown eyes. Her mother pulled her away as soon as she saw us, as if there was a risk of contamination.

Maybe I've spent too much time watching women cry – after Christopher died my mother did little else for two years. Maybe it was knowing that my dad went to the redwood forest to grieve that first made me so susceptible to vulnerability in a man. To be raised to contain your emotions and fail now and then – when it mattered: that touches me deeply.

Philippe looked up at me through tears he did not try to hide. 'I don't know her anymore,' he said. 'The last I heard, she hated me.'

'But you didn't hear it from her, did you?' It was as if I was on one of those fairground rides that thrusts you into one corner only to snatch you away in the opposite direction, the type that makes people vomit. I was furious with Philippe but not about this; right then his distress was more painful to me than my own. Isn't it always like that when you love someone? The relationship between parent and child is unlike any other; it's the only one both parties embark on sight unseen, no going back. I had only ever seen it from one side, but I knew it all the same. 'Did Brigitte say what the problem was?'

'No, she was ranting and raving. Probably using me to fire herself up for the courtroom. That's how she always used to be.'

This was an intriguing insight into Philippe's past. Whatever my faults, nobody could call me a ranter. More of a bottler-upper. I was such a pleaser that I was forever apologising, even to people who bumped into me in the street or trod on my foot on the Metro. At work I was known for my Anglo-Saxon calm and common sense, which to me were not qualities but the only way to be. It was staying within certain parameters which enabled me to function, avoiding extremes. I suppose it comes back to putting things in boxes, building walls around them.

It makes sense that people who've been through traumatic experiences feel a need for control in everyday life.

I know I do it but I've never thought about why, or about the price I've paid.

'It'll be okay,' I told him. 'It's good that Vanessa can turn to you in a crisis. I'll get the spare room ready.'

'Thank you,' he said, grasping my hand. 'I knew I could count on you.'

As I opened the window and folded back the bedroom shutters to air out the last traces of my mom's perfume, I thought how extraordinary it was to be such an intrinsic part of someone else's life. Automatically factored into their equations, even at a time like this.

Philippe and I had been together two months when I took a trip to the UK to visit Emily, planned before we met. At the Gare du Nord he handed me an envelope as we said our goodbyes. The anticipation was so exquisite that the Eurostar was almost at the tunnel before I opened it.

Toute mon âme se consume à t'aimer. Tu es mon unique pensée.

(My entire soul is consumed with loving you. My only thought is of you.)

Words, Victor Hugo, Philippe wrote. *The feeling, mine.*

I gave a little gasp of joy, fingers flying to my lips. The woman opposite smiled.

And although it couldn't possibly be true any more, nor did it feel completely false. The scent of jasmine reached me from the courtyard wall, always more intense in the hours of darkness. I might not be enough for him, but we still had something.

10

'Where are you going?' Philippe asked when he saw me pick up my bag.

'I told you,' I said. 'Back to Nico's.' That was incredibly stupid. For me to gauge his reaction to hearing that name Philippe would have had to be completely calm. In reality he was so agitated I'm not sure he even heard me but I backpedalled just to be on the safe side. 'To the butcher's, to get another steak.'

He glowered as if I was one of his trials.

'For God's sake, Alexandra, do you seriously think the three of us will be sitting down to dinner and polite discussion?' He shook his head. 'You really know nothing about teenagers.'

That was a stinger but I suppose it was also true. There were awful retorts I could have made but Vanessa was a separate issue to whatever Philippe was up to. It's strange how life can bob along evenly for years then all of a sudden several things blow up in your face. They were just too much to deal with at the same time.

Philippe and I were adults. Once I'd established what was going on in our marriage we'd either work it out or...

I couldn't actually face the possibility that we wouldn't. But his daughter was very young when her parents split, a pawn in a vicious game until Philippe had called a halt to it. It's hard to have your world upended at a formative age.

I overcooked the meat and we chewed our way through it mostly in silence, our attempts at conversation faltering after a couple of short rallies. As the evening wore on, Philippe texted Vanessa several times and got no reply.

'Would you just call her,' I said in the end.

When he did, he got a recorded message saying the number was no longer in use. As far as I knew, the last time he'd used it was when he called her on her sixteenth birthday and she either couldn't hear him or hung up, neither of us was sure which. I saw my husband diminished by pain that night. I felt it.

But at a certain point, everyone starts to question their parents' version of events. The fact that Vanessa had fallen out with her mother gave cause to hope that she was old enough to think for herself, to give her father a chance at last. It was both a good sign and a twisted way of looking at it. For her to even think of coming here and Brigitte to allow it was a development we were still struggling to take in. You'd think there would be a million places a teenager would rather go than to an estranged parent who'd always been painted as a bastard.

Even now I had never seen anything in Philippe that would justify that. His behaviour made him weak and disloyal, not cruel or evil. It caused me anguish because I loved him. It was shocking because I saw him as a good man. Right now I could hardly stand to see him so drawn and tense, lighting one cigarette from another, something I'd only ever seen in the movies. The smoke was bothering me so I rushed to clear the table. In a plastic bag on the kitchen counter was the tub of sauce that would have lubricated the steak, helping us choke it down. Unrefrigerated for too long, it had started to separate and was now translucent around the rim. But the craving for the fresh, green taste of tarragon was too much for me and I picked up a used fork and shovelled an enormous blob into my mouth with the handle. It was greasy and rancid and had me retching into the sink, running water to disguise the sound.

By the time I'd finished in the kitchen, I was beginning to wonder if this business with Vanessa was a nasty wind-up on Brigitte's part, although there was no obvious reason for her to start playing games with Philippe after years of wanting nothing to do with him. She earned good money as a lawyer and wouldn't even accept child support, which struck me as unnecessarily vindictive. He was now slumped on the sofa with his nose in the latest Houellebecq novel but his eyes wandered away blankly into the corner of the room more often than he turned a page.

I was about to go to him when there was a commotion in the courtyard, which would have to have been quite loud to reach us this clearly on the fourth floor. I opened the kitchen window but because of the awkward angle I couldn't quite see the participants in an increasingly fraught exchange.

'*Mademoiselle*, you are not allowed...' came a man's voice. Well spoken and formal, it could have been one of several of our neighbours, most of whom we knew only to greet in passing on our way in and out of the building.

'Oh, shut up and let me pass! My dad lives here.'

There was a metallic clang as something made contact with the recycling dumpster.

'Philippe...' I said, without looking away. He joined me by the sink as a figure came into view from the entrance archway and started peering up at the windows, the heavy door to the street closing as the offended party left the building. The sky was scored with fading silver slashes as darkness fell.

'*Oh putain*, it's her!' Philippe said, covering his face with his hands. 'I'd better go down.'

He was the first to reappear, puffing as he pulled a bulky wheeled case out of the elevator. He told me she'd refused to get in with him, although it would have been a little close for comfort, it was true. The doors closed behind him but it stayed on our floor. We stood there staring at it expectantly like a pair of idiots.

'Surely she must know to press the call button,' I said eventually.

He turned to me as if to say *I really don't need this from you*. Then his expression changed. When I looked over my shoulder, Vanessa was standing right there, towering over me. I hate to think of the first look she saw on my face.

How could anyone go from making so much noise to moving so silently? I had my answer when I noticed her boots, which had bouncy rubber platforms at least four inches thick and went up to the knee with dozens of buckles. An odd choice for thirty degree heat, but maybe there wasn't space for them in her suitcase.

This was as bizarre for her as it was for us, I reminded myself.

'Vanessa! Hi, I'm Alexandra. Come on in,' I said, full of fake cheer. An American would normally have said 'welcome' at this point.

Inside the apartment a gust of wind made the kitchen window bang and I just made it to the door in time to stop us being locked out. Vanessa snatched her bags and barged into our home without waiting for us to lead the way. Philippe was right. I knew nothing about *ados*, as the French call teenagers. *Ado-lescents*. It sounds sinister, somehow. You look at them, the older ones adult sized but only partly formed – and have no idea what they're capable of, still less what they're thinking.

Vanessa had never been to the apartment but before I could suggest she put her case in the guest room, she'd dragged it into the living room, ruckling the antique Persian rug to reveal the anti-slip webbing underneath and tons of dust and crumbs. I clenched my fists behind my back to stop myself from straightening it, knowing for sure that teenagers didn't care about dirt. For some reason it was Geneviève I thought of at that moment. Strange and messy things never happened to her. You could bet there was no crap under *her* rugs.

Vanessa let the case go and it fell flat, the extended handle missing a vase in the unused fireplace by a matter of inches, not that she noticed. She hurled herself onto the sofa, showing no interest in her surroundings, allowing me the chance to take her in. Maybe Philippe was doing the same. I could not imagine what it must be like to look into the face of a person who wouldn't exist if it weren't for me.

Both of her parents being from the south, Vanessa had a dark Latin look about her but whereas there was previously some resemblance to her mother, a tiny Rottweiler in stilettos, that had gone now. She didn't look much like Philippe either, other than in her unexpectedly tall and heavy build. Her dyed black hair was unwashed and her face caked in the wrong shade of foundation, which drew attention to her bad skin. But the poor girl was having a rough time and I could see that one day she would emerge from this phase to be absolutely stunning. Her eyes, rimmed with thick kohl and smudged mascara, already were.

'Would you like something to drink?' I asked. 'We have juice, water, maybe a Diet Coke...'

'Vodka.' That was the first word she ever said to me. *Vodka.*

Philippe gave a tiny nod. My mom had polished off the Finlandia so I resorted to some cranberry Absolut we'd been given and never opened. The ice cubes splintered as the liquid crept into the space around them. You could get drunk on the vapour. I only poured two glasses. 'I'll give you two some privacy,' I said. It was late and lying flat on my bed in a darkened room felt like an outlandish fantasy.

'No, Alexandra,' Philippe said sharply. 'Stay, please.'

'This has nothing to do with her,' Vanessa said, before repeating the phrase in English for my benefit, which offended me more.

'You know I speak French,' I said. Well enough for her to understand me and demand vodka. She waved her hand as if I was an irritating fly, presenting Philippe with a dilemma. He could get off to a bad start by reprimanding her rudeness, or he could let it go. I made a throwaway gesture of my own. This didn't need to be any more difficult than it already was.

'So,' he said, trying to smile at his daughter. I lingered, still hoping to slip away, but he motioned to me to join him. He was afraid of her and I bet she knew it. 'Why don't you tell us what this is about? Your mother didn't explain.'

I wished he wouldn't speak to her that way. His slow, patronising tone seemed calculated to annoy her, as if he were talking to a child half her age.

'The stupid bitch,' Vanessa spat out. Her droplets of saliva sat there on the glass table, glistening.

She was daring Philippe to contradict her and prove himself a liar. But she didn't know him any better than he knew her. He was smarter than that. 'That doesn't tell me much,' he said.

She sniggered before turning to stare at me. 'You're nothing like her. I suppose that's something.'

I laughed openly, which wasn't good. How she thought she could tell I wasn't a bitch by looking at me, I did not know. 'Your English is excellent,' I told her. Unusually, I wouldn't have guessed from her accent she was French. We both sounded mid-Atlantic, like those actors who can do American convincingly without being the real thing: Hugh Laurie, Cate Blanchett, Charlize Theron. My mother frequently complained that I sounded British, referring more to my turn of phrase. It was hardly surprising.

'English is the language of the struggle,' Vanessa said.

'What struggle?'

She gave me a pitying look. If I needed to ask I was too dumb to deserve an answer. 'Do you think this is sustainable?' she asked, making a global sweeping motion with both arms. It wasn't clear what she was referring to, but I was pretty sure the answer was no.

11

Geneviève was very keen to get her hands on our new book. Unlike Henri and Philippe, her taste tended toward the traditional and conservative, as nobody who had visited their apartment could have doubted. There must have been hundreds of its kind in the area, rarefied private spaces exuding the taste and refinement of a historic monument you'd pay to visit, like Edith Wharton's house, but on a miniature scale. It couldn't have been much fun for an only child to grow up in this environment, so enriching in one way, so sterile in another.

Geneviève had the dual benefit of ample funds and time on her hands and although I couldn't recall her paying for a copy – or handling cash at all, actually – her enthusiasm for our twice yearly publications benefitted Editions Gallici in a way that was hard to quantify. To the left of the fireplace in her living room was a huge book-case where a sizeable collection of our titles took pride of place. Thanks to her, several distinguished art critics with aristocratic names now acknowledged almost everything we brought out, giving us prestige and publicity that money couldn't buy even if we had it. There was something admirable about Geneviève's patronage of the arts. She existed on a superior cultural plane where it was irrelevant that the rest of the world was hooked on gadgets.

I was keenly aware that it would only take one volume she didn't approve of for her support to wane, but with Alain at the helm severed limbs and knitted genitalia wouldn't be making an appearance anytime soon. It didn't surprise me that Geneviève was interested in religious icons; like many residents of the 7ᵗʰ arrondissement she was deeply Catholic, to the point of attending Confession every Friday. She made me promise to let her know the second the finished copies came in – never angling to see anything before the final, perfect version, which suited me because I was protective of the galleys, which had a fragile embryonic quality. With their typos and slightly off colours, I was as reluctant to subject them to scrutiny as I would have been to serve a half-baked cake.

A week behind schedule, the shipment had finally arrived from Italy, where printing costs were lower. My excitement was as great as ever; I loved the smell of the cardboard boxes, the sound of the Stanley knife ripping through the weft of the packaging tape as I hovered over my colleague Viane, whose job it was to send the copies out to subscribers. I could never resist warning her not to damage those on top with the blade. 'Not at a hundred euros a go,' I joked, although that really wasn't the point. She laughed, something my colleagues did a lot around me but not in an unpleasant way. At least they thought I had a sense of humour. As the only foreigner in the company, my foibles were put down to cultural differences, of which there were many. They all knew I couldn't help it. We gathered around to coo over the book, overcome by the quality of the end product. The job held no greater moment, the reward for up to a year's hard work. None of us was in it to get rich.

I waited for things to calm down before taking a single copy back to my office and clearing the desk, as if preparing for some kind of ceremony. I ran my hand across the low-gloss dust jacket before resting the spine flat and allowing the book to fall open at a random page. Closing my eyes, I let my weight sink into the chair.

I had never felt so exhausted. For days my thoughts had been spiralling between my mother, Philippe, Jean-Luc and now Vanessa, like hands spinning uncontrollably through the quarter hours on some demonic clock. Longing to think about something else, I took a deep breath and went in search of sustenance. There was a sensual dimension to any new book, doubled when it was one of mine. They had a smell by which I could have identified them blindfolded in a store (not that many places stocked our titles): a strange blend of the woody and the chemical, not even particularly pleasant.

People often remarked that I loved my work and it was true. I felt a tiny thrill every morning at the fall of my foot on the white stone steps leading to the offices. I cared far too much about the covers we agonised over, the feel of the smooth, heavy pages, the perfect layout of text and images. To love what you do for a living is rare, my work the only real passion I was capable of. That wasn't a reflection on Philippe. It was a reflection on me.

It might have been different if I'd been willing to get help before now but I never wanted to. I was adamant about that even at the age of ten. Not very Californian of me, I know. Thirty years on, even the Europeans have started to talk. In Paris seeing a *psy* has become so fashionable that people discuss it openly, competing over whose issues are the most interesting, whose therapist the most perceptive and profound. Who's the most *damaged*. I was lucky to find you. You were so kind that time back at the beginning when I couldn't stop crying, so patient on the days I spent more time looking out to sea than talking. There aren't so many of those now. You don't say much, and when you do it's mostly to ask questions, but knowing you're listening is the reason I can finally hear myself.

That afternoon I was having trouble keeping my eyes open thanks to our latest house guest. So much for teenagers and their headphones; Vanessa's music had throbbed through the flimsy wall between the spare room and ours until gone two in the morning, Philippe and I so unsure how to deal with it that we did nothing. The neighbours below had banged on the ceiling in the end, so now I'd have to apologise next time we met in the lobby or the street. It took at least another hour to drop off after that.

Thinking about sleep during the day is asking for trouble.

I woke with a jolt followed by a ripping sound in my right ear when I moved my head. My cheek had been stuck to a page of the book by sweat, drool or maybe just the oil of my skin, leaving the thick paper damp and buckled. There was a tear an inch or two long parallel to the spine, made before I realised what was happening and peeled it away from my face.

Fortunately nobody could have seen me. The door to my office was closed and when I went out, my colleagues were gone; they didn't live to work, especially on a Friday. The younger ones celebrated the start of the weekend at a bar in the Marais which I passed on leaving the office. Alain went home to his wife, Viane and Lisette rushing off to see their two-year-olds and free the nanny they shared in the 11th arrondissement.

I headed for the bathroom sensing something wasn't right. A deep crease in my cheek was correcting itself in front of my eyes and blue and red ink had transferred to my skin in a purplish blur. When soap and water didn't work, I only succeeded in removing the dye with an entire packet of Kleenex and a tube of hand cream. That was the best solution I could come up with as the survival kit I schlepped with me for every eventuality (migraine, diarrhoea, period) had never had to cater for anything like this. Once I'd cleaned it off, I applied a fresh dusting of face powder. My eye make-up needed only minor repairs. I brushed my hair and with that, order was restored.

I've always been hard on myself, on principle. But at that time I was conscious that I needed to give myself a break for once, take it easy over the weekend and try to get my head around things. I was under a lot of stress, after all. Philippe would want to see the book and I wanted to show him; there it was again, that need to carry on as usual. It helped me believe everything *would* return to normal at some point, that one day all this would feel like a blip, insignificant in the context of our life together. Back in the office, I closed the covers. It was as if nothing had happened.

12

The sight of him in the reception area brought me to a standstill. The others must have left the door unlocked, thinking I'd soon be on my way out. No visitors should have been there at that hour.

'Hello,' I said, instantly failing in my attempt to sound relaxed.

Jean-Luc Malavoine turned away from the display cabinet where he'd been perusing the spines of some of our latest releases whilst texting. I smiled at the formality when he held out his hand, more suited to a bureaucrat than someone his age. But it was natural that he might feel embarrassed after the episode in the restaurant.

Here we were again, alone. 'Have you recovered from your journey? You're looking...' I cut off, unable to summon a single word I could consider saying out loud.

'...better?' he suggested, blushing and trying not to laugh. 'Yes, thanks.'

'So what brings you here?'

This time the way he looked at me was unmistakable and I didn't care in the slightest why he was in my office. Geneviève and Henri were nice-looking but it didn't seem feasible that they could have produced someone this gorgeous. Jean-Luc's smile had an open, unguarded quality, his eyes bright as seaglass, at the confluence of blue and green. His brown hair was streaked with light and needed cutting. A pair of sunglasses hung from the breast pocket of a plaid shirt rolled up to the elbow. Energy pulsed off his tanned skin. *Life.*

'I'm here to collect a book,' he said eventually. 'My mother was going to come by, but I told her I was going to be in the area...' He caught my eye to check that I was on board with this obvious lie. The complicity he was assuming made me nervous. Geneviève and I were supposed to be friends, unless he'd heard otherwise. And what on earth made him think it was okay to act like this with me? I put my hand to my face, the ink stain replaced by a deep flush, as if he knew every thought I'd had since that night, every dirty little thrill.

'Of course,' I said, '*Icons*! The copies arrived this afternoon, in all their glory.'

The stack of boxes was still occupying one side of the reception area, which was darker than usual because they were partially blocking the windows. One box was open, the flaps sticking up. 'Do help yourself,' I told him, resolving to stay exactly where I was. For me to get the book I would have had to cross the room into close proximity with him, to edge my way round the Danish sofa in curved steel and black leather, which had been returned to its usual spot following the delivery. This was the grandest part of the Editions Gallici offices, in the style of an elegant

76

salon with wood panels and an ornately carved desk. It was no secret that I found the addition of a piece of ultra-modern furniture preposterous; I had never seen anyone attempt to sit on it. But in order to reach the boxes Jean-Luc pushed it aside with his foot like an abandoned toy. Whilst his attention was diverted, I let my gaze dwell on him, absorbing everything I could. His physical presence wasn't down to size – I'm five foot four, fairly average, and since I was wearing heels he was only an inch or two taller than me, but in perfect proportion, with just the right amount of muscle for a slender athletic frame. I found myself wanting to know what he looked like without the clothes, a thought I had never had about any man in such brazen terms. When he turned around I had the unsettling feeling he really *could* read my mind from my expression, if his was anything to go by. Knowing. Flirtatious. The way a woman likes to be looked at. It scared me how damn good it felt.

But not in *this* situation, for God's sake, not him and me. That didn't compute. A voice in my head – my own quiet, sensible voice – was asking me *what is wrong with you?* I tried to stay calm by telling myself he'd soon be gone: he had his copy now; I'd look behind the reception desk for a bag to put it in and send him on his way. Given that we'd seen so very little of each other in the past, it wasn't as if I'd need to actively avoid him.

But he showed no sign of leaving. Instead he leaned against the desk, opened the book and started leafing through it as if he were interested, and by this point I'd convinced myself that nobody outside this building ever would be. He frowned slightly, squinting to read the captions. Forgetting my scruples of not two minutes ago, I crossed to stand next to him, curious to see what he would choose to linger on. I watched his fingers glide down the edge of the pages with the lightest of touches, turning them so as not to leave any trace. It was beyond me not to imagine them on my skin. I had to stop myself from fidgeting, hyper aware of all the places I like to be touched: my shoulders, my breasts, the inside of my thighs and where that leads.

After a while he looked at me. I hadn't realised quite how close we were, our personal space intersecting. If I could feel his breath, he must be able to feel mine. '*Bravo, c'est magnifique!*' I thanked him, dipping my head modestly as if I had created every one of the treasures myself. 'Have you been there?' he asked.

I hesitated over the reason I hadn't travelled to Romania. 'There didn't seem much point, unfortunately. The religious order is extremely secluded. The author managed to wear them down but they would never have allowed a woman into the monastery.'

A woman. How I wished I hadn't drawn attention to my gender and yet it wasn't as if he hadn't noticed. I doubt very much that Jean-Luc Malavoine would ever have looked at a man the way he was looking at me. I was staring at him too. I couldn't stop.

'You're American, right?' he asked. I'd almost forgotten we were having a conversation and tried to collect myself.

'Yes,' I said. 'From California, way up in Del Norte County. Don't suppose you made it there.'

'Oh, I did. The redwoods? God, the west coast is stunning.' As he said this he closed his eyes and his expression took me aback, stirring up my own feelings about the place I grew up. He'd switched to English without even appearing to notice and for once I didn't mind. The combination of American inflexion with a strong French accent was so sexy that if he'd decided to recite the endless list of footnotes from the book I would happily have listened.

Things look and feel so different when you unhook them from what they usually mean, when you stop agonising and angsting and give in to pure instinct. *Sensation*. There was a change of pressure that would have registered on a barometer. *Desire*. It circumvents logic. That's not an excuse. It's just the way it is. *C'est comme ça.*

'At spring break I hitchhiked the whole way,' he continued. 'Well, most of it, from Seattle back down to LA.'

'That must have been an experience,' I said, pushing aside visions of a different experience altogether. 'Isn't hitching a bit risky?' Way to sound boring and middle-aged.

'It was amazing. I stopped for a few days to see the giant redwoods. Can't remember the name of the town;

79

it had this little lighthouse that looks like an actual house with a bright red roof.'

'Gosh, what are the chances? That's Battery Point, really close to where I grew up.'

He smiled, pleased. 'And do you know LA?'

'Can't say I do. Only been there once – I've been in Europe a long time. Where were you?'

'Santa Monica. You know Diebenkorn, the Ocean Park pictures?'

Of course he would know about art. If only he'd stop talking about things that drew me in so I could say *I was just on my way home…* At the same time, it was a relief to direct my errant thoughts to the respectably neutral topic of abstract expressionism.

'I love Diebenkorn! Such outstanding use of colour. There's an earlier painting where the street rises up on the way to the ocean – you can't see it but you know it's there. I once counted seventeen greens in that picture—'

In a wordless interruption Jean-Luc leaned toward me. This wasn't fantasy any more. It was wish fulfilment.

13

I felt Jean-Luc's hand in my hair, pushing it back. I turned my head away, I don't know why; undeterred, he began kissing me, starting at my collarbone. As he worked his way up, I couldn't wait for our mouths to meet. I was wearing a slim skirt with a silk blouse which allowed a tasteful suggestion of expensively engineered lace, nothing too revealing. But I felt naked before he slid his hands under both of these layers, shaking as I unfastened his belt. There was even a French accent to the sharp exhalation he made when my palm brushed against his hard-on. The same word can be used for the intimate body parts of a man and a woman and it leaves nothing to the imagination: *le sexe*.

The centre of my body had shifted from my head to that exact spot in an overpowering flood of anticipation. He was looking around for a place to do it. I didn't care where; I was thirsting, as if I would die if I didn't get it. Jean-Luc drew back to look at me and honestly, I felt like the most desirable woman alive. I kicked off my shoes; he undid my blouse, slowly, those eyes at first swooping back to mine between buttons, finally unable to look away.

There was the desk, the floor or the stupid black sofa, finally good for something.

As we gravitated toward it, I remembered just in time to double-lock the door that led from the stairway. He wouldn't let me go; his warm hands moulded to my breasts. On the rug in the reception area, the pieces of clothing we'd pulled off each other were already inter-twined.

I reached to guide him. He pushed my hand away. The first time was urgent and frantic, just so we could breathe again. After that, things slowed right down and showed no sign of stopping.

I was going to say *things like this don't happen to me* but it wasn't like that. Life had dealt me plenty of crap in which I had no say. But I *did* this and I don't deny it. Sure, at the time it felt like I had no choice but that would be dishonest. Too convenient. Most of us encounter sexual temptation at some point. There's always a choice – it's just easier to discount the options we don't like and for me that was saying No.

We gave that sofa the workout of its life and when I lay back on it afterward, shattered, but in a completely different way from before, it felt nothing like the first time with any other lover. There was something touching about the way he looked at me when it was over and a trace of self-satisfaction I couldn't hold against him. Not after *that*.

I was glowing and blinking in astonishment. So this was what people meant by *amazing sex*! Was it purely chemical, a rush of endorphins sating an appetite?

This is hard to admit, but doing it with Jean-Luc made sex with Philippe seem to lack a crucial dimension, even at its best. I swear that revenge for his cheating couldn't have been further from my mind. Not consciously. Let's face it, if the area of the brain that evaluates decisions had any say in this I would never have done it.

For once in my life, I didn't think at all. I did it because I wanted to, it really is that simple. For the first time, I did something spontaneous and wild. Slutty, some would say. Something I didn't stop to justify or analyse from every angle. Jean-Luc wanted it too. He started it (which I never would have) and he liked what he got. But that was a bonus. That day I was out for my pleasure, to satisfy a desire stronger than I had ever known. And now there was a shimmering at the edges of my world. It had never looked like this before.

Jean-Luc was twenty-three years old. It was me who should have known better, that much is clear. I was past the age at which anything can be gently written off to youth or inexperience, probably some cougar conquest that he'd brag about to his friends. That wasn't a nice thought. But then I had a worse one. More a case of being uncomfortably reminded, because it's not as if I didn't know. I'd fucked Geneviève's precious son.

14

Jean-Luc dressed quickly. Before leaving he bent down to kiss me on the mouth but it felt like a classy sign-off, perhaps a rather sweet attempt at gallantry. Maybe he thought I did this all the time – I'd offered no resistance. The door was once again unlocked and still there I lay, unpleasantly warm and sticky now the rush had worn off, crashing to earth from an unprecedented height, arousal dissolving into body fluids. Scrunched up tissues snatched from a box on the reception desk lay on the floor and after picking them up I dabbed between my legs with wet toilet paper, longing for a shower. The sofa would need a thorough wipe-down.

I was going to be late home now even if I took a cab. I had no idea what Philippe was doing but lately that was often the case. For all I knew my husband could have been screwing the mysterious Nico next door while I'd been going at it with *the son of his oldest friend*. I made myself focus on this excruciating detail.

Shit. It wasn't going to be easy to draw a line under this. Philippe and I had both turned into lesser versions of our true selves lately but I had outdone him by some margin. Whoever Nico was, I didn't know her and it was undoubtedly better that way. And this lurking awareness that our transgressions weren't like for like would surface every time I resorted to *if he's doing it, why can't I?*

I searched in the mirror for signs of what I'd become in the space of a single half-hour but of course there were none. Where did I go from here, invent an excuse? If I needed one it wouldn't be hard to make something up on the day the book had come in. Taking it home would make for a good diversion. Would I tell barefaced lies or say nothing at all (which seemed to be Philippe's favoured option), hoping that he didn't notice anything untoward, or he didn't actually care?

I was surprised how much this last thought upset me. We'd turned each other's lives around, only for it to come to this?

The ride home was scenic, along the Quai de la Tour-nelle with a view across the Seine to Notre-Dame but right then it could have been any road, anywhere. I rarely took cabs, never having adjusted to the improvement in my material circumstances that came with marrying Philippe. Part of me was still living next door to Christine in that walk-up off République, buying a few groceries from the Franprix on Boulevard Magenta going towards the Gare du Nord. I often used to see the homeless man whose entire life revolved around one bench and two of those huge IKEA bags. One time I realised he was mastur-bating under cover of the blue plastic and I was disgusted, even though you couldn't see anything. Others passed by without noticing.

Whatever my former position on the morality scale, I had shifted a few degrees. What Jean-Luc and I had done was inappropriate in more ways than I cared to think of but it *was* between two consenting adults, I reasoned, trying to allay the panic tightening my ribs. It was not premeditated on my part – I'd had uncensored daydreams about him, sure, but completely without intent. The idea of anything *physically* happening between us would have made me laugh out loud. Now it had, I tried to convince my upright American self to view my lapse in context. In this city infidelity was not universally regarded as wrong, no matter that I'd never gone native until it suited me. The cab driver kept sneaking glances in the rear view mirror. In my reflection in the glass, my silent beratings gave me the stony, concentrated look of someone plotting a terrible crime, when in fact I'd taken the first step on a dark path where I was in danger. But it wasn't too late to turn back. As long as nobody found out, nobody would get hurt.

I told the driver to let me out in rue Saint-Sulpice – it's silly but I don't like them to know where I live. I shoved a fifty at him and he muttered at having to give me change. 'Your bag,' he reminded me wearily. Through the open door of an upmarket travel agency came the buzz of a cocktail reception in full flow with trays of work-of-art canapés laid out and a group of tanned *bobos* swigging at

flutes of Prosecco surrounded by posters of faraway desti-
nations.

On the landing outside our apartment, I fumbled in
my bag for the keys like a doppelgänger who hasn't quite
got the hang of their parallel life. So I looked like the
same person as ever, but if I could do something so out
of character, what else might I do? My encounter with
Jean-Luc seemed unreal, as if it had all been in my imagination, although my previous sexual fantasies now seemed
rather tame. I could do better in real life! What I'd just
experienced was comparable to only one other revelation
that I could recall: my first ever orgasm made my body
feel like a house of miracles to which I'd held the key all
along.

I dumped my bags in the hallway with a deep sigh
and straightened my clothes as best I could. There was
no sign of Philippe, nor of his daughter, though she had
certainly left her mark. Our cleaning lady, Majoula, came
on Fridays so the place would be nice for the weekend.
The money I'd left for her was gone from the mantelpiece
but there was no way she'd been in: the sofa cushions had
been disturbed and replaced the wrong way round and the
smaller striped silk ones lay all over the floor. As I bent
down to rescue them a collection of soda cans and beer
bottles came into view, several of them tipped on their
sides, liquid oozing onto the parquet and into the rug.

My lower back twinged, informing me how it felt
about being subjected to an energetic sex session with a

man *seventeen years my junior*. I began to examine this from every angle to see which looked the worst.

The age difference between Jean-Luc and me was equivalent to the whole of Vanessa's life, not that she had anything to do with it, I just happened to be cleaning up her mess at that moment. Or to put it another way, I was her age when he was born, so technically old enough to be his mother, though that made me feel bad for my prudish seventeen-year-old self, still a virgin and teased at boarding school for being so uptight. That poor girl would rather have died than spread her legs for some guy who'd just walked in the door, no matter how hot he was. The generation gap (give or take) felt like the most damning detail but I found it surprisingly easy to dismiss because I was so much younger than Jean-Luc's mother. When an image of Geneviève popped up in my head I groaned. For Christ's sake, who was I trying to kid? (Myself, and it wasn't working). I doubted there was anywhere it would be considered acceptable to sleep with the child of a friend, not even done with college, let alone the son of your husband's best friend.

I ran a bath, the water no more than warm as the afternoon's blazing temperatures had barely dropped. There was no reason for me to tidy up after Vanessa – so what if Philippe saw what she'd done? In the short time since she'd arrived I'd found a reason to be glad of our uninvited guest: as a distraction.

I balled up my work clothes and shoved them in the laundry hamper: the dry-clean-only skirt, the delicate silk blouse which had lost a button, right on the chest, wouldn't you guess, letting the fabric gape open. Quite an eyeful – no wonder the taxi driver had been staring, though that wasn't the only possible explanation.

The smell of sex had followed me home, clinging to my skin, an elixir equal parts me and him. I sank into the water before I could change my mind about washing it off, plunging my head under and letting my hair stream out around me. The day I took the lilies to Geneviève I'd had that strange out of body experience where I pictured myself freaking out and felt liberated by it. As I contemplated the gulf between my afternoon and reality, it was the exact opposite, like I was in prison.

I scooped up the foam in my hands, soaping my aching limbs. I pressed my palms into the arch of my back and under the curve of my bottom but made sure not to touch myself *there*, letting the water swirl around. It was a little sore but I didn't mind. I knew I'd have to forget but for now my body remembered. Forty was late to discover there were layers to sex that I hadn't known existed. The water was cold by the time I got out of the tub. I pulled a comb through my hair and brushed my teeth. There. Clean and fresh all over.

But it was only skin deep. I couldn't shake the impression of new vistas rolling out in front of me, an altered state of being. The first fix is usually free, the one that gets you hooked. The rest you pay for.

15

I put on a light summer dress and was about to lie down when there was a simultaneous trilling of the theme to *American Beauty* from my phone and tablet, both in the living room. I never ignored my mother's attempts to reach me, feeling that if I did she would be able to witness my decision to reject her. There would have been a certain symmetry to that but still I couldn't do it. I pressed to accept the Skype call, pausing for the time it took to conjure a smile onto my face. As her only child I owed her that much; I'd be devastated if my daughter ever felt that way about me.

Her pixelated image hung on the screen for a few seconds, her voice slow and dragged out, and then there she was, in all clarity. I positioned the screen at a distance on my dressing table and sat down on the bed.

'Look at you, all wet! Did I get you out of the shower?'

'No, not at all,' I said, rubbing the ends of my hair with a towel. 'How's it going?'

It used to be bad enough that we didn't have much to say to each other on the phone but it was harder than ever since Mom had discovered Skyping was free. First she gave me the lowdown on her disrupted sleep patterns and lack of appetite and then she carried the tablet to the back porch to show me the broken catch on the rabbit hutch, as if I could do anything about it at five and a half thousand miles.

'Ask Lenny if he can fix it,' I suggested. The neighbour we'd had growing up still lived next door, though I always wished he'd move away, just like I wished we would have. Lenny was the one who'd nearly drowned himself in the search for Christopher and the one who'd carried him home, putting an end to my behind-the-sofa hope that if they couldn't find him, the worst (which nobody would say in front of me) could not have happened. I'll never forget the wrongness of my brother lying there, gone. The stench of the ocean in our living room, the runnels of seawater across the wooden floor. My mother howling as my father paced up and down, up and down, two people who belonged together instantly split in two.

I could never stop thinking how different things might have been between Mom and me if not for that day. She'd given up on her Parisian alter ego since returning home and without the red nails and the posh cigarettes, she looked tired and older than when I had her here in the room with me. Despite everything, I missed her. One way and another I'd been missing her most of my life. I read that by the time you hit twenty-five you should stop blaming your parents for anything. They didn't mention it the other way around.

'Are you okay, Alexandra? Something seems a little off with you today.'

I averted my gaze from the screen, frantically blinking back tears. The towel would be a giveaway.

I was desperate to talk to someone and there was nobody I could dream of telling. Not only did Philippe and I share most of our friends in Paris but they also knew the Malavoines, or knew of them. My best friend Emily lived in England and was married with three children, belonging to another world entirely. The same was true of my expat tennis partners, whom I'd seen only twice since my operation – one was the daughter of a Baptist preacher but the others would be just as horrified at what I'd done.

It was bad enough when it was just Philippe behaving badly. If only I'd had you to talk to back then. *If only*. I could say that about so much of this.

That afternoon I had done something shocking that I didn't understand and knew was wrong and wished I hadn't. It felt like nothing would ever be the same.

Or, Jean-Luc and I had done something crazy and passionate and incredible that I didn't regret at all.

I find myself doing this sometimes, cleaning up my account, although it doesn't help anyone. The second voice was always louder; truer, as if I'd accidentally uncovered the secret to being fully alive. I wasn't sure I could survive without experiencing that feeling again. I'd gorged on it but was left feeling famished.

My mother made it through the days on a diet of booze, smokes and pills. If she'd been here I'd have asked for a Valium to block everything out until I could pull myself together. I used to take pills myself but in the end I always choose pain over feeling nothing. That's not living.

'It's complicated,' I said. 'You know how it is.' I hoped that was sufficiently vague.

She snorted. 'Tell me about it.' It may be a rhetorical expression but I knew she was expecting something more. I faced the screen head-on and made a conscious effort to look her in the eye.

'You were right about Philippe,' I said, staying true to the theme of marital problems but not telling her anything she hadn't already guessed. 'He *is* cheating on me.'

My mother gave a melodramatic grimace of sympathy, as if I were a stranger on a bus boring her with a sob story. 'I know how that feels.'

For fuck's sake, I wanted to say. *Just this one time, could something be about how I feel?*

'I'd rather not talk about it,' I said, as the image began to break up. A message flashed up on the screen saying 'poor connection'. And then it was gone.

16

There was some tortelloni in the fridge: made in some factory, shrink-wrapped in thick plastic, the sort of food you buy hoping there will always be something better. And usually there was, but not tonight. Philippe would be disappointed – I normally made a special effort on Fridays if we weren't going out to eat. There were so many good places on the doorstep, his new favourite serving robust dishes from the southwest using every last part of the duck, mine an upmarket Vietnamese which did a delicious and fragrant *pho*. I put the pasta on the counter and a pan of water on the stove so Philippe would see that I had plans, however unappetising.

I took hold of the corkscrew the wrong way, pinching my fingers hard, but eventually I succeeded in uncorking an excellent Louis Latour. Philippe had visited the vineyard in Burgundy and this wine always put him in a good mood. I raised the cork to my nostrils and breathed in so deeply it made me shudder. My senses were heightened, still.

There was a hammering at the door and as soon as I opened it Vanessa's eyes fastened onto the bottle in my hand. 'Oh, cool,' she said. 'I could do with a drink after the day I've had.'

This just proved how undignified and futile our apprehension and pussyfooting of the night before had been – acting like a doormat with this girl was asking to be trampled.

'And what sort of day *have* you had?' When Vanessa went to speak I wagged my finger at her and she closed her mouth again. 'Because I've had my cleaning lady on the phone in tears. I don't know what on earth you said to her but she thought she'd been fired. Majoula is a refugee with three children to feed.' My tirade left me out of breath. Being taken to task was becoming a habit for Vanessa, pissing her mother off and now me in quick succession. She looked hostile and abashed at the same time. 'It wasn't hard to guess what you spent the money on. You left this place like a pig sty and by the looks of it you've had plenty to drink already.' I stamped on the pedal of the kitchen bin and the lid sprang open on the bottles and cans, neatly separated for recycling. Of course I'd cleaned up in the end; I couldn't not.

'They're not all mine. Some are Philippe's,' she said.

I told her to sit down and pressed my hands together in a supplicating gesture until I realised what I was doing. 'Why are you here, Vanessa?'

'Because my mother kicked me out.'

'I know that. But why *here*?'

Her mouth twisted. 'Because Philippe's my dad and I don't have anywhere else to go. I know *you* don't want me here.'

I winced as she chewed at a nail and tore off a fine strip of skin from the tip of a finger, then spat it out into thin air. I gave a sigh. I didn't *not* want her here. As things stood, I would have been downright alarmed if she were to leave. And besides, something about Vanessa got at my heart, however mad she made me. 'If your dad wants you here I honestly don't mind, if we can agree on a couple of rules. But first can I make a request? Do you call your mother by her first name?'

'No,' she said. 'That bitch. I call her nothing.'

I did my damndest not to smile. 'Then don't call your father Philippe. Call him *Papa,* like anyone else. That would mean a lot to him.'

She produced a sound halfway between a splutter and a sneer.

'You said some of these drinks were his. So he's been home and gone out again?'

'*Dad* and I had a row,' she said. 'He went for a walk in the... that park down the road.'

It bothered me that Vanessa couldn't put a name to the Jardin du Luxembourg, to realise that Philippe and I were playing Mom and Dad (because I'm pretty sure we both felt like impostors) to a kid from an affluent suburb who didn't know her way around the city. Still, the Sixth wasn't exactly gritty, even if the park was full of people pounding their frustrations into the dust.

This wasn't a great outcome for the first time father and daughter found themselves alone, although it was crazy to think my presence would have made a difference.

'When did he leave?' I asked.

Vanessa had no concept of time – she didn't even wear a watch. 'Dunno. Couple of hours ago, maybe.'

Despite the warmth of the evening, I shivered to recall what I was doing a couple of hours ago. Already I was conscious of the line separating my *before* and *after* selves, one still attached to a familiar continent, the other totally adrift.

'Did you go looking for him?'

Vanessa looked down with such dejection that I decided to get off her case. Next to her feet a half-bottle of vodka was poking out of her grotty shoulder bag, one of those cheap ethnic ones with tiny fake mirrors and sweat-shop embroidery. I reached to pull it out and placed it on the table.

'Sounds like we've all had quite a day,' I said, careful to change my tone. 'But whatever the problem is, vodka isn't going to help. Is drinking the reason your mother's mad at you?'

Vanessa flipped again. 'If you really want to know, I got in a fight with this stuck-up girl for fucking her boyfriend.' I internally replayed what she'd said and attempted a *go on* face. 'She was spreading lies about me at a party at the weekend, so I gave her a black eye. Nobody gives a shit what she did to me.' She lifted up her hair to show me long red scratches down the side of her neck and a nasty deep one on her shoulder, practically a cut, that had started to heal in a bumpy scab with several millimetres missing.

'That's not good,' I said, inadequately, given that my thought was *How dare they do that to you?*

'She's only the Chief of Police's daughter,' Vanessa went on. 'My mother knows him through work. She wouldn't have gone so ballistic over it otherwise. But I'm glad she kicked me out.'

'Really? Why?'

'Why do you think? So I don't have to see any of them! I thought it was over between Boris and that *petite connasse*. I thought he liked me.' She shook her head. 'Turns out he only did it to make her jealous. Before this, everyone at school just thought I was fat and ugly. Now I'm a fat ugly slut who doesn't wax.'

Vanessa didn't defend herself against their verdict. It was so easy to picture the beautiful, smug faces of the other players in this sorry tale, laughing at her expense. She probably wasn't even sober when it happened.

'Is anyone calling the boy a slut?' I asked. Do they ever?

I went to sit next to Vanessa but when I tried to take her hand she snatched it away, glaring. 'Why am I telling you this? Like you care.'

I don't know which of us was more surprised at the intimate turn of the conversation. We had taken the first few steps to being something to each other, never mind that I'd never applied for the position of stepmother. The first time Vanessa brushed me off it felt like insolence. Now, less than twenty-four hours later, it stung.

Hunger won out and after eating the pasta we flopped down in front of a mediocre movie about a man threatening to throw himself off the Roosevelt Hotel in Manhattan. The vodka remained unopened and the red wine was still breathing on the kitchen counter. Neither of us would take refuge in alcohol. It really was the most unlikely day for me to start setting an example to the younger generation.

On the TV screen, police officers scurried about on Madison Avenue with a huge inflatable mattress that I bet never saved anyone in that situation.

'God, don't you wish he'd get it over with?' Vanessa said. It was such an awful thing to say that I couldn't help laughing. I felt the same about Philippe walking through the door, even though I dreaded seeing him after what I'd done. I was in for a long wait. He'd texted to say he was having a drink with a friend of ours who ran a bistro in Montparnasse. Translated, this meant dinner and a late night. He didn't ask after his daughter despite having abandoned us to each other's company when we were no more than strangers with strings, and yet by recent standards it was something that he'd told me anything.

Vanessa and I both kept dozing off until I finally nudged her, turned off the TV and announced that we should go to bed. The day that would change the course of my life was over.

17

It did occur to me that Philippe and I were now quits.

He was in bed when I woke, facing away from me. I watched his ribcage expand and contract as he breathed slowly, peacefully, unaware that our marriage was heading for the rocks. For the first time in weeks it was raining heavily and my plan to go out running was ruined. Being at home wasn't making me feel warm and safe. What I needed was a place to be alone with my thoughts. A place that *wasn't* home.

Like many residential buildings in Paris, the top floor apartments in ours had a *chambre de bonne*, a tiny maid's room, in the attic. From the street the minuscule mansard windows looked like old-fashioned matchboxes perched crookedly on the roof. It was a sign of times past that these rooms could not be accessed from within the apartments they belonged to, nor from the residents' stairwell containing the elevator. The person who used to spend the most time on their feet was also the one who had to trudge up and down five flights at the start and end of every day.

As I did, with my own burden. To reach our attic room I had to let myself out of the apartment, go down to the entrance hall, past the elevator shaft and through the door leading to a tiny light well and the little-used staircase, its bare treads worn into crescents and covered in thick dust; the hefty service charge didn't run to keeping this area clean. I started to sneeze and by the time I was halfway up my eyes were streaming and I could hardly breathe. Disorientated by the endless spiralling, by the time I reached the top it wasn't clear whether I was facing the street or the courtyard. It was so long since I had been up here that I hesitated over which room was ours. There were two others, plus a truly horrible bathroom I never wished to see again. The cost of living in Paris had created a market for these cramped spaces that many owners were keen to exploit but these particular garrets remained unloved, forgotten and not a little creepy.

I picked the wrong door and although I got the key into the lock, it wouldn't turn and required several minutes of frantic jiggling to work free. Finally I got into our room, which was pokier than I recalled even though it only contained a few storage boxes from my single years between Jonathan and Philippe. After Jonathan dumped me I moved to Paris, hoping that because everything would feel so different, I'd feel different too. I'd swapped first continents then countries to get to this point and now the one good chapter of my life risked being cut, torn up, screwed into a ball and tossed in the wastepaper basket. Or radically amended on the grounds of plausibility, because *a woman like me would never do something like that.* Jonathan was a writer, so I know about this stuff.

Philippe liked a lie-in on weekends. On a normal Saturday I would go running, shower, take him coffee and then we'd have sex because we were mostly too exhausted on weekdays. There had to be a reason for us *not* to on weekend mornings and me hiding up here was not going to work.

I'd slept indecently well, all things considered. My body was still thrumming with the intense satisfaction of the day before, a good kind of ache. If there were only a way to disconnect that pleasure from all the strictures and structures that said it was wrong: marriage, respectability, that boxed-in feeling the middle years can bring: *Is this it? Surely this can't be it?*

Evidently it didn't have to be.

I'd come out wearing a long cardigan over my summer pyjamas: I'd heard French friends laugh pityingly at adults who wear anything in bed but Philippe and I always had. I had never wondered before if he slept naked with Brigitte. It was a reasonable assumption they had a more exciting sex life than he and I had of late; it appeared to have been an attraction of opposites and if the number of rows he'd hinted at were any indication there must have been a lot of making up. They *were* together for twelve years. Plus he was younger then, of course – I'd never had any previous cause to reflect on the difference that could make.

Scuffing the dirt off a space on the floorboards with my flip-flop, I sat down in one of the few parts of the room with a straight wall, hugging my knees in toward me, finding the hammering rain on the roof right above me sensual and stirring as I thought of Jean-Luc, *mon amant*. He really knew what he was doing for someone so young – I couldn't decide which part of him I'd most enjoyed where. My nipples hardened, my mind fooling my body into thinking it was about to happen again. Nobody had ever made me come that hard.

I told you I was going to be frank.

It felt like an aberration, something that should take years of practice. And maybe that's all everything had been up to now. My right hand dipped into my pyjama bottoms but I pulled it back as if I'd been caught stealing.

I could torment myself and make Philippe suspicious by making some excuse not to sleep with him. He was understanding when pain or bleeding prevented it, as it frequently did in the run-up to my surgery, but I couldn't use that as an excuse now. His daughter staying with us wouldn't work either; he'd scoffed at me that time during my mother's visit. Families do live in close quarters.

Or I could take this mood, this longing, back to our bedroom and see if it could be put to use. One theory about infidelity is that it can reignite the pilot light of marriage. Honestly, the things we tell ourselves.

I went down from the maid's room and took the elevator up to our apartment, not wanting to tire myself out. There was no sound from Vanessa's room and when I looked through the keyhole – I was losing my grip on acceptable behaviour – her large shape occupied the bed like a rock.

I entered our bedroom with a big mug of coffee in each hand, mine full almost to the top with steamed milk. Before Philippe had the chance to finish his, I'd undressed and was rubbing myself against him, grasping at the erection that soon resulted. He looked pleased and rather taken aback – he usually made the first move. I never used to be the slightest bit forward with men. As I was writhing around, I asked myself what the hell I was doing – trying to be a better fuck than his lover? I felt like an actress playing a whore – not one step removed, but two.

Sex with Jean-Luc felt more natural than this. It even felt less wrong because I really wanted him and I really *didn't* want this. Philippe's eyes were closed as I moved up and down on him – if he had been watching surely even he would have guessed there was a problem. As it was, I'd have to put up a billboard in our bedroom saying *something is wrong with our marriage* for him to realise.

Philippe sometimes found it difficult to finish with me on top, where gravity was not in his favour. He rolled me over and with a groan more pained than ecstatic, he shuddered and collapsed heavily onto me, sending a blast of hot breath down my neck. I'd known from the start I was going to have to fake my orgasm and in the end I didn't even get to do that. That there had been nothing in it for me didn't seem to be a consideration. I nudged Philippe off of me and we both just lay there, staring at the ceiling.

I hadn't only gained a taste for something I couldn't have. Any desire for what I did had gone. My entire body was prickling with discomfort and as I felt him leaking out of me onto the sheets, freshly changed the night before as if my indiscretion had taken place right there, I had never felt so utterly empty inside. I had made this bed.

18

Some things you can predict. Almost everything that matters, you can't. When Alain and I decided to hold the launch of *Icons* at the gallery owned by my husband and established with the Malavoines' backing I didn't foresee that I would have recently cheated on Philippe with their son.

Any other venue would have been a great excuse to spend time away from the office, where I constantly relived the scenes with Jean-Luc, especially when passing through the reception area. Instead I had to visit the gallery with Lisette to finalise all the details and risk Philippe hovering around. It was Lisette's job to order the sparkling wine and canapés but there were always fiddly logistical issues to overcome. That was the price for an interesting venue and we always aimed to match the location to the theme of the volume. *Icons* had been tricky in that regard – naturally no Orthodox church would have admitted alcohol-infused culture vultures, half of them revealing vast expanses of cleavage, arm and leg.

My reservations were of another kind.

Philippe adopted the white cube format favoured by small private galleries – nothing to compete with the arte-facts, easily painted another colour when the need arose, then back to white again. The current exhibition was of abstract work by Nasim Asradi, a Muslim artist inspired by unrest in the *banlieues*, and consisted of steel and vinyl wall hangings and metalwork displayed on movable plinths. It was a bold move on Philippe's part to represent someone whose output was this challenging and politically moti-vated; to his frustration its success had been more critical than commercial and several of the key exhibits remained unsold. The people who could afford them didn't want to think about that world.

When Lisette and I arrived, Philippe was nowhere to be seen. His assistant Suzanne was taking a call so we wandered around sizing up the space. The exhibit to my right looked like a torture instrument with glinting razor blades along the edge of each spike that you could easily miss if the light didn't catch them. I looked at the label: *Incineration, 2014* – €9,800. Next to it was the red dot that meant SOLD.

Suzanne wobbled her head as the person on the end of the line droned on. She ran a purple talon down a list of export duty figures and gabbled a few in a manner that suggested the discussion was at an end, then purred a few multilingual pleasantries before hanging up.

'Russians!' she said. 'He's the broker for the guy who just bought *that*,' she pointed to the knuckleduster I'd been looking at. 'They shell out for this stuff and think it will rock up at their mansions the next day as if by magic.'

'Well, I hope you feel differently about Romanians,' I said, keen to get the meeting underway and get out.

'So, a visit from *Madame le Patron*,' Suzanne said to me. '*Quel honneur!*'

'Oh, would you stop it!' I said, laughing. 'It's a good thing I'm not your boss. I don't envy Philippe the job of keeping *you* in line!'

Suzanne liked this and treated me to one of her killer smiles. She was twenty-nine and so sexy she could even turn a woman's head. Her hair was cut in a short asymmetric style which always looked like she'd just left a salon. Half-French, half-Vietnamese, she'd got the best of both with a slim, firm body and generously sized breasts that were, as far as could be judged, perfect. And it wasn't hard to form an opinion as they were on permanent display in a transparent black top. She had a closetful, not to mention an enticing collection of lingerie.

I didn't kid myself for one moment that this had escaped Philippe's notice when he hired her but Suzanne flirted with anyone she pleased, even me on occasion. Where her intentions lay was a matter for speculation but from the occasional comment she let slip I suspected she was keener on wealthy Russians than she cared to admit. It must be fun to get up every morning and be her.

'It's a shame, this would have been the best wall to project the images,' she said. Suspended between a pair of handcuffs joined by an unfeasibly long chain was a swathe of pleated light grey vinyl that reminded me of those folding bathroom doors in RVs and motel rooms too cheap to have a real one. It even had the same nasty smell as when I was a kid. I looked at the label: *Fuck your Jesus, 2013* – €15,000. No SOLD dot.

This was not good, not good at all. In fact, it was positively indecent to hold an event celebrating images of Jesus Christ and the Virgin Mary in a space that was also home to this object. I'd missed the *vernissage* because I was convalescing when the exhibition opened and Philippe's offer to host our launch had come as a huge weight off my mind. It was too late to do anything about it – we'd just have to hope that nobody noticed.

'The other wall will be fine and we'll do the speeches over there too,' I said, not least because it would encourage the guests to face the other way. Lisette handed the USB stick to Suzanne, who disappeared into the office. Within moments the room was all aglow. The three of us stood transfixed – luckily you didn't need to believe in God to be moved by the beauty of the icons.

Lisette and Suzanne were discussing where to set up the bar and the book display but I had other things on my mind. As usual, we had no idea how many guests to expect: the way it normally worked was that some succumbed to a better offer and plenty who had declined or failed to reply turned up because they found themselves in the area and decided to grab a few drinks for free.

As it was summer and icons were 'not sexy', as Suzanne put it (it's a miracle she was capable of saying those words), we had gone overboard and invited far more than we could comfortably accommodate if most of them showed up. Plus there was the author to contend with – Professor Bernard Ioanescu's ego ideally needed a room of its own. He would be furious if it was unpleasantly crowded so nobody could see him and twice as piqued if hardly anyone showed up.

'What the heck is that noise?' I said, looking around me.

'Isn't this the music you wanted?' Suzanne's attempt to pull a hideous face made her look like Audrey Hepburn. Lisette and I exchanged glances. When we decided to play a soundtrack of the monks chanting as mood music, we didn't know they sounded like this.

'Doesn't really say *party*, does it?' said Suzanne.

'Well it *is* called Lamentations,' Lisette said, examining the original CD, which had been lent to us by Bernard.

'You're right, it's not the mood we're aiming for,' I said. 'Some of the Romanian chants I've heard are beautiful and a little more... uplifting. I'm sure we can come up with something else.'

The silence that filled the gallery when the dirge was turned off was heavenly in its own right. Raising the music issue with Bernard Ioanescu was just inviting him to be difficult. This is what YouTube was for.

Within minutes an otherworldly set of voices filled the space like the colour from the images: light, melodic, hypnotic. My eyes closed and for the first time in weeks

I felt a sense of peace. Within seconds it was interrupted by the loud ringing of my phone.

It was Geneviève. Jean-Luc had left without the book.

19

Philippe patted his face with a towel and the spots of blood brought him back to the mirror. He always took ages over a wet shave and must have cut himself when I yelled at him for occupying the bathroom when I wanted to get ready for the launch. As if that was a crime in his own home.

He caught me gently by the shoulders and dipped his head to catch my eye. He'd seen me like this before; not *this* agitated, fortunately, but sometimes I was so tense and unreasonable I even annoyed myself. Maybe it was in my favour that he used to be married to a fiery woman like Brigitte. He was generous enough to put it all down to my hormones rather than a fundamental flaw in my personality. Right now he put it down to big-night nerves.

'Don't get stressed, Alexandra,' he said. I love the way he says my name, which he never shortens, pronouncing it with a soft *ss*, almost like Italian. 'You know it's not good for you. Everything's going to be fine.'

He only knew his half of the story, of course, but how could he act as if nothing had changed? He wrapped me in his arms but it felt all wrong. The best thing about the two of us never was the sex – it was everything else. But now the trust was gone and I could no longer conveniently hold him accountable. Breaking away, I took a pack of dental floss from the cabinet and sawed away at my gums until they bled. It shouldn't have taken me this long to ask myself if Philippe was unhappy with me. Maybe neither of us was suited to marriage after all – we weren't making a very good job of it. I spat diluted blood into the sink and sluiced it away.

But if Philippe could be kind to me despite my tantrum, I owed him something in return. 'How are things with you and Vanessa?'

'Better than yesterday,' he said, smiling. 'We just got off on the wrong foot. Maybe I was expecting too much. She may come along to the launch – I thought it would give her a chance to show she can behave.'

Or not. My laugh sounded slightly hysterical even to me. He gave me an odd look. 'Please tell me you're joking.'

'I see,' he said. 'You think she's an embarrassment.' His mouth hardened and it became apparent that I had yet another rival for his loyalty. He may not have raised Vanessa but she was still his daughter. He could say what he liked about her – I got no say at all.

'That's not it. I just think she'd be bored with nobody there of her own age.'

He accepted my hurriedly concocted explanation. The chances of Vanessa showing up seemed remote. She wouldn't know an icon as anything other than a symbol on a device.

Replaying the call with Geneviève in my head was driving me crazy. Without any idea what Jean-Luc had told her, or if she even knew he'd come by the office, I had to pretend there was poor reception and immediately called Viane at the office to get a copy couriered to the Malavoines' home. I had no idea whether Geneviève believed me but told myself she had no reason not to. I had said nothing to incriminate myself. I was sure of that. *I hadn't, had I?*

As if my anxiety needed fuelling, my mother had Skyped me and insisted on seeing what I was going to wear. I'd picked a similar style to her red dress in a vibrant kingfisher blue but I wasn't altogether happy with it, even less so after Mom had her say. The cut was less flattering than hers and I'd gone for the more generous of two sizes, mindful that any tightly encased flesh at the event would invite unwelcome comparisons with Suzanne, who had a ten year, twenty kilo advantage over me. Not that it was a competition.

Mindful of the *tits or legs* rule, I'd opted for the first, setting off the deep V neckline with a simple pendant on a long chain. I could have turned up wearing almost anything. It was my responsibility that everything should go well but I wasn't the star of the show.

Laughing out loud is supposed to be a good way to reduce tension but Philippe would have thought I was off my rocker and nothing seemed remotely funny. I practised a welcoming smile in the mirror, wishing I was more in the mood. Alain and I weren't the most charismatic party hosts: my accent made me self-conscious about public speaking in French, fraught with nerves until that part was over and unable to eat for hours before. Like Geneviève, Alain was posh and rather aloof, but being extremely well connected he could be relied on to steer Bernard around the room and make introductions. That left the dutiful mingling – two hours of the same minute-long conversation on repeat – and the dreaded opening speech to me as the editor. Since I knew so little about Romania I planned to keep it very short. Sometimes I am still that frightened little girl hiding behind the sofa. On such occasions I would look around me at the confident, vivacious people bonding and networking, and wonder if everyone has to live with this fear of being found out; wishing the inside matched up to the outside. It's a comforting idea that at least half of us are faking it.

'Do you need me there early?' Philippe asked. When I assured him we didn't he headed for the sofa and picked up his novel from the side table. I pushed away a memory of Jonathan's bestselling début, in which a thinly disguised version of me plays the neurotic wife and mother.

Since Jean-Luc, it was impossible for me to be as angry as before with Philippe. I wanted to resolve the bad atmosphere between us before leaving, to go into my big night with the feeling of having my husband on my side, something I had never previously doubted. I gave Philippe a quick kiss, which turned into a long one, the kind that usually led to sex. He tried to pull me onto the sofa; I laughed and said he'd wrinkle my dress. He ignored me, threading his hand through the gap in the layers of fabric to caress my leg. 'But you look so *good*,' he said. It felt like a long time since he'd looked at me that way.

There'd been such *tendresse* between us that fall evening by the river, in knowing we were heading home to make love. I went over to the mirror above the fireplace and applied a coat of the deep red lipstick my mother had left behind, after Geneviève suggested she try a softer shade. I could see what Philippe meant. There *was* something new about me, something visible. I eyed myself suspiciously and received a knowing look in return.

20

It was a good idea to stop micro-managing Suzanne and Lisette and let them get on with their job. The window display at the gallery was spectacular, drawing passers-by as the gold of the icons caught their attention. Inside, the loop of images from the monastery transformed the space, the brutal edges of Nasim Asradi's pieces consigned to the background, plinths relegated to the corners to make it easier for the guests to circulate. I stood contemplating the unmistakably Middle Eastern features of the Orthodox Jesus and Mary, which made far more sense than the north European versions usually seen in France. Soon the chanting coming through the speakers would be drowned out by animated chatter but for now it had a heart-searing sweetness.

Suzanne and Lisette looked at me expectantly and I could feel myself beaming as I complimented them on their hard work. Behind the drinks table was a tall shaven-headed black guy I didn't recognise, wearing a blinding white shirt and a long waiter's apron. I drew closer to Lisette and said in a low voice, 'Why are we using outside help? There was no budget for that.'

'Dédé's a friend,' Suzanne said, far too loudly. 'He offered to do it for the contacts.'

It was clear from the way Dédé was looking at Suzanne what kind of contact he was hoping for but I was happy that anyone considered this the place to be. All we needed now was a roomful of others who felt the same.

'Philippe told me his daughter was staying with you,' Suzanne said. 'Is she coming tonight?'

'Oh, I don't think so. It's not really her scene,' I said, as if I had a clue what Vanessa's scene was.

'I never knew you had a stepdaughter, Alexandra!' said Lisette, surprised that I could have kept this from her. 'How old is she? Where does she live? What's she like?'

I smiled at the questions. 'Vanessa's seventeen and she lives with her mother in Neuilly.' I searched for the right words to describe her, recalling Philippe taking offence. 'She's got attitude. Very much her own person. You never know, maybe she *will* turn up and you'll get to see for yourself.'

Lisette was satisfied. In her best dress, I noticed the tell-tale curve to her belly, just like the first time. She'd probably find it easier to tell me now she knew about Vanessa. My colleagues knew the reason for my absences and were no doubt capable of piecing it all together. When Lisette brought her firstborn into the office she didn't tell anyone else, 'You don't have to hold him'. And once she'd said it – with the best intentions, I knew – I didn't feel I could.

Suzanne was modelling a new hairdo with bright purple streaks in the front. Stunning, and didn't she know it. With her figure it was never a choice between tits and legs. She was wearing a high-necked, incredibly short silver tube dress with tiger-print Louboutins, which made her tan legs go on for ever. A familiar sight in Paris, the subtle ostentation of that red sole always amused me, the upmarket equivalent of leaving the price on. I had no idea how much they cost, only that she shouldn't have been able to afford them on what Philippe paid her. The shoes I was wearing cost two hundred euros and the first few times I wore them it made me feel ill thinking about it. At eleven I wore the same shoes for over a year and by the time my mother noticed, they were three sizes too small.

A cab drew up and Alain and Bernard got out. Bernard surveyed the room with an air of satisfaction.

'We're all set,' I told them.

'Great,' Bernard said. 'Let's just hope someone turns up.' That was self-effacing from the man who'd taken umbrage when I mentioned his excessive use of semi-colons with all the tact I could muster.

The storms of the last few days had cleared the air and it was a glorious summer evening. A few people I recognised had walked past the window several times peering in, killing time. I went over to bid them come in and gave Dédé the signal to begin pouring. After all my doubts I was filled with a sense of belief: in *Icons*, in the future of Editions Gallici, in the future, period. I could do this.

The gallery began to fill, the noise level rising incrementally. When he arrived, Philippe smiled at me across the room, not wanting to interrupt me in work mode. Only he and Alain had any idea how much it mattered for this edition to be a success. The guests clutched their glasses and exclaimed at the icons flashing and lingering on the walls. Suzanne had curated film installations in her previous job and without me asking she had transformed a boring slide show into its own artwork. She grinned when I looked her way. I should have known if anyone could make icons sexy, she could.

You can say what you like about Parisians – and doesn't everyone? – but I respect their dedication to beauty and pleasure. The talk was not of real estate and stock prices but colour, texture, technique; travels to the east, places you could see Byzantine-influenced sacred art in France such as the Sacré Cœur and the hilltop basilica in Marseille, where I barely lasted ten minutes because all around me were memorials to victims of shipwreck and drowning.

The pulse at the base of my throat wasn't going to ease until I'd got the speech over with. I looked at my watch – we'd agreed seven o'clock and that left only five minutes. Bernard was deep in conversation, describing a shape with his hands, of a Romanian domed roof, at a guess. The thought of starting the official proceedings without Geneviève and Henri concerned me and I was about to ask Philippe if he knew where they were when they breezed in, with none other than critic Pierre de Longueville and an elegant woman with a silver-grey chignon.

I clasped my trembling hands together as I went to greet them. Geneviève's smug expression suggested she regarded this as a personal victory – she had invited Longueville to every launch since she and I met, thus far without success. He was all charm as she introduced us, smiling modestly as I babbled about how delighted we were. Bernard's face lit up like a child's, knowing what this meant: Longueville had already been sent the book and he did not stoop to hatchet jobs. He either shone the light of his approval on a work or it passed unacknowledged. The woman was his wife, Marina, who was explaining her half-Romanian ancestry to me. Paris is full of people who are half this, half that – another reason I liked it.

'How interesting that you have chosen Greek Orthodox chanting,' she said, although by now the music was hard to hear. 'You do realise this is not Romanian?'

Bernard hadn't noticed anything amiss but I couldn't blame him for our blunder. With the most impeccable timing, Dédé approached us with a tray of drinks. Marina took a glass and handed one to me as if she were the host, laughing in the same deep throaty way she spoke. 'Look at your face! I am teasing about the music, can't you tell? Such things do not matter. There is only one God.'

As she and her husband spotted people they knew and headed off to join them, Geneviève touched my shoulder and raised her eyebrows. 'You're welcome,' she said, before I had a chance to speak, resentment making me clam up for longer than she was willing to wait. It was beneath her to take all the credit – they were here because of *our* book and their links to Romania. Did the woman think nothing was beyond her influence? If she did, she couldn't have been more wrong.

21

Philippe is right: it's never the things you fear that come to pass – so there's really no point worrying about the future. For a time, I stopped, because the future itself had become inconceivable to me. When I started coming here I was doing well if I could imagine getting through the day.

I needn't have worried about my speech for the launch of *Icons*. The great turnout made me rise to the occasion. Leaving the notes I had made in my bag, I made a virtue of not having been to Romania by saying how much Bernard's book made me want to go, to a murmur of assenting voices. When I stepped away from the microphone a Romanian journalist was waiting to accost me, offering to personally escort me to his country whenever I wished.

His effusiveness was delaying the start of Bernard's speech, which gave me a welcome excuse to disentangle myself. As soon as Bernard began I saw how he had won the monks over. He held the room rapt with his reverence for the icons, his respect and affection for their creators and guardians. When a photo of the mitred and heavily bearded monks came up on the wall his joke about them not being responsible for the angelic singing we had been listening to got a lot of laughs. He described bringing these little-known treasures to a wider audience as the high point of his career. He said some very generous things about me and even gave a mention to our next title on Baudelaire as art critic. This was a man I had worked with on and off for a year and had thought was an asshole. It was only later that I found out who my real friends were.

Bernard was drawing to a close when the raised voices of some teenagers on the street made him look toward the open door. Unfortunate timing for Jean-Luc Malavoine, who happened to step into the gallery at that precise moment. The only good thing was that nobody was looking at me. Fear and excitement share a lot of the symptoms brought on by seeing him again: racing heart, light head, clammy hands.

I'd been so anxious about seeing Geneviève that it hadn't occurred to me that *he* would turn up uninvited. I'd been reenacting our encounter in my head but I hadn't anticipated ever coming face to face with him again. Jean-Luc raised his hand, in apology for his lateness no doubt, but it was the gesture rock stars and big actors use to acknowledge adulation and there weren't many ordinary people who could have pulled it off without appearing utterly ridiculous. Geneviève's moue of mock disapproval turned into an indulgent maternal smile. Her boy was here.

But he looked right past her and Henri. As the gathering broke into applause at the end of Bernard's speech Jean-Luc scanned the front of the room intently, not being very subtle about it. Before he had a chance to spot me, I headed to the drinks table to check that there was still plenty of wine left. It seemed we had a celebration on our hands.

The wine was there but it was Lisette being mother. 'Where's Dédé got to?' I asked.

She went to reply then changed her mind, concentrating on pouring as if it were a life-or-death task. I didn't need to ask where Suzanne was.

I slipped down the corridor to the kitchenette and beyond it the gallery's only toilet, at some distance from the exhibition area. This was fortunate, as was the fact that nobody had needed to answer a call of nature during the speeches. From inside came the unmistakable sound of two people vigorously enjoying each other's company.

I tapped on the door as loudly as I dared and rushed away, appalled to find myself feeling turned on as well as pissed off. I didn't get five paltry minutes to relax and enjoy the unexpected success of the event. If there had been a rear exit it would have been tempting to make a run for it. But there was no way out of this.

Dédé was back at his post when I returned after turning the music back on, Lisette now selling the book with the pile beside her shrinking fast. I hadn't thought many guests would want to schlep something of that size to dinner but the heft and the hefty price tag were evidently worth it for a virtual visit to Romania, a feast for the eyes and a religious experience for those who so desired. There was a small line eager to get their copies signed by Bernard, who was wielding his Mont Blanc with a flourish.

Suzanne was willowing through the dense crowd with two wine bottles with cloth napkins tied round the necks, topping up glasses. When she shot me a glance I tried to smile naturally. Thank God she didn't know who had caught them *en flagrant délit*. I didn't want to be a hypocrite.

Philippe wound his arm around my waist, taking me doubly by surprise when I turned to him. 'Look who's here!' he said, beaming at Vanessa beside him. Despite looking far from sure she wanted to be, she'd clearly made an effort. She'd washed her hair for once and was wearing heels and a tatty lace dress that was undeniably fetching despite being too small and revealing an amateurish tattoo on her upper arm.

'It was so nice of you to come,' I told her, hoping she got what I really meant: *Thank you for doing this for him.*

Philippe kissed me, whispering, 'Congratulations! I told you everything would turn out well.' Across the room, Jean-Luc had his back to us, talking with his parents and the Longuevilles. When Suzanne reached them, she seemed in no hurry to move on. Now that some of the guests had stepped out onto the street to smoke it was easier to hear the music and snatches of conversation.

'It's extremely kind of you to invite us,' Longueville told Geneviève, 'but I'm afraid we have other plans.'

His wife Marina came over to me. 'What a wonderful party!' she said. 'I have known Bernard Ioanescu for twenty years.' She weighted her words, as if I didn't get the warning message from her penetrating gaze. 'He is a great art historian and the book is splendid. But it's not good for anyone to always get what they want.' That extraordinary laugh again. Did she think I was sleeping with Bernard? She certainly didn't need to worry about that.

Was *she*? There was nothing I could say with both my husband and hers within earshot, although they were lost in a lively discussion. 'We must go, *chéri*,' she told him. Longueville looked at his watch. 'We'll sort this out tomorrow, Philippe. But consider it a deal.'

'What deal? What's he talking about?' Geneviève demanded, as if she had some automatic right to know. A person of her standing should know that if you bring people together you have no control over what subsequently happens between them.

'Get the red dots, Suzanne,' Philippe said. 'We just sold *Fuck your Jesus!*'

There was a titter from those nearby, who gathered around to examine the wall hanging. I took advantage of the distraction to check out Jean-Luc, who had gravitated toward the youngest people in the room, some doctoral students of Bernard's from the Sorbonne who seemed to have adopted Vanessa. It hadn't occurred to me that she and Jean-Luc might even remember each other from long ago – at the very least they knew *of* each other. As I watched, Jean-Luc turned away from her and stared at me from across the room as if we were alone together. That he could be reckless was about the only thing I knew about him – apart from the obvious – but if he kept this up someone would notice. People have antennae for that; I realised from seeing Dédé and Suzanne together and from my embarrassing exchange with Marina de Longueville that I was developing one of my own, where previously I had been oblivious to others' sexual peccadilloes. Maybe it was something you could only gain by joining in.

Finding herself excluded from the crude banter, Geneviève collared her son and guided him in my direction. 'You two haven't had a chance to meet properly,' she said.

22

There was no escaping it this time. As Jean-Luc stepped forward to kiss me on both cheeks, I stood with my hands pinned to my sides. The smell of him reminded me of the first time we touched, making the tiny hairs stand up on my arms and all across my shoulders.

'Alexandra had to get this magnificent book biked to me in the end,' Geneviève said to Jean-Luc and then, to me: 'He offered to fetch a copy from your office on Friday—'

My brain whirred in panic until I concluded she wouldn't be reacquainting us if she knew we'd seen each other since the restaurant. The pattern of her Hermès scarf was searing itself into my retinas, my eyeballs aching from the effort of not staring at Jean-Luc. Not that it helped. I shifted my weight from one foot to the other, pressing my legs tight together, trying not to think what I was thinking. Not to feel so disgracefully carnal.

'I'm sorry to have put you to the trouble,' he said, lightly. 'I bumped into some old friends in the Marais and we went for a drink. By the time I left them it was too late.'

Okay, this was good. We'd be safe enough with small talk. 'So, you're back in Paris for a while?'

'That's right. I've missed it.'

'We are planning to make the most of him,' Geneviève said. 'Visits home have been low on the list of priorities.' What was so unusual about that? If the subject had come up between her and *my* mother – a possibility I did not discount – they would have agreed on this wholeheartedly. 'Can you believe he claims to be exhausted after California? From what I gather, he spent most of it diving.'

The meaning of the look he exchanged with his mother was indecipherable but its animosity took me aback. 'Oh, come on,' he said, weary now. No wonder he liked to steer clear of *Maman* if she treated him like a teenager.

'Still, diving!' I said. 'I've always wanted to try it.' I'd probably have said the same if he'd talked about jumping off a cliff. My post-speech glass of wine was almost empty and I was finally starting to relax. If they were going to bicker amongst themselves it was less likely that I would put my foot in it.

And it wasn't me who did.

'Your father and I met Alexandra's mother when she was over from California,' Geneviève said. 'She was with us the night you arrived home.'

'Does she still live in the place you grew up?' Jean-Luc asked me.

It was a general enough question that could have come from anyone, but something about the way he asked strongly suggested prior knowledge. Geneviève picked up on this immediately, looking from one of us to the other. Jean-Luc hadn't even been introduced to my mother and had supposedly never so much as had a conversation with me. At least he hadn't mentioned the red lighthouse at Battery Point.

'Yes, actually,' I replied. 'A small town at the very opposite end of California to where you were.' I proceeded to explain my origins in excessive detail because naturally *he did not already know this*. Over-elaborating is a classic liars' mistake and I wasn't even lying. Then again, there are so many kinds of lies. Barefaced. White. Transparent. Lies of omission. Deliberately giving a false impression.

By now, for some unaccountable reason, Jean-Luc was holding forth on North Pacific currents and weather systems, all of it more technical than I could easily follow but still I listened, entranced. I was used to the physical presence of the ocean, its representation in art and literature, not to thinking of it as something that could be explained. He sounded odd, like an automaton or the disembodied voice on the severe weather warnings that cut in on American radio stations. I almost started giggling when I realised what he was playing at. And sure enough, his mother, unfamiliar with the area and the science, was soon bored into submission and went to find Henri.

To avoid being seen alone with Jean-Luc, I excused myself, saying there were a few people I needed to say hello to before everyone started to drift off. The next time I looked around the room, he was gone.

The last few stragglers were upending their glasses, still deep in conversation. I sent Philippe and the others ahead to claim the table Geneviève had booked at a nearby Italian restaurant, without asking any of us if we wanted to eat dinner with them. My mumbled excuses for remaining behind went unquestioned because in a small company like ours everyone had to pitch in. As I placed some dirty glasses by the sink, Lisette followed me in with a few more.

'Are you still here?' I said. 'Go home, seriously. Suzanne can deal with this in the morning. Get a cab, you look exhausted.'

She gave me a little smile and patted her waistline. 'You guessed, didn't you?'

'Yes, I guessed. Congratulations,' I said. 'That's wonderful news!'

From the kitchen I heard the last guests call their thanks and goodbyes into the empty, echoing space. I leaned against the wall and closed my eyes, craving a moment alone in order to face the second half of the evening.

Before long I looked up to see Jean-Luc standing there. 'You came back,' I said, pointlessly.

'It's okay,' he said. 'They've all gone. I locked the door.'

As he came toward me I extended my arm like a traffic cop. I couldn't handle him coming any closer.

Now *that's* a lie.

'What made you come here tonight?' I said. 'In front of my husband and your parents. Surely you must realise—'

He touched my face as if he hadn't heard me, like the first time, threading his fingers through my hair. I didn't notice him breach the boundary I had set until it was too late. We were kissing deeply, a klaxon sounding in the back of my head that my body couldn't seem to hear. It's not easy, the moral high ground, especially if you've discovered you prefer the underside. He backed me up to the counter, pressing himself hard against my hip, and from behind came the muffled shattering of wine glasses in their thick plastic crates. I pushed him away. The more I tried to talk myself out of it, the more I wanted him.

So I'd have to try talking *him* out of it.

'I can't explain what happened on Friday,' I said. 'I don't know what got into me.'

He burst out laughing and I heated up so violently my face must have matched the colour of my lipstick. His juvenile humour should have brought me to my senses; and it did in a way, just not the right way. I was trying to give him the brush-off; instead it felt like foreplay.

'You haven't been thinking about me?' he said. 'Because I haven't been able to think about anything but you since that night in the restaurant, and then Friday... It's driving me out of my mind.'

'Of course I've been thinking about it.' I deliberately said *it* instead of *you* but it sounded more loaded, not less, as if I thought about sex constantly the way men are supposed to. 'All I mean is that it shouldn't have happened. I'm not blaming you. You're young and you were trying your luck. It was up to me to say no.'

'You regret it?' he said, with a look of dismay that dismantled me.

There was no simple answer to that. 'Listen, for what it was, it was fantastic.' It didn't seem fair to let him think he'd put in an unsatisfactory performance.

'So *what was it?*'

My mind filled with explanations which would sound sad and desperate. I couldn't tell him he'd caught me at a vulnerable point where lots of things in my life were up in the air. I couldn't tell him – and probably didn't need to – that he'd caught me like a bitch in heat. Ashamed as I was, I secretly liked this new, disinhibited version of myself. I admired her ability to let loose. 'It was just sex, Jean-Luc. A crazy, spontaneous one-off. These things happen.'

I was trying to be delicate to spare his feelings but my woman of the world act wouldn't fool anyone. I've never liked one night stands. My biggest problem was that I couldn't bring myself to say that the encounter had meant nothing to me. Maybe he would have dropped it if I had.

'I've slept with a lot of girls,' he said, apparently unfamiliar with the concept of *too much information*. I noted 'girls' and wondered what it meant that I was not one. And then I had my answer. 'But I've never felt a... connection like I did with you.' It thrilled me that he had to search for the word to describe it. He looked at me, suddenly unsure of himself, and I felt an overwhelming surge of emotion wrapped in sensation. 'Are you saying it's always like that?' he asked.

I shook my head. Just as there are various echelons of lying, so it is with betrayal. And although we did no more than hold each other this time, it was the greater betrayal by far.

23

The others were in high spirits when I finally joined them on the terrace of the Italian place near Saint-Germain-des-Prés, slipping into the vacant seat opposite Henri.

'Here, Alexandra, we saved you some.' Philippe fished the bottle of champagne out of the ice bucket next to the table and poured me a large glass, managing to drip just as much water over the tablecloth. 'Another!' he called out to the waiter. I wasn't hungry but ordered the plate of antipasti, which was some of the best in the neighbour-hood. It suited me fine that they were drunk, except for Geneviève, who is naturally the *must not lose control* type. Mercifully she was on my side of the table at the other end, so not only could I not talk to her, I couldn't see her very well either. None of this was happenstance, of that I was certain.

This should have been such a great night for me, for all of us. We had never held a launch which generated this kind of buzz, for the title I would least have expected and just when we needed it most. Bernard and Alain were beside themselves with excitement. Philippe was still brimming with delight over the sale of *Fuck your Jesus* to Pierre de Longueville and was in his element rubbing Henri's nose in it. Henri had advised him against representing Nasim Asradi, thinking it a big risk, but now offered congratulations, slapping him on the back like a giant bear, saying, 'You were right not to listen to me this time, but don't make a habit of it!' Their close friendship seemed a rare thing between men; there was nothing they wouldn't do for each other. I felt tremendous affection toward Henri for the part he played in Philippe's life, seeing him through some hard times before I was there to take care of him. It touched me to see them together, their dark heads greying now, to hear their Niçois twang. They laughed at the same things. It was only their choice of wives that set them apart – I could only speculate about *other women* but it wasn't hard to imagine Henri resorting to the occasional indiscretion. The Malavoines had been married for ever so maybe it was different for Geneviève, but I didn't feel my marriage of five years could compete with our husbands' friendship. Philippe had known her a long time too and she could be very short with him sometimes, or lump him and Henri together as if they were the same person.

'If you must keep referring to that monstrosity at the gallery, could you at least leave out the deplorable name?' she said, mortified by stares from a family of Spaniards at the next table, although the teenage son was finding it very funny. Philippe's apology sounded more humouring than sincere to me but she accepted it. Following the Longuevilles' strategic getaway and the display of tension between her and Jean-Luc, Geneviève had to be as keen as I was for the evening to end.

After dinner we set off in opposite directions, Philippe and I heading toward Saint-Sulpice in near silence, first through streets of crowded and noisy bars and restaurants then deserted ones lined with designer stores. We liked to pause and admire window displays which caught our eye – they always looked more dramatic in the dark. When one of us stopped, the other did too. In one window of the Annick Goutal perfume store a huge fork of lightning with a dozen tributaries advertised a new fragrance. Philippe did nothing to hide his preference for the image on the other side of the door, of a topless young woman with her arms draped sensuously across her body. She was slim and small-breasted, hipbones jutting out above low-cut jeans. She was nothing like me.

Did she remind him of Nico? The questions that had been boiling away in my head were no longer just mine to ask. Unless I confessed to my infidelity, what right did I have to demand who Philippe's lover was, what it was like when he touched her, whether his feelings went beyond lust? If we could have this unspeakable conversation, there was a chance our marriage could survive what we were doing to it. If it didn't, we could find ourselves back where we used to be, but older, more disillusioned than ever, maybe deciding our lives weren't meant to be shared with anyone. I'd just told Jean-Luc I couldn't do it again. You can only use the *moment of folly* excuse once. How would Philippe feel if he found out I'd been with another man? I couldn't stand the idea that he would be okay with it.

I was pretty sure he wouldn't, and if he found out who that man was he wouldn't believe me capable of such unscrupulous behaviour. He was forever teasing me for my Anglo-Saxon rule-keeping and fair play, the way I'd rather ask for change than leave a stingy tip and scold him for parking where it wasn't allowed. He wouldn't be so amused to find I'd done a U-turn on something that mattered.

When we got home he wanted to make love, his good humour unaffected by my inability to share it. God forbid that he was suggesting sex in an attempt to rescue my mood. Blocking out the imprint of Jean-Luc against me in the kitchen, first I resisted Philippe's attempts to pull me on top of him, then the light pressure of his hand on the top of my head. The thought of that made me gag. His ardour noticeably diminished by now, I performed – I can think of no other word – a blind hand job, delaying looking at him until the final moment. My speed increased with the urgency of his breathing but it seemed to be taking for ever and was making my fingers and my elbow ache. I looked just in time to see him open his eyes with a startled expression like he didn't know what was coming. My hand escaped just in time but some got on my nightdress. I got up from the bed and peeled it off like I'd been sprayed with battery acid.

I did not sleep; how could I have when a few miles away, someone lay awake thinking of me? Someone who said he could think of nothing and no one else. Jean-Luc had laid his head on my shoulder when I told him it was just a little crush and it would pass. Now I was lying *and* patronising. The truth is, I was cheating on them both.

24

The next morning I lost my footing in the Jardin du Luxembourg as I took a curve on the west side too fast. My leg slid out from under me and I crashed down, breaking the skin on my left calf and embedding the dust and germs of a hot summer into my flesh. There were fewer runners than normal. The sky was grey and over-cast, typical of the days when Paris seems to say, *It's not all la vie est belle, my friend, make no mistake about it.*

At the sound of rapid strides slowing to a halt I turned to see none other than Mr Coffee/Quickie crouching down to enquire after my welfare. '*Aïe!* Are you okay?'

My leg was an ugly sight. The gravel which hadn't broken the skin had left a bumpy pattern around the weeping mess in the middle. I made a face and tried to get up but it stung like hell and my ankle was throbbing. In the end I did need the man's help to stand. Ignoring protestations that I would be fine, he walked me very slowly back to the gates where our previous exchange had taken place. He told me his name was Daniel and I reluc-tantly told him mine.

'What you need now, *Alexandra*, is something to take your mind off it…' There it was again, that flirty gleam-in-the-eye tone that suggested we'd both be missing out if we didn't follow our outdoor exertions with some more behind closed doors. Maybe he thought I would do it to be polite.

'You know, I really don't,' I said. 'You've been very kind but could you possibly find someone else to hit on? How about her?' I pointed as a toned twenty-something in tiny shorts passed us, a long blonde ponytail bouncing out the back of her baseball cap. Nobody raised an eyebrow about a man with a much younger woman. Barely a week had passed since the first time this guy tried it on with forty-year-old me, not setting his sights too high. Then I'd been offended that I could pass for a woman who *might*. Now I was a woman who *had*.

Philippe had left me a note on the dining table that read like a telegram.

REVIEW FIGARO BRAVO KISSES

If it hadn't been for my injury I would have run to the nearest *tabac* for the newspaper, but I booted up my laptop and there it was: an impressive spread in the *Littérature* section, our biggest by far, complete with Bernard's photo, the book jacket and another of the icons. Pierre de Longueville had struck exactly the right balance between aesthetics and religious significance. Lisette called to say she was fielding calls from journalists who suddenly wanted interviews with Bernard after ignoring our press releases for weeks. A TV arts channel was offering to pay for him to return to the monastery with a film crew. Turned out icons were about to become cool and we had absolutely no idea. 'I thought we could set up the reception area as an interview room,' Lisette suggested, since we couldn't afford to do it in a hotel. 'We'd have to station someone downstairs to make sure nobody barged in, but I think it could work.'

I told her I'd be at the office as soon as possible.

Extracting specks of dirt and grit from my skin with tweezers was a horrible job but I got through it, grateful that my tetanus shot was up to date. My wails must have been louder than I realised because Vanessa stumbled out of her room, glaring. 'What the—?' She saw my leg and screwed her face up. 'Yuck!' she said. 'That is *gross*.'

'Thanks for the sympathy, Vanessa. I didn't set out to do this.' The wound was finally clean and painted with iodine, which just left the rest of me. 'Somehow I've got to wash – I can't go to work in this state. Especially not today.'

I pulled my hair into a twist and fastened it. Not great but it would do. There was no way I could shower without getting my leg wet. Vanessa was chewing the inside of her mouth. 'Take a bath and prop it up on the side,' she said, before swanning out.

As I was in a hurry I only ran enough water to cover my body. Getting in wasn't difficult but as soon as I did, I saw that getting out with my bad leg on the outer edge was going to be impossible. When Philippe and I had the bathroom remodelled we didn't think we'd be needing grab rails any time soon.

I had just realised I was going to have to ask for Vanessa's help when she walked back in without knocking. Irrationally, given that she was about to see me naked, I crossed my arms over my front. I'm not proud of this, but I was relieved she wasn't a waif like the girl in the perfume ad.

'I've come to wash your foot. This one,' she touched my big toe. There was a pause long enough for me to know this was nothing to do with my injury.

'What is it, Vanessa?'

'I didn't only come to the party for Dad, you know.'

'I know, I was pleased you came. You coped really well – it's not easy when you don't know anyone.'

'That was a good thing! It made a nice change from being slut-shamed. It's all over Facebook what happened with Boris, but you're the only one who knows the whole story. My mom didn't want to know – she never has. But I can talk to you.' Abandoning my modesty, I covered my face as my shoulders began to shake.

'Oh, shit,' she said. 'Did I make it worse? If it hurts that badly you should really take something.'

25

Normally I would have been delighted to see Emily in Paris but I'd never been good at hiding things from her. She's been my only real confidante ever since I turned up at Coldwater twelve years old, foreign and friendless.

After several days my leg was still not in great shape. The grazes were itching as they began to heal and my ankle ached, although it hadn't warranted a trip to the emergency room. Over the years I'd come to dislike hospitals more and more after having my pelvic organs scraped, lasered and unstuck in London, New York and twice in Paris.

I certainly couldn't make it to our meeting place on foot. Walking around a city is like the movies: a million fleeting moments, there and gone. The Metro is more like the theatre: individuals sharing a confined space for different periods, their physical presence, expressions and silence as eloquent as anything they might say. Once on the train, I didn't even consider getting the novel out of my bag, knowing that I'd only read the same line over and over. I'd recently purchased Grégoire Delacourt's *La liste de mes envies*. How many times had I seen that title without it striking me in any way, the idea of listing one's desires? I wasn't sure I'd ever truly had any and now it wouldn't be a list. There'd only be one entry.

Instead I looked at the people surrounding me: glued to their phones, staring into space, living their lives. I've always wondered what it must be like to be in someone else's head, how it would feel to be a good person with a clear conscience, who's never mean or bitter, who's never caused anyone pain. There can't be many people like that, can there? Or maybe I'm fooling myself. Maybe there are. Emily is like that.

I ask myself if, on average, other people are happier than me. I don't mean since all this, of course, but in general. How joy feels to them. Sadness. Grief. We all have a pent-up invisible interior and yet we're constantly taken aback when someone springs a breach and it comes flooding out, sometimes when it's too late. Take my mom and me; nobody would have the faintest idea what we carry with us. Before I was old enough to want a child I'd seen what it was like to lose one. It's still the worst thing I can imagine. I almost don't have to.

As lost in *rêverie* as I was *en réalité*, I almost missed my stop. The restaurant where Emily and I were meeting for lunch was uncomfortably close to Malavoine territory; it wouldn't have been my choice but she was on a tight schedule. With ten minutes to kill I lingered in front of the Wall of Peace at the south end of the Champ de Mars and looked at the forest of pillars, feeling empty of the reflections they were designed to inspire, for all that I was greatly in need of serenity. I'd been morphing into some-body new at such a rate that I hardly recognised myself. Sharing the blessing of a doting mother and two older sisters, it was Emily who initiated me into every aspect of being a woman – how could she fail to notice?

Ahead of me a man was walking a large white poodle which was oblivious that it was shitting within view of one of the world's most famous landmarks. The owner didn't stop to pick it up.

To my left a group of men in their early twenties were bantering and kicking a ball about like big kids. Anxious not to be caught staring, I snuck a few glances at them from behind my sunglasses, trying to establish whether I'd had a buried penchant for younger men all along. They were a typically Parisian mix: fair, dark, Arab, black, a couple of them very good-looking. The bare-chested ones with T-shirts hanging from their belt loops were honed and muscular. The Moroccan-looking one, the smallest, gave me a cheeky smile and apologised when the breeze sent the ball my way with a cloud of dust, making me leap sideways. They were full of energy and exuded a kind of brutish masculinity that I registered without being stirred by it. Before Jean-Luc I doubt I would have paid them any attention at all.

At the brasserie Emily had chosen there was one table left on the terrace and I was debating whether to take it when she appeared. My eyes pricked and I hugged her for so long she had to tell me to let go. 'I hope your friends don't mind me dragging you away,' I said. It was a birthday trip for one of them who was turning forty.

'Not at all. I'm relieved not to have to stand in that queue for the Eiffel Tower. They know I've done it before.'

Emily and I came to Paris together on a school trip in 1989, my first visit to France. The tower was brightly lit up for the bicentenary of the French Revolution and we were fifteen years old, the perfect age to appreciate such glitziness. Everything was as glamorous as we'd hoped and it made London seem so grey and drab. The language I'd loved already, but that was the day my love of the country took hold.

At Emily's insistence, the waiter brought us two glasses of champagne and after he'd stopped by three times to take our order, we agreed to stop talking and concentrate. In the end we ordered four dishes that sounded good and I said Emily could take her pick when the food arrived. I'm not fussy – at school I would often finish hers.

As the menus were removed, I picked up my glass and realised I'd downed half of it in one. 'So who are you here with, anyone I know?'

From the way Emily pressed her lips together I instantly knew that one of them was Jonathan's sister. She and Emily were college friends and set me up with him when we were both living in New York. Abandoning my plans to become a real American, I'd moved back to England to be with him. He was so persuasive that I convinced myself it was romantic not to get married until we were expecting a baby, not realising he meant *unless*. He'd done me a favour in the long run. If there's no love, there's no point in pretending.

Before I could forget I handed Emily the gift for my goddaughter. It was a top from Zadig & Voltaire with the metallic rivet wings on the back, an extravagance, but one I knew she'd love. Cassie was born not long after Jonathan and I broke up and Emily knew I needed something in my life that stood a chance of working out. And it did; I adored Cassie, now eleven, visiting them in England at least once a year. And Cassie loved to show off about her American godmother who lived in Paris.

Emily chose the terrine with fig chutney, leaving me with six Cancale oysters. It would have been like her to crack an aphrodisiac joke, but I was spared. As I squeezed the half lemon wrapped in muslin, my mouth was watering already. The acidity of the Muscadet we'd chosen complemented the mineral saltiness of the oysters to perfection and a syllable of delight escaped me as I tipped my head back, feeling the sun on my face. These days I was more open to pleasure than I would ever have believed possible.

26

It must have felt like twenty questions. I grilled Emily about her weekend in Paris, the children, her family, who took me in countless times in the school break when my mother didn't come through with the plane tickets my father paid for.

At the time I just got on with it because that's what kids do. But when I look back it's like someone wrenched my heart out with their bare hands and pummelled it before putting it back. And although I got used to it, it never became my normal, not when we used to be a family who baked cookies and went to the beach and took long walks in the forest. The Olympics were held in Los Angeles in the summer of '84 and as I danced and turned cartwheels along the trunks of fallen redwoods my dad put on his hopeless American accent: 'Representing the United States of America, Alexandra Folgate of Crescent City, California.' It's rose tinted, I know, but I only remember good things from *before*.

Emily told me her husband was being made redundant but had some leads so they weren't overly worried. My mouth pulled when she said, 'life goes on.'

Well, yes, you can always fall back on that one. Except that it doesn't, not always.

The chicken and the salmon both looked delicious, so we swapped plates halfway through, something I wouldn't even have done with Philippe. We attracted one or two amused glances but I was past caring. It had taken me ten years to realise I was living in a city where beneath a veneer of conformity a lot of people did exactly what they pleased.

We were never going to get through the whole meal without Emily asking about me.

'So are you feeling better after the operation?'

I was, so much so that I'd started to take it for granted. 'The doctor said I'll be fine for a while now. The new fish hook will help.'

Emily smiled – for different reasons we were both fans of the T-shape miracle gizmo. By this point I was desensitised to gynaecological indignities and having instruments and devices inserted into me, but it wasn't a subject I cared to discuss over lunch.

There really are a *lot* of things I don't like to talk about.

The book! I hadn't mentioned *Icons* yet. The monastery were allegedly considering a documentary presented by Baptiste Genevois. He knew no more about icons than I did before editing the book but it wouldn't occur to anyone to doubt his authority. Male TV presenters didn't have to be young or attractive though he certainly was and very engaging with it; the ideal choice to bring a niche subject to life, with Bernard as the main expert interviewee. There was a growing hope that none of us at Editions Gallici was willing to admit to – that it might all work out. We could do a mass market tie-in and the effect on sales would be dramatic. Emily was smiling and nodding a lot. 'And then are you off to Nice as usual?'

I hadn't given our vacation a thought but the prospect of Philippe disappearing down south – hopefully taking Vanessa with him – flashed up in my mind first like a mirage, then something from which I needed to be rescued. Which was the lesser evil, to go or to stay behind?

'Because of *Icons* we can't shut up shop completely like we usually do – it's unlikely anything will happen before September but someone should be in Paris just in case. It looks like I'm that someone.'

'So is Philippe going without you?' Seeing my expression, Emily's eyebrows dipped: it was a minute adjustment but I knew she was on to me. '*Oh*,' she said. 'Last time we spoke I thought there might be something wrong.'

She'd sprung her Paris trip on me the day after the launch and I'd had to deal with back to back conversations with her and my mother. In the circumstances it wasn't surprising my behaviour seemed a little strange.

'The atmosphere's so tense with Vanessa staying,' I said. 'She and Philippe argue all the time and guess who ends up in the middle? He told her she reminds him of Brigitte, the way she's always spoiling for a fight. She can't stand her mother so that didn't go down too well.'

'Maybe that's the only way she can deal with the whole situation. It's never been easy on her, has it?'

I was quick to agree. I'm not sure any of us can help the way we are, especially at seventeen. 'But Philippe's right about how volatile she is, even with me. One minute she's sharing very personal stuff and she was lovely when I hurt my foot. Then yesterday it was back to shouting and calling me an interfering control freak. She's either really affectionate or really spiteful and I never know which it's going to be. It's like you used to say about yours when they were small – she's desperate for attention and there are various ways of getting it.'

Emily listened knowingly. Though everything I'd said about Philippe and Vanessa was perfectly factual it made a liar of me. It was *a* reason, but it wasn't *the* reason. The terrace was emptying around us in the lull between lunch and the exhausted tourists' afternoon pit-stop, the tables a mess of balled-up napkins, breadcrumbs and red wine rings. I persuaded Emily we should order something sweet to follow.

'Philippe and I are having problems,' I blurted out before the dessert had time to arrive. 'He's having an affair.'

In our friendship it used to be Emily who said and did the unexpected. If we'd been in England or the States she would have known how to react: the way most people would react. Her hesitation didn't surprise me – nobody ever really knew where I was coming from, and I wasn't sure either: I'd never considered myself properly American or British, and I certainly wasn't French. Emily looked around as if seeking confirmation of our whereabouts; a city with customs she didn't understand. She was still a tourist here; God knows what I'd become.

'Oh no, Alex,' she said. 'How did you find out?'

'My mother helpfully pointed it out to me during her visit,' I said. 'You know how she is. But I'd had my suspicions for a while.'

'Are you sure it's true?'

'Yes. Her name is Nicoletta. I called her number from the office – I don't know what I was hoping to achieve. Anyway, thank God she didn't pick up – there was a voice-mail message in Italian and I could only make out a couple of words. She has a sexy voice, kind of husky,' I added, piling my miseries high.

'What are you going to do?' Emily glanced at me. 'I mean…'

'Is it normal here? Are you asking if I'm okay with it?'

The muscles jumping on her forearms showed me Emily was making fists in her lap. Criticising someone's partner – even your best friend's – is a risky business. Loyalties are the joists hidden deep in a wall: where they lie and the direction they take invisible until you take a sledgehammer and see what's holding the whole thing up.

But Emily was ever the diplomat. 'I've always liked Philippe,' she said, 'I can't believe he'd do this. You're so good for each other. I thought you were happy together.'

'I thought so too. I didn't notice it had changed until it was too late.'

Emily came round to my side of the table and hugged me. That's how we first became friends, when we had neighbouring beds in the dorm and she couldn't stand to hear me cry at night. 'You know how dreadful I was feeling last winter, and all the worry about work at the same time and then the surgery... All of that was tough on Philippe and he has problems of his own. There's been a huge hike in the rent on the gallery and the gamble he took on that exhibition has paid off in some ways but not others. He's been there for me more than I have for him.'

'But that doesn't make it okay to cheat on you! Why are you making excuses for him?'

Returning to her seat, Emily attacked a profiterole like she was spearing his balls. I could have left it at that but hypocrisy spoils the taste of chocolate and cream. One of the few people who really cared about me was about to question whether she knew me at all.

It's very liberating that I don't have to worry about what you think of me. You didn't know me before, you don't know me outside this room. Our starting point each time is wherever I am.

I took a deep breath, knowing I was about to see Emily's face change. 'I've slept with someone else too.'

'You did *what?*'

'I wasn't planning on telling you.' And this was why. Emily looked like a detective who's just stumbled across the tiny detail that tilts an investigation the other way. When it transpires that the victim is herself not blameless.

'God, Alex, I was surprised about Philippe but this! Sorry,' she said, holding up her hand, 'I need a moment to take this in.'

When it was just Philippe screwing around, all was black and white. I liked it better that way.

'You'd better tell me about it. Were you getting your own back?'

'I *was* distraught about Philippe, but it wasn't like that. It was just the one time. I mean, not that it makes a difference, of course. I shouldn't have done it at all.' Now I blew out hard. 'You must think less of me, but it's a huge relief to get it off my chest.'

'Look, I can't lie. This is a shock. But you must have felt so betrayed. What you did is understandable, in a way. He was doing the same. You're only human.'

We're all so *pitifully* human.

'Who was it?'

'Someone much younger. He came on to me. The attraction was very strong.'

She tilted her head, studying me. '*How* much younger?'

I winced. 'He's twenty-three. I know, I *know*!'

'Bloody hell! Please tell me it wasn't your intern?' she said.

'No, absolutely not!' Wow. My best friend was ready to believe anything of me now. I moved on quickly from my indignation, given the further details I wasn't prepared to reveal.

'Is it someone you're going to run into again?'

'No. Well, I already have, unexpectedly. He knows I think it was a mistake. You're always saying I overthink everything. Not this time I didn't.'

'So it's not going any further?'

'No, definitely not. I've told him so. I could hardly complain about Philippe if I was doing it too.' My lapse was superseded by my resolve, which had a satisfyingly moral feel, if only because it placed me above Philippe, who kept going back for more.

'That's just as well. Because whatever's wrong with your marriage both of you having affairs isn't going to fix it. This really isn't like you.'

The times I've heard that. Maybe because she was reassured that I wasn't about to destroy my entire life, Emily gave in to curiosity, lowering her voice with a guilty expression.

'So, what was it *like* doing it with someone so young? I'd be terrified of them seeing my body. You're going to tell me he's unbelievably gorgeous, aren't you?'

'That's part of the problem. He really is. He made me feel so *good* about myself. It was the best sex ever, totally off the charts. Unfortunately!' We were both laughing helplessly now. 'Payback time for all your stories,' I said. 'Bet you never thought *that* would happen.' Emily was into sex way before me and she never used to hold back on the detail. One way and another, I had a complex about it before I got started.

'I'm even more worried now. I mean, if it was *that* good...'

'It was better.'

Now Emily gave me a stern look. 'Listen, I'm pleased for you. Oh dear, that sounds awful! But I can tell you're

157

tempted to do it again – if you could see the look on your face.' My gaze cut away to the table. 'But you can't! You and Philippe will get through this somehow. I've seen how things have changed since you got together – you have to try and talk things over, go to counselling if you need to. You'd be risking so much compared to this kid. He's only *twenty-three*, for crying out loud, all he wants is a good shag! This is just a game to him.'

That's what I thought, at the very beginning. But when I recalled what passed between Jean-Luc and me after the launch, I almost argued back. Emily was wrong about something else too. The part where she said I had the most to lose.

27

It was an unknown number but I knew it was Jean-Luc. And knowing he could only have got mine from Geneviève's phone I could hardly bring myself to read the message, looking all around me even though I was alone in the apartment.

It would have been best for him not to contact me at all, although I hadn't specifically asked him not to. Strange as it may be for someone in my line of work, I've always been wary of words. The written kind can leave a trail or fall into the wrong hands. And spoken words are live ammo that can damage things between people, shrapnel lodging in the memory with the potential to break loose. *Don't you call me Mom.*

Not that thoughts can't be as lethal, but if they remain thoughts and you can keep the lid on, you're only harming yourself. Well, the lid's off now.

Must see you, only to talk. JL.

Oh, please, as if *I* was the one born yesterday! I stared at the solitary speech bubble. The only sensible option was to press delete and make like I'd never received it. My finger hovered over the screen (I wasn't of the thumb generation); I was standing in the same spot where I'd spied on Philippe, scrolling through his exchanges with Nico. If I replied to Jean-Luc it would become a conversation like theirs, and about what, exactly? I'd said what I had to say, or rather, all I could. I wasn't in a position to go sending messages like *I want you*.

Jean-Luc looked tired at the launch, as Geneviève mentioned, and older than before. I'd put that down to the smarter clothes he was wearing that night: black jeans, linen jacket, a blue shirt open at the neck. But what if it wasn't just a line that he'd been lying awake thinking about me? He was on the verge of tears when I told him I had no intention of sleeping with him again. I imagined a terribly French star-crossed love story in which I was no more than a bit part: maybe he'd just been ditched by the girl of his dreams in LA and had returned to Paris broken-hearted. The romp with me was supposed to get it out of his system but it turned out more complicated; he didn't just like the taste of my mouth, my breasts, my *sexe*, he liked *me*. It wasn't for long but we did talk first, about art and monasteries! He liked my body just fine but it couldn't realistically be the main attraction for someone his age who'd 'had a lot of girls'. Maybe he did need someone to talk to. Vanessa had confided in me.

I might have a gift with younger people I never guessed at. Or maybe individuals who were a bit unbalanced sensed that we had something in common.

Jean-Luc would be staring at his phone, waiting for a reply. When I tried to picture his surroundings it brought home to me how little I knew about him. What did he do all day apart from *think about me*? When he said that, I believed it. If I didn't answer he might feel I'd been using him for sex. Unwitnessed as I was, my face caught fire. If there was something serious on his mind it was better that he spoke with me than end up telling anyone else what had happened. I'm foolish enough to do stupid things but not enough to be unaware of the consequences. The idea of me as a predator was ridiculous but I was well aware how this might look. The one combination that wasn't big in Paris was the older woman and the much younger man. *Go figure.* And where Jean-Luc and I were concerned that wasn't the worst thing about it.

Once I crossed that line between respectability and this new incomprehensible place, I couldn't win. My feelings were as strong as Victor Hugo's when he wrote those beautiful lines to his fiancée, Adèle; as real as Philippe's when he copied them out for me to read on a train. But it wasn't romantic, poetic love consuming me to the point that I could barely function.

Philippe had shown no sign whatsoever of being in the throes of passion or crisis. In fact, it was his disconcertingly normal behaviour that allowed me to spend so long in denial. If he really thought cheating on me was no big deal then I was wrong about what we had together. Maybe I'd been wrong about everything all along. It wasn't as if I could explain my detour out of character. How was it possible to care about my marriage and be so powerfully attracted to another man? My best friend had warned me not to do this, not because she judged me but because she could see better than me where it was headed.

I had to find the courage to talk to Philippe. As Emily said, reciprocal infidelity wouldn't solve anything. At one point in my attempts to exonerate myself I even blamed Christine for planting the idea in my subconscious. *Nothing to stop you doing the same.*

Except that it wasn't the same – I can't seem to do anything the easy way. If it was revenge I wanted or sex on the side I could have gone to a bar in an unfamiliar neighbourhood and responded to a stranger's advances – I got those looks sometimes. He'd fuck me several ways, I'd forget my old hang-ups and suck him off, let him come on my face if that's what he wanted. Afterward, I'd dress silently in his apartment or hotel room and steal away without him ever asking my name. Tawdry. Dirty. Just like me and Jean-Luc, in theory.

However hard it proved – and I never doubted it would be – I had to get over this episode with him before I could face Philippe. If I wanted our old life back, I had to let these fantasies go and start behaving like my old self. Too bad if it wasn't the real me. I didn't know myself the way you're supposed to by forty, and if this was how it felt, I wasn't sure I wanted to.

A good twenty minutes had passed since Jean-Luc texted me. I decided it was best to get it over with. OK, *now. Where?* I replied.

Our apartment was a generous size, a hundred and twenty square metres in Paris-speak. Spacious until it comes to pacing, that is. By the time I had circled the living room and hallway five times it felt more like the maid's room up in the attic. I considered going up there – those confines had become intimately associated with this whole mess. But I couldn't risk it. There might not be a signal and what's more, I didn't have the energy. That afternoon I was seeing the author of our Baudelaire title. It was a routine meeting but this was my career, which suddenly seemed less precarious than the rest of my life, the one thing that anchored me. No doubt the great poet would have found my scruples comically tame, what with his laudanum addiction and predilections for debauchery and vice. They had, however, killed him.

28

When Jean-Luc's second text arrived I couldn't help thinking of sandy-haired Daniel from the Jardin du Luxembourg, he of the conveniently located love nest. Inexplicably, the rendezvous Jean-Luc had given me was on the western edge of the 19th arrondissement. Still, it was vastly preferable to anywhere I risked bumping into Geneviève. Paris isn't very big to start with and a small world gets smaller when you have something to hide.

On the Metro a young woman wearing vertiginous nude stilettos and three clashing shades of pink was conducting a furious argument, barking into her phone in an Eastern European language, letting go of the chrome pole to slice through the air. I left the train in a wave of people heading one way, to be replaced by another, everyone struggling with cases and strollers, feeling an urgent need to be somewhere we were not. Where were we all going? Back to work, on vacation, shopping. It was too late for lunch. To meet a lover: to kiss them passionately and not care who was watching, to tell them it was over and that it wasn't them.

That's how it had felt with Jean-Luc after the launch. I wasn't just saying it was a mistake and I couldn't do it again. It felt like I was telling him it was over. Why had I agreed to see him when there was nothing else to say? I could only hope I'd wake up and pull myself together.

I changed lines and emerged at Stalingrad, the area itself a battleground in its chaos and ugliness, with traffic pouring in from every angle. It was also swarming with people, some heading for the canalside beach that the City set up, along with the main one on the banks of the Seine, for those who didn't have the means or sense to leave for the summer.

The address Jean-Luc had given me was off the rue d'Aubervilliers, close to the railroad leading out of the city to the northeast. This was a very different Paris from the *beaux quartiers* I knew or even the nearby Canal Saint-Martin, where I used to take solitary Sunday afternoon walks before it became a mecca for hipsters. The place I was looking for now was next to a kebab joint frequented by scowling men who were leaning against the wall smoking and staring at me. Outside someone had dumped an ancient bathtub and toilet with the word *merde* scrawled across the lid. The doors were open and a young man greeted me as he wheeled a moped with a pizza delivery box out onto the street. A fusion of samba and French rap coming from different apartments filled the neglected courtyard, accompanying another heated discussion in a language I assumed was Arabic. As I searched for the right staircase, two contractors dressed in dusty work gear emerged from one of the lobbies hauling the cracked sink which would complete the set on the sidewalk. They too stared at me, standing there with my briefcase.

I needed to go where they'd come from, they told me, right to the top. It was like being back on the servants' staircase in my building but even more treacherous. After my running accident I was still nervous and had no choice but to grab the filthy banister as I went up, dirt ingraining my palm. The wooden stairs were worn diagonal on the lower floors. On the third I passed an apartment which had been completely gutted, with bare electric cables dangling from exposed beams. Nothing about the neighbourhood or the building made me want to stick around.

'You came.' Jean-Luc hadn't shaved in days, reminding me of the night he showed up in that restaurant, eclipsing a roomful of people who had to try. When he pushed the hair out of his eyes I had to turn away like someone was shining a flashlight in my face. He looked more devastating every single time.

Who knows how long we might have stood there, drinking each other in.

'Can I come in?' He stood aside and I skirted past to avoid any physical contact although as I'd already found out, with him it didn't have to be sex to drag me in deeper.

'Do you live here? It's quite a contrast to the Seventh.'

He gave a sniff of contempt. 'I lasted a week at my parents'. It's so dead round there – and then there's my mother, she's always preferred her fantasy version of me. This belongs to my friend László. Do you smoke?' he said.

I hoped he was talking about tobacco because there was a distinct aroma of weed in the air. When Jean-Luc offered me a light, I took the book of matches and did it myself to dispel the reminder of Philippe the evening Vanessa arrived. 'I can't stay, I have a meeting this afternoon.'

Hearing my tone, I belatedly hit on a plan: to substitute Jean-Luc's fantasy version with the real me, accentuated for effect. Brusque and frosty, borderline rude. Nobody could find that sexy.

And anyway, who asks their lover over without picking up their dirty laundry? The deep blue shirt he'd worn to the launch was lying on the floor with several pairs of socks and boxer shorts. My resolve evaporated at the memory of his sculpted backside as I'd watched him dress: in the flesh, skintight black cotton, faded denim.

Gosh, it was hot in this place.

It was a studio, with dishes piled in the sink and a wall of floor-to-ceiling bookcases eating into the space. The bed was made up with fresh white sheets I bet he'd brought from the family home. It wouldn't do to stare at it but nor could I trust myself to look at him for more than a second at a time.

He didn't speak and I didn't dare ask what he'd wanted to say. We'd started with passionate, graduated to tender and now it was plain awkward, worse than ever because this time I'd chosen to come here. It was a mistake. Another one, but still reversible: all I had to do was walk back out the door. A door that no longer existed. So much for the hope that seeing him would make me snap out of it. That had only worked in part: I *was* shocked and ashamed. I was also still here.

'It was me who started this and I take responsibility,' Jean-Luc said, out of nowhere. 'I'm sorry you regret it.'

Oh, God help me, he'd been in therapy. I held up my hand, my heart clanging with indignation at the suggestion that anything had been *done to me*. It wasn't a seduction of one by the other. I was damned if anyone was going to absolve me of my half share.

'As I recall, we both got pretty carried away,' I said. 'Neither one of us was doing anything against our will.' By now we'd spent more time discussing it than doing it. 'Let's just agree to keep it to ourselves. Then we can both move on.'

So much for telling Philippe. It wasn't strictly necessary.

Jean-Luc's eyes lanced me. 'But I don't want to move on,' he said. 'And I don't think you do either.' I didn't have to say anything for him to know he'd hit home. 'You wouldn't be here if that's how you felt. If you'd ignored my message or told me to get lost I would have respected that. You don't feel guilty because you wish we hadn't slept together. You feel guilty because it's what you want and you are scared.'

I put my bag and briefcase down on the floor and rubbed at the muscles in my neck and shoulders. Sometimes it's only when the weight is lifted that you feel the pain. And the fear. He wasn't wrong about that. He wasn't wrong about any of it.

There was no point avoiding his eyes when he seemed able to see right into my head. I felt my grip loosen as I surrendered to that mesmerising green-blue and the relief of not fighting any more. And where my head went, my body was quick to follow. He'd sat down on the other side of the room but it was as if he were right next to me, his breath warm and inviting on my cheek, my collarbone. The wanting started small and rippled right through me.

'It's good to be scared,' he said. 'Fear makes you feel like you're really alive.'

Until now it had only ever had the opposite effect on me.

Despite my considerably longer stay on this earth, I could find no answer. When I went to speak it was as if I'd forgotten how. Lying to Philippe would prove incredibly easy but I couldn't lie to Jean-Luc. I didn't try.

'Everything you say is true,' I said. 'I don't know what to do about it.'

I was hoping my capitulation would bring him across the room. There was nothing cocky or triumphant about his smile – he just looked so happy. He wasn't going anywhere, waiting patiently until I made up my mind.

As if my mind had any say.

'We both know what *I* want,' he said, opening his hands. It sounds crude, but I was struck by how earnest he was. What Jean-Luc wanted was not the issue. He was free, with a summer to spare. I pictured him at Philippe's age, telling a future son about his brief fling with a married woman, a foreigner. In those stories I was supposed to be the one who 'taught him a thing or two' though that profile didn't fit at all. 'Mysterious', yes. 'Unreachable', in almost every way. *But mon Dieu, underneath that calm exterior...* Believe me, I was amazed to find myself so in thrall to sensuality, finally a fully-grown sexual being.

It made no sense then, nor will it ever, but I did still love my husband. That should have been the beginning and end of it, I know. It should have been enough. If I didn't care about him, it wouldn't hurt so much that he was seeing another woman behind my back. Philippe was the only man who had brought me lasting happiness. I hated the thought of causing him pain, and yet I elbowed it aside.

There was no comparison between the nature of my dealings with him and Jean-Luc. Right then, in that cramped little studio, despite the doubts I'd previously held and my knee-jerk attitude to adultery, separating love and sex *did* make sense to me – they might be best together, but there were other ways. As long as this thing with Jean-Luc remained purely physical it could go in a box on a lower shelf. The main event – my marriage – would not be affected.

I actually convinced myself of this at the time. It's amazing how any situation can be moulded to the shape you want to see. I read somewhere that humans aren't naturally monogamous, that exclusivity is a convention stemming from the pressures of society, religion, economic necessity. Some find it too hard to live by, against their nature. They can't see the advantages of fidelity, or they are greedy and want the comforts *and* the kicks. Here I was, not so decent and conservative after all. I had trouble dismissing the shadow version of myself because it excited me. She was hedonistic, assertive, impulsive; the rare woman who indulged her desires, regardless of cost or consequence. Objectively it was appalling; in the moment, electrifying. I wanted more danger. More euphoria. More me and him together, as much as I could get.

The desire of my body for Jean-Luc's would have been more than enough to propel me across the room. But what made me do it was the sense that he stood on cliff tops with his arms flung wide to a storm, while I had always sought a cave to cower in.

Jean-Luc didn't just make love like the world was about to end. It was how he did everything. I had a lot to learn.

29

After my meeting Philippe was in one of his morose moods, which went with the end of an exhibition, too self-absorbed to notice anything amiss. Neither of us was hungry, so I took a bath. I finished the last few pages of my book before immersing myself in visions that reminded me of the previous time I lay there with perfumed water lapping at my limbs, not knowing if I'd ever get to feel that good again.

Well, I did. For all my resolutions, I wasn't strong enough in the end. I was no better than Philippe after all. Jean-Luc remembered everything that turned me on the first time. He already knew that if he made me come first I would hover there the whole time our bodies were in motion. I'd never been able to *feel* a man come inside me before. Maybe I still couldn't. Maybe it was just the intensity of the way he looked at me in that penultimate moment.

The next morning Philippe picked a convenient Saturday to sleep late, still snoring rhythmically when I returned from my run. I wasn't going to risk waking him – normally he'd be eagerly awaiting our weekend conjugation by now – so I wrote him a note to say where I was going, and left as quickly as I could.

The bells of Saint-Sulpice were booming nine o'clock as I set off on the short walk to Le Bon Marché. Sèvres-Babylone was one of my favourite corners of the city. The streets were quiet at this early weekend hour, a few small dogs being walked by the old ladies you see so often in Paris, bent almost double, wearing coats and cardigans even in the warmest weather. I stopped for a brief chat with Mathilde and her bedraggled terrier, Alphonse. We first met when she was ahead of me in the line at the post office and I tried to defuse an argument over whether she'd been short-changed. The mistake was likely hers but the man behind the counter was so mean I couldn't just stand there. I was never entirely sure if she remembered me.

I pushed open the door to the Grande Epicerie, one of the city's best grocery stores, with the usual relish. Philippe and I were comfortably off, as opposed to *friqués*. Unlike its regular clientele, we couldn't afford to shop here often so every visit felt like a treat. I always visited the American section with the sense of committing culinary treachery. Any foreigner browsing here would assume that Americans have a bizarre obsession with condiments and items as far removed from raw ingredients as could be, for the offering mostly consisted of chemical-laden sauces and salad dressings, with very little that a French person would deign to call food.

I never missed the chance to sneak in a couple of boxes of Kraft mac and cheese. My homemade version – much refined over the years with French hard cheeses and a dash of white wine in an homage to fondue – was superior in every way but I had a sentimental attachment to this unlikely delicacy. Along with saltine crackers and grape Kool-Aid it is practically all I lived on between the ages of ten and twelve, which is to say between Christopher's death and leaving for England. That was my father's idea of a solution when he turned up and saw the state my mother was in. *Look at her, Carolyn. This can't go on.* And to me: *It's for the best, darling. Boarding school will be an adventure.*

The middle school counsellor had been calling my dad in Brazil because Mom wouldn't pick up the phone. And she'd made it clear her next call would be of an official nature. When I arrived in Kent to find Coldwater as dark and creaky as a storybook haunted house, I was the only one who liked the food. It was hot and filling and best of all I didn't have to go buy it or cook it myself. I was so skinny the anorexics tried to befriend me, before backing off in disgust. One time I accepted a bet from my classmates to lick the plate clean after a second helping, checking first that the staff weren't watching. It took almost three years for me to fill out and develop some curves.

My mind was turning to perfect flaky almond croissants when I sensed someone close by. Invading my space in a way that was making me uptight.

'How's the leg?'

I stood up, the mac and cheese being at the bottom of the display, to see Daniel from the park standing there, his eyes roaming over every part of me *except* my left leg.

'It's healing well, thank you. I've almost forgotten about it.' I didn't want him to think there was any favour outstanding.

'Ah,' he smiled, looking down at my shopping basket. 'We share a weakness, I see.' He made a point of using the expression *péché mignon*, 'sweet sin', which always sounds far more exciting than what it's being used to describe. I could have sworn I saw him lick his lips.

I was genuinely surprised at his taste, until he informed me he was Canadian. He spoke regular French rather than the indecipherable Québécois, which needed subtitles in the movies. Now he'd told me, I could hear a slight accent I'd not noticed before. I didn't ask where he was from or anything else which would prolong the encounter, which felt more uncomfortable than usual despite the fact that today we were both fully clothed and not panting or drenched in sweat. He was more handsome than I had realised.

Bumping into him was the limit. I was trying to stop myself spending every minute thinking about Jean-Luc, which was difficult enough. I was trying to get out of having sex with my husband. And here I was attempting not to be drawn in by Daniel's shameless flirting, although it must be said that he was rather good at it. His lack of subtlety was deliberate to get women to laugh. We all want someone who'll make us laugh.

'So, will I see you out running again soon?'

'Actually, I managed two laps this morning. Starting back gently.' Since there was nowhere in the neighbourhood as pleasant and convenient as the Luxembourg to go for a run, it would not be possible to avoid him.

'I'm glad,' he said. 'I've missed you.'

I glanced away and saw a woman in the neighbouring Tex-Mex section take a sudden interest in a jar of jalapeños.

That made me smile. That and the weird, spacey way I was feeling before Daniel even showed up. 'That's very sweet of you to say,' I replied, so as not to sound utterly charmless. His persistent attentions may have been irritating but the other woman's reaction made me realise I was flattered by them too. 'But I should tell you, I already have a... I have a... I mean, I'm married.'

Sometimes you just are not safe from what's really on your mind. Panicked by how close I'd come to saying *I already have a lover,* it now sounded as if I might be lying about my marital status. I sought to grasp my wedding ring as evidence but went for the wrong hand. Daniel laughed and shook his head.

'I think you'll find it's *here*,' he said, taking my left hand in his. By now, the only possible option was for me to laugh, excessively. And go bright pink, which would only get worse the more I thought about it.

When Geneviève rounded the corner she found me laughing, blushing and holding hands (albeit very strangely) with a man who wasn't my husband *or* my lover, although what she saw would do nothing to contradict the latter interpretation.

'Geneviève! How lovely to see you!' We exchanged kisses. The look she gave me exists in every language.

I took a peek at her basket, which contained a small bottle of one of the single estate Italian olive oils displayed close to where Daniel and I had bumped into each other. It was a reasonable assumption that Geneviève would have lingered over her purchase rather than grabbing the first bottle she could lay her hands on. This wasn't Monoprix.

For the love of God, how long had she been within earshot?

Daniel flashed a smile at us both in a *don't forget me* kind of way.

'Geneviève, this is Daniel. We sometimes see each other running in the Luxembourg. He's from Montréal.' I couldn't summon the words to describe my relationship with her.

Before entering Philippe's rarified world, *her* world, I wasn't familiar with diplomatic ploys such as mentioning common ground when making introductions. It works well when you need to walk away and leave the other people to it. And it's also a lifesaver when you want to do just that but have no choice but to stay right where you are.

Daniel and I exchanged the most transient glance as he greeted Geneviève. She knows Montreal and Daniel, who may have been from there or from some tiny fur-trapping village a thousand miles away for all I knew, played along beautifully. He chatted a bit about the city but kept coming back to running, making it sound as if that, rather than chasing women, was his main interest in life. He said he'd done the Toronto marathon and was not only training for New York in the fall but would soon be moving there, after spending three years in Paris.

Geneviève was clearly rather taken with Daniel despite being of the common belief that physical exercise (other than sex, although she probably included that) was vulgar and unnecessary. Daniel was delightful with her and now I'd seen how well he could pick up signals when he wanted to, I was curious to find out what he did for a living. Geneviève asked him.

He was an actor. Aren't we all?

30

As I checked the mailbox I gradually identified the shouting, which I'd heard as soon as I came in off the street. Instead of picking on one of our unsuspecting neighbours, this time Vanessa was yelling at Philippe for all she was worth and getting the same treatment in return. I stood still for a moment, the last of my high ebbing away. Philippe had hardly ever raised his voice in the time we'd been together. By all accounts Vanessa's mother had known how to push his buttons but the man I'd married didn't have especially strong opinions or a temper. Right now he sounded incandescent with rage. Despite the volume I couldn't make out what he was saying but I wouldn't have wanted to be on the receiving end.

Tempting as it was to head right back out again, I approached our staircase still clutching my groceries, a handful of junk mail, a letter from the doctor's office and an incorrectly addressed envelope from the electricity company. I wouldn't have taken Philippe's name even if I could pronounce it and still went by Folgate. *Mme Darrousier* would have been a better wife to my husband, of that I was quite sure. Having absented myself from what should have been the good times that morning, I wouldn't shy away from supporting him in times of trouble, even if he was heartily contributing to them. There had to be a reason.

The two of them took it down a notch when someone in one of the other buildings opened a window and told them to shut up. This was the third time we'd annoyed the neighbours and if it continued we would soon find ourselves regarded as undesirables. What might pass for normal where Jean-Luc was living wouldn't be respectable in the neighbourhood where senators from all over France kept a Parisian *pied-à-terre*. We only lived here because a friend of the Malavoines let Philippe have it cheap for a quick sale when they were both getting divorced.

'*What* is going on?' I was in the hallway and nobody heard me. When I went into the living room Vanessa was jabbing a finger at her father, mad eyed, hair all over the place, wearing nothing but a huge man's T-shirt, which left a lot of bare flesh on view.

'*C'est toi, le con,*' she said. *You're* the jerk.

I didn't have sufficient experience of watching French people row to figure out what was going on. It was beyond belief that Philippe would speak to his daughter like that, and in any case, he'd used the masculine form.

Registering my presence now, Philippe pointed at a tall blond boy standing in the doorway to the spare room wearing jeans, a pink shirt and a smirk. 'I'm out of here,' he told Vanessa.

'Damn right you are! Make it quick before I sock you one.' Philippe was breathing in snatches as if he'd run up all four flights of stairs to the apartment. I feared for his health – at fifty-two he was at that dangerous age for a man where a single instance of over-exertion or extreme stress can be fatal.

'You don't have to go, Boris,' Vanessa said, glaring at her father.

'*Boris?*' I glared at the boy now. 'Actually, he really does.' I flung open the front door and took up position next to it until he got the message and left, still with that irritating smug expression.

'I can't take much more of this,' Philippe announced. Ignoring the balcony, he went to the other window and leaned far too heavily on the low decorative railing that was the only thing between him and the street below.

'You're fucking well not the only one!' Vanessa slammed the door to the spare room so hard that a picture in the hallway fell off its hook. After all that, the silence was ominous. Philippe and I looked at each other. With pure desperation, in his case.

I took a breath in. 'Well, I guess it's my turn to say the same. Something's got to give around here.'

Philippe gave an enormous shrug, his hands held up and out like he was holding something long and tubular. 'You deal with her then, I just can't. I'm beginning to see what her mother means. She's absolutely impossible!'

I tapped quietly on Vanessa's door in the sincere hope she'd tell me to fuck off. She asked who it was and told me to come in. She was lying on the bed with her hands behind her head, making the T-shirt ride up over her belly. There was something touchingly childish about her faded red underpants and lack of embarrassment about her body – for all that it was unmistakably that of a grown woman. What was going on in her head lay somewhere in between and that's what made this so hard. The fact I knew nothing about teenagers obviously didn't help.

I never used to gesticulate before I moved to France. It has its uses. Maybe my hands drew a question mark in the air. They did something that she understood. 'He won't listen to me,' she said. '*Dad* just won't listen.'

'I'm not defending him shouting at you' – I thought I'd start with that – 'but you need to try to understand why he's upset. Parents have views about friends sleeping over. To him, you're still his little girl, remember?' I kept finding myself embroiled in their inability to communicate, wishing there was some way they could get back what they'd missed of each other.

She turned to face me and I had to gather myself to go on. I couldn't make it better but I had to do something. 'Am I right that Boris is the boyfriend of that girl you got in a fight with? Because if so...'

'It's not what either of you think,' Vanessa interrupted. 'Boris was in the city with some *potes* last night. He got separated from them and didn't have enough money to take a cab home by himself. He didn't even get here until three a.m. Everyone always wants to think the worst of me.'

182

'That's not true at all.' *Nobody gives a shit what happened to me*, she'd said when she showed me those scratches. But I did. I asked, and what's more, she told me. And then she told me nobody else knew, as if that meant something, when maybe it was just me wanting to feel needed. To believe there was one small area of my life where I was doing good.

'The point is that you can't just do as you please and that includes letting someone we don't know into our home in the middle of the night. And you can't keep winding your father up – it's driving him insane. To be honest, it might be a good idea for you to patch things up with your mom. It can't be any fun for you staying here.'

Finally I'd said something she agreed with. 'There's a weird vibe in this apartment. It feels kind of empty, like no one really lives here. You and Dad are never together, or even if you are, you don't talk to each other any more.'

Vanessa reminds me of *my* mother sometimes. It might be the lacerating frankness. And as for those scary powers of observation: how bad must it be for her to have noticed the deterioration between Philippe and me in a few short weeks? She'd never even seen us together when things were good. 'Well, you might have something to do with that, Vanessa. You're absolutely right, there has been an atmosphere since you arrived.' She didn't come back at me as I expected, looking down like a dog that's used to being hit. 'I'm sorry,' I said. 'I didn't mean that. I'm new to this, remember.'

Vanessa peered up at me in surprise through the gaps in her hair before shaking it off her face. I waited to see how she would exploit my admission of weakness, not that she'd needed me to point it out.

'I can guarantee that my mom doesn't want me back. I've "embarrassed her professionally". Anyway, she's about to go to Sicily with her new boyfriend and there's no way she'd let me stay in the house on my own. I guess there are squats, if I ask around...'

I smiled at the mischief in her voice; even Vanessa got bored of arguing. 'Now you're just being silly,' I said. 'But what about when September comes around? You can't live here and go to school in Neuilly.' I could say the words but even the near future was such an abstraction that it was like discussing life on another planet.

Vanessa pushed her lower lip almost inside out. There was something unnervingly feral about this girl who'd been catapulted into our lives. She had quite a repertoire of unflattering facial expressions and her approach to personal hygiene was lax. This room needed airing out. How that preppy little shit could have stood to spend the night in here was a mystery. He set more store in personal grooming than Vanessa did.

She sat up on the bed and looked right at me. 'Who says I'm going back to school? You can't beat the system from within.'

I sighed with exhaustion and sat down gingerly on the edge of a chair strewn with clothing. It wasn't my place to tell her what to do. 'Don't you *have* to go back to school?' I asked. It was a genuine question. I knew very little about the French education system. I'd have to ask Jean-Luc. Vanessa sniffed loudly and shoved me off the chair, before pulling on a selection of the clothes I'd been sitting on, including a pair of shiny patterned leggings I'd hoped would 'go missing' in the laundry.

'I'll be out late tonight,' she said, squeezing a length of cheap orangey foundation onto her finger and proceeding to plaster it on without washing her face. 'Just so you know.'

As I left the room I hesitated, as if it were an afterthought. 'So where are you going?'

It was an eloquent look she gave me. It said: *don't push it.*

31

It was only seeing the poster marked LAST DAYS on my way home that reminded me I had tickets for the exhibition at the Marmottan. I meant to ask Suzanne but like so much else, it had slipped my mind.

Philippe groaned when I mentioned it – the Impressionists were not to his taste, too popular and bourgeois. Like Henri, he preferred the kind of art that most people don't even think *is* art. We were alone in the apartment now Vanessa had taken off. 'I'm not in the mood,' he said. I wasn't either. I wanted to see the paintings, which were from private collections all over the world and rarely on display. But not with Philippe. Not now. As things stood, spending time with him was asking for trouble, the chances of us enjoying each other's company remote. After his row with Vanessa, I felt an unsettling mixture of revulsion and pity for him. Adding my own variations on guilt and euphoria after going back to Jean-Luc, the balance came out in Philippe's favour. But only just.

I sat down on the end of the sofa and pinched his cheek lightly, registering the platonic nature of my gesture. It was a show of affection you would more likely give a chubby-cheeked baby than a weary man, his skin a bit slack to the touch, less so to the eye.

'Come on,' I said, hoping to enthuse myself as much as him. '*Ça te changera les idées.* It'll do you good. There are bound to be seascapes.' My gaze travelled to the painting over the mantel as I thought again of the night my mother told me what I already knew in the depths of my heart. How different things might have been if she hadn't forced it out into the open.

But not as different as they look now. Saying all this out loud is making me see everything in a new light. My only hope of finding a way to live with it is to face up to what happened in every detail. Even if I could wipe my memory, I wouldn't. And there'll always be someone to remind me.

As I hunted in my bag for the exhibition tickets, the reality of the crisis we were facing hit me so hard I could have vomited into it. Rushing to the bathroom, I sat on the toilet longer than I needed to. When I blotted the tissue between my legs, in a moment of sheer despair I even considered touching myself, not because I felt like it, only as a respite from the turmoil in my head. Every unwanted thought unleashed a dozen more.

Once again I did not do it. I wanted no lesser pleasure than the kind Jean-Luc gave me. I was still reeling after the second time. I may not have felt the connection he talked about that first afternoon, too caught up in the physical, but when I did it was a tenfold magnifier.

Sometimes I tormented myself with an alternative version of that scene, the kind of pointless anxiety I'm prone to, as if actual events weren't enough to worry about. What if I'd rebuffed Jean-Luc, gently, saying *I'm not so sure that's a good idea.* What if I'd slapped his hand or even his face with *How dare you? What the hell do you think you're doing?*

To think that I could have missed all this. The question wasn't how *he* had dared.

Philippe was marching up and down the hallway, jangling keys in his hand, the keyring wrapped round his middle finger.

'You sure you want to drive? Won't it take for ever?'

It had started to rain and despite the fact that I grew up on the west coast with its hundred permutations of cloud, rain and fog, there was something uniquely depressing about Paris in wet weather. The prospect of being holed up with Philippe in our car, with its low roof, the windows closed and the wipers whipping, induced such claustrophobia that I would gladly have wasted thirty euros to forget the whole thing.

But when Philippe remembered where he'd left the car – he didn't use it much and often it was only the letters announcing traffic or parking fines that reminded us we owned a vehicle – it was boxed in, a gap of approx-imately two inches at either end. '*Putain!*' He kicked the outer rear tyre half-heartedly, attracting jeers from a pair of passing teenage boys.

'*Dégagez!*' I roared at them. We both seemed to have lost the ability to speak at normal volume. The kids looked afraid of me, an unlikely lunatic in my loafers and belted tan trench, and they wasted no time following my advice.

Philippe managed a glimmer of a smile as we headed for the Metro after all. 'You know, I think you're becoming more French, Alexandra,' he said. To get to the museum in the 16ᵗʰ arrondissement we could either change twice, at Montparnasse and Trocadéro, which would be heaving on a Saturday afternoon, or take a longer ride to the western limits of the city and change just once. Philippe regarded himself as either Parisian or not as it suited him, but where transportation was concerned, his decision took precedence over mine. Or at least it usually did. Today he touched his card on the reader and followed me meekly onto the Line 10 platform, direction Boulogne – Pont de Saint-Cloud.

This line was never crowded. We sat down and Philippe moved the edge of my coat from his seat. Every minute act which would normally happen on autopilot acquired a kind of inverse frisson, sharpened by the contrast with my *liaison dangereuse*. But whereas every touch or glance between me and Jean-Luc was charged with excitement, with Philippe it was like padding around knowing there are landmines underfoot.

Opposite us sat a young couple with a boy of about three years old wearing the same Senegal football shirt as his dad. As the parents talked, the child kept up an animated dialogue between two My Little Pony figures with tinselled manes, either in another language or more likely in fluent gobbledygook. He gave each of the animals a distinct voice.

'Isn't he adorable?' I nudged Philippe, thinking the child's innocent joy would lift his spirits as it did mine.

Philippe, who hadn't noticed, looked at him affectionately then turned to me with a sad smile. 'You would have made a good mother.'

It upset me that he would bring this up in a public place; he *did* know how I felt about that but because of where we both were when we met, it was not something we'd gone into. I didn't know if he was trying to hurt or console me, another doubt I would never have had in the past. Over the years I'd arrived at a place of acceptance where I could see parents with their children and not be skewered with anguish over what was denied me by nature, fate; whatever you wanted to call it, it was nothing personal. I'd always felt there was a certain justice to not getting everything I wanted and that it would be wrong to fight it, asking for too much. I'd trained myself not to care about those who think the life of a childless woman has no meaning – what did they know? At least the fact that I'd wanted children and not been able to have them exempted me from judgement, if not pity; doubly so in France where women who didn't have children were thin on the ground.

Jean-Luc had put his finger on it before he really knew me: I kept my emotions at a distance out of fear. I've come to see control – not just self-control, all kinds – as an illusion. There are threats from outside, from random occurrences, other people's unpredictability. And occasionally, without warning or provocation, distress would crash through the barricades I'd put up, sparing only the last fibres holding me together. But trying to be stoic and philosophical only gets you so far. Of course I felt sorry for myself, but I had a pep talk for the relapses, to remind myself how much worse things could be, as if loss – or happiness, for that matter – can be calibrated. As if downward comparisons are ever any consolation. My mother once held up her fingers in air quotes when speaking of the "grief" of infertility. You might think I'd have moved on from that now but it hasn't lost its sting.

I should have done this years ago. I was always afraid talking would make it worse and the irony is that it took everything getting worse to bring me here. But pain is its own entity – it exists regardless – the talking a release. Like a confession.

Something hinted at my sorrow that day on the Metro because Philippe went on to explain: 'You're so much better at handling Vanessa than I am. I wasn't expecting it to be easy, but she has no respect for me and after today, well…' He pulled a face that frayed me at the edges and as I looked at him I thought *I feel too much for you to be doing what I'm doing to you.*

'It'll get easier in time, don't beat yourself up. It's a good sign that she feels safe enough to act out with you.

Vanessa loves a good rant,' I said. 'And you know she can be just as vile with me.'

Opposite, the young couple were arguing now, the man pointing to the child, then snatching the glittery pony toys out of his hands. 'This is *my son*,' he said to his wife. The child shared her beauty and right now, the same bereft look in his eyes. 'You say you'll put a stop to this when he goes to school? It'll be too late by then!' Now the woman and the little boy were crying shiny silent tears.

'*Crétin!*' Philippe muttered loudly, as the train pulled into our station. I pulled at his jacket sleeve as the doors opened, before he could get into yet another argument. But I had misjudged him, as it seems I often did. He turned to me as we walked up the steps toward the exit. 'There are so many ways you can screw a child up,' he said. 'How does anyone ever end up normal?' He'd picked the wrong person to ask.

When we got to the exhibition, Philippe was more his old self. It was hard to equate him lost in contemplation with the man on the edge I'd been seeing lately. As I'd hoped, the seascapes made him impatient to be back on the Côte d'Azur. There was one of a bay which he remembered exploring with his brothers and Henri when he was a boy.

Some of my happiest childhood memories are of playing on the beach, before I became an only child.

32

An affair in its early stages is disruptive. As well as all-consuming, it is time-consuming. The hours accelerated when Jean-Luc and I were together and stretched out endlessly when we were apart, even though we were finding ways to meet almost every day. Philippe and I were seeing less and less of each other without too much need for subterfuge. Having grown up outdoors, neither of us liked lingering in the apartment in the summer. He was working his way through the complete works of Modiano and Lemaître, whiling away hours in one of those metal chairs with the punishing backrests in the Jardin du Luxembourg, cooling off with a swim at the Piscine Saint-Germain. We used to talk about what we were reading all the time; now we barely talked at all.

In truth, everyone in my life was fading out but Jean-Luc. Alain and his wife were taking a long summer break in Bordeaux after the birth of their first grandchild, the rest of my colleagues content to wind down and work shorter hours in anticipation of *le grand départ* and well-deserved vacations. It had been a testing time for all of us.

I told Jean-Luc not to send me incriminating texts, although to be getting any from him was incriminating. It wasn't that I feared anyone seeing them – Philippe had never shown any interest in my phone and I'd changed the settings so that new messages didn't beep or flash up on the screen. It was simply more erotic, the anticipation heightened, when we kept to time and place.

The moment our next assignation was arranged it flipped the catch on my imagination, anticipating the how, where and when. I had trouble sitting still, the best kind of tension ramping up inside of me until I could hardly bear it. My ability to concentrate had deserted me – I was supposed to be editing our next book but I could find no fault with anything. On examining sumptuous colour plates of works by Delacroix and others, I could picture nothing clearly. Everything around me was bright, saturated but slightly out of focus. I was in a state of permanent intoxication.

I heard Jean-Luc's footsteps on the stairs. It was his first (and only) return visit to the office and he tapped softly on the door despite knowing I was alone; it was another very hot day and I'd sent everyone home early. We headed straight past the Danish sofa to my office. My visceral craving for him still took me aback. It reached the most insensate parts of me: fingernails, tooth enamel, the ends of my hair. He touched me everywhere.

We fell back onto the rug, our breathing raw with release, fractionally out of sync. The stillness of the afternoon insinuated itself into my bones as I lay beside him, the sun warming our skin through the window panes. He turned to kiss me, which I wasn't used to once it was over. 'You look happy,' he told me. 'And so beautiful.' He pronounced it *beauty-full*.

I propped myself up on one elbow, my bare breast skimming his upper arm. 'So do you,' I said. Beautiful really was the word, and he was no less masculine for it. 'Being home agrees with you.'

A shadow crossed his face. I thought I'd said something wrong until I realised it was a swallow circling the courtyard. It flew past once more before soaring to rejoin the sky. Since I was a child fascinated by eagles, I'd envied birds the power of flight, without dreaming I'd ever have the faintest notion how that felt.

'What time is it?' I asked.

'What does it matter? We're not in a rush.' He paused, and with a shyness I hadn't seen before, said, 'You could, you know, *talk* to me sometimes.'

It embarrassed me that my instinct to pounce and rub myself all over him was so transparent. Of course we talked sometimes but now my mind was blank. We exchanged looks and burst out laughing, as if conversation was more inappropriate than our usual pastime. 'So, what do you want to talk about?'

The flare of panic as he lost his nerve was visible, the hand nearest to me shaking until he steadied it against his leg. 'I don't know, anything. *Parle-moi en français,*' he said.

'*Non!*' I said, doing it anyway. 'My French is horrible. Correct, but horrible.' I couldn't think how to say *I can't*

get my tongue around it. Even if you know them, colloqui-
alisms sound ridiculous in a foreign language unless you
speak it like a native.

'I like it,' he insisted. 'Your French sounds more British
than American.'

'That's because I learned it in England.'

'Say my name!'

That was narcissistic but I went along with it, articulating the words which turned hoops in my head. Besides,
there *was* only one way to say his name – even my mother
could manage it. 'Okay, *Jean-Luc!*' I put on a gravelly
voice. '*Comme tu veux, Jean-Luc.* But only because it
doesn't have an R.'

He grinned. The fact is that I would have done
anything he asked. Overcome with self-consciousness, I
switched back to English because I'd thought of something that had been troubling me from the very start.
'Have you been with an older woman before?'

Now Jean-Luc frowned as if he didn't quite get my
meaning. 'No,' he said, in the end. 'Why are you asking
me that?'

'But is it something you'd thought about, before us?
I mean, you wouldn't be the first young guy to be
curious...'

My jaw tensed in an effort to silence myself. So far age
had sketched only faint lines on me, but now whenever I
saw young women in the street I was assailed by their fresh
skin, their perfect boobs and cute little asses. I imagined
the smiles they gave their boyfriends being for Jean-Luc,

their laughter aimed at me, amused but without malice, for I was no threat to them. What could he possibly want with me, when he could have that?

'Jesus Christ, Alexandra!' He smacked himself hard in the forehead. '*All* women do this! You take something beautiful – especially yourselves – and look for something to be wrong. Nothing's ever right as it is.' Neither of us was happy any more. Bridge-like lines appeared between his eyebrows when he was thinking: two vertical, one across the top, so serious, like the day he'd made me face my fear to the sound of squealing trains on tracks. When he went to speak, they disappeared. 'I like that you are *bien dans ta peau*, probably more than if you were younger. You like this body you have, I can tell. You're not hung up on appearances. There's more to you.'

The French have that expression too about being comfortable in your own skin. It's not literally about liking or accepting your body but as I lay there on my side, with Jean-Luc running a finger from the hollow at the centre of my chest, down over the soft roll of my belly and slipping between my legs, I realised he was right. My medical problems had always made me feel unfeminine, emphasizing my deficiencies as a woman. I hadn't been to the beauty salon since my latest hospital visit and had let the hair grow back naturally. I'd heard young men didn't like that but it didn't bother him.

'So I don't seem old to you?'

He made a faint tutting sound. 'After so long in Paris you are still so Anglo-Saxon about this! A woman can be beautiful at any age. Just relax.'

'But there must come a point where—'

He could just have laughed it off but he pulled away, reaching for his shirt. 'What turns me on is up to me. Don't try to tell me my fantasies. Would you like it if I did that to you?'

A giant surge of alarm rose up my chest and into my throat. 'No,' was the only sound I could make.

'I don't understand why you're doing this. What do you want me to say?'

I made some pathetic gesture of helplessness, pressing back tears.

'*Tu me plais et c'est tout.*' There's something so direct, so unmistakably sexual about the French way of expressing attraction – it has pleasure rolled in before anything has even happened. I *pleased* Jean-Luc even when he was furious with me, just as everything about him aroused me, even his anger. Especially his anger. It made me feel powerful that I could provoke such passion and intensity of feeling. It frightened me, and just as he'd said, it made me feel gloriously alive.

He wasn't going to let it drop. 'I don't care about your age, my age – do you realise there are parts of the ocean floor that are one hundred and twenty-five million years old? Maybe I should care that your husband is my father's best friend, but I don't. Fuck it! Life is complicated, so what?'

He hadn't seen enough of it to know what an understatement that was. I envied him the confidence of youth, of thinking it will only increase, when often it's not like that at all. The more I've experienced, the harder it is to make sense of anything. I'll never know how much of that's the same for everyone and how much is just me. Not that I'm special, I've just never met anyone who's been through all the things I have.

We were both fully dressed when he came back to me, staying at an unnatural distance. He wasn't just insulted by my downgrading us to some clichéd rite of passage; he was wounded, and I was shaken by the fragility beneath the skin. My insinuations were unjustified, offensive, when we took such pleasure in each other's private shapes and sounds: his soft gasp of anticipation when I started to touch him, mine at the stroke of his tongue. My ankles crossed behind his back; the momentary loss of symmetry in his face, reconfiguring in that afterward smile. This was intimate knowledge – and so was knowing how easily he hurt.

'You know, we're not as different as you think,' he said. I wasn't brave enough to ask what he meant.

'I'm sorry,' I said quietly. 'I'm still getting used to this. Next time we'll talk first. I mean, really talk, about anything you want.' Because nobody says they want to unless they have something to say.

He hesitated and I figured there was at least a 50:50 chance he'd say *Actually, you know what...*

For good and ill, what he said instead will be the last memory to leave me. There've been times I wished I could forget it, still more when I risked dying a physical death if I lost sight of why it started, what it became, the way it engulfed us; if I stopped believing it meant something, verging on everything when we were alone in a small room. No clocks, no years, no nothing. Just us and the sea and the sky.

'If you'd turned me down that first time I would have left Paris the same day. Because it would destroy me to be near you and not have you.'

33

Packing up an exhibition was Suzanne's least favourite part of the job at Galerie Darrousier. For a start, she didn't get to dress up – most of her clothes were designed to be seen in, or through, not for any practical purpose. Knowing she'd be fed up, I took a detour via rue Mazarine on my way to work. The gallery was officially closed on Mondays and there would not be another exhibition until the fall now – like much of Paris, it was about to enter summer shutdown. Suzanne was wearing Converses, leggings and a figure-hugging tank top and looked like a teenager without the usual flamboyant make-up.

'Look at you,' I said. 'When you're not even trying!'

I made us coffee. Philippe complained about Suzanne's caffeine habit; within days of being hired she'd rejected the crappy jug and filter in the kitchenette and insisted she couldn't function without a Nespresso machine. She got through at least ten capsules a day.

The floor was covered with crates full of packaging materials. 'You arrived at just the right moment to help me take this down,' she said, referring to the now infamous wall hanging. 'I had him on the phone earlier giving precise instructions.' Hands full, she cocked her head at the photo of artist Nasim Asradi on the wall. 'He was threatening to come and do it himself.'

'Perhaps you should have let him. He's very good-looking, don't you think?'

'Not as much as *he* thinks,' she said. 'That's a deceptive photo. Catch him in profile and his nose is twice the size.'

'Not everybody can be blessed with your perfect proportions, Suzanne!'

She paused for a moment, scrutinising me. Surely she wouldn't actually say it?

'Your eyes are a *tiny* bit close together, Alex.' She slid her thumb and index finger back and forth in front of my face. 'A centimetre, tops. It's not a big issue. You look good.'

I laughed because the usual rules of tact didn't exist for Suzanne. I was flattered that she'd ever given my attractiveness a thought, although according to an American magazine article my mother had shown me, women do this in female company whether they realise it or not, constantly reevaluating their place in the hierarchy. Whenever Suzanne bent down her tank top scooped to reveal a fuchsia satin bra that barely covered her nipples. Without a shred of self-consciousness yet deeply self-aware, she wore her sexuality like an outrageous dress that nobody could fail to notice.

We carefully lifted the vinyl hanging off its moorings and pleated it as per Asradi's instructions to retain the exact folds. Of all the exhibits it had the shortest distance to travel and would be at the Longuevilles' house by lunchtime, although I strongly doubted it would ever grace any wall there.

'Tell you who *is* super hot,' Suzanne said.

I smiled inwardly: did she think Dédé was going to be news to me after the night of the launch?

'Jean-Luc Malavoine!' She gave a seductive growl. 'So moody and mysterious. I wouldn't say no to some of that!'

Dread must have turned my face blank. If I'd looked down I swear I would have seen my heart thumping through my blouse.

'You know him, don't you? I saw you talking.'

'Barely,' I replied, examining the chain links between the handcuffs. 'He's been away at college for most of the time I've been with Philippe. But Philippe's known Jean-Luc all his life, obviously. He and Henri go way back.'

Our task completed, I straightened up and busied myself removing some polystyrene packing peanuts which had attached themselves to my trousers by static, my gaze now directed firmly toward the floor. I did all of this *ve-ry slow-ly*. One at a time. Trying to breathe so neither of us could hear it.

Gradually my heart rate stabilised. Reminding Suzanne that the connection was my husband's and conjuring up images of Jean-Luc's childhood was a smart move, which left me out of it. I'd averted trouble once before just inches from where we stood when Geneviève had brought Jean-Luc over to talk to me at the party. Just as well I seemed to have an aptitude for thinking on my feet, because if he and I were going to keep seeing each other, I was going to need it.

If. Days had passed without me hearing from him.

Suzanne was watching me. For her, nothing I'd said exempted me from commenting on Jean-Luc's appearance. Usually I found her assessments of men as objects (or if they were honoured, works of art) wickedly amusing but that kind of badinage required me to join in. So I went for another deflection.

'I was convinced you meant Dédé! There was some strong chemistry between you two that night,' I said, in a teasing, gossipy tone that sounded quite unlike me. Suzanne grinned suggestively. 'Dédé and I are just friends...'

I interrupted before I could hear the French for *friends with benefits.* 'Sorry, Suzanne, I really need to get to work. I've got tons to do while it's quiet.'

Maybe it was for the best that I couldn't tell anyone what was going on backstage in my life. Any confidante would have had to tolerate me twisting every single situation or remark to be about the object of my desire, like a besotted teenage girl oversharing every new experience. But this actually *was* about Jean-Luc and all I could do was feign indifference. I took the coffee cups back to the kitchen where he and I had embraced like tragic lovers about to be torn apart by war or sickness. Or prior commitments. Everything made me think of him, simply everything. Since the first mention of his name it was as if he were right with me in the room. I was washing the coffee cups on autopilot but there was something else I didn't fully register at the time: if it became more than sex, I was breaking my own ground rule.

If it wasn't already over.

I made it to the door of the gallery, keenly anticipating the freedom of walking up the street toward the Seine, unaccountable to anyone for my innermost desires. 'You still haven't said what you think of Jean-Luc,' Suzanne said, making me feel I was under observation. This girl didn't give up easily. It was knowing that, in addition to the strong suspicion that she could have any man she wanted, which made me say it, looking her right in the eye without smiling.

'He's nothing but a spoiled momma's boy. I mean, if you think that's hot…'

As I stooped lower, her pretty face fell.

34

I mined Jean-Luc's words for comfort, wishing I could rewind to that moment: *It would destroy me to be near you and not have you.* If I never saw him again, it was something to have made someone feel that way. Emotions reared up inside me like coiled beasts fighting: a sense of culpability, of loss. It took a long time to arrive at the only logical conclusion for his silence. With my shallowness I'd sown doubts about what he was doing with me where previously there were none. He'd left Paris: for the south, for the States, anywhere I was not.

As it turned out, he hadn't gone anywhere. Back at the studio a week later, we fell into a long and wordless clinch. There was something tentative about the way he touched my face all over, right down to the arch of my eyelids, as if we were new to each other. I couldn't fully grasp what was going on between me and Jean-Luc but I couldn't seem to go without it.

'Can you believe I was halfway through a text to you when I got yours,' I told him.

'You were? What did it say?'

'Well, two-thirds, to be precise. It said *I miss—*'

He planted his face in his hands and when he looked up, he was shaking his head and smiling, signs of the same elation and relief I felt.

'You just said the same as usual...' I said.

'Well, it's true,' he replied. 'I do spend a lot of time thinking. And especially about you. I kind of lost it last time. I thought I'd scared you off.'

'Funny, because that's exactly what I thought I'd done. What I said... it wasn't about you.'

'Anyway, it was worth it,' he said. 'Now we know we are not scared.'

I was still terrified but it was absolutely worth it. I lay back on the bed with my eyes closed, arms up by my head as the tension unspooled, my breasts lifting and spreading across my rib cage. 'Want one?' I heard him say, and before I saw what he was offering Jean-Luc handed me a beer, his fingers dripping with condensation that he wiped on his jeans. I don't drink beer but the concept of things I didn't do had ceased to mean very much. My mouth was dry and it was refreshing and lemony, more pleasant than I'd anticipated. I watched Jean-Luc drink from the bottle, the sheen on his lips transferring to the back of his hand. We hadn't even kissed.

He lay down beside me, leaning on one elbow.

'You look exhausted,' I said. 'You're not sick, are you?'

That prompted a pained expression. 'I work nights at a gas station up by the Porte de la Villette. It suits me. I never sleep much anyway.'

I didn't get why the Malavoines' son, whose masters in the States must be costing a fortune and who loved the sea, would come all the way back from California to work in a gas station in Paris. 'But surely you have other plans for the summer?'

He looked toward the window and sighed before turning back to me. 'There's no point. Nothing ever goes the way you plan.'

For all Suzanne's lustful designs on Jean-Luc, she wasn't wrong about him being moody. He looked and sounded profoundly gloomy, in a way that was also touching and sexy. That is not easy.

'Are you about to start quoting John Lennon?' I paused when he didn't react to my attempt to be chirpy. 'You do know what he said…?'

'Yes. I can quote lots of people who died before I was born. I expect you can too.'

'Sorry.' I was always saying the wrong thing. 'I didn't mean to make light of…' I didn't *know* what, but something was eating at him.

'It's okay. It's not anything you said.'

'Your days must be a bit strange. What time do you start work?'

'Sometimes ten, usually midnight.'

'So you can still go out in the evening if you want. Do you have friends in the neighbourhood?'

'Sure, there are people I can see,' he said, with complete indifference. 'But that's not why I came back.' I briefly thought he was going to satisfy my curiosity. 'I watch László's place,' he said, looking around the studio as if entrusted with guarding a château. 'My boss pays good money. It is enough.' He reached for my shoulder. 'With you, it is more than enough.'

Now we kissed, slowly, gently, without the frenzy. There was a delectable indolence to drawing it out, switching to a slower setting. My body's urgent demands abated, for now.

As so often when a horizon opens in my head, I thought of the ocean. 'Tell me about your west coast trip. You must have seen so much more of it than I have. I was sent to boarding school in England after my parents split up.'

I would not be who I am if I'd stayed in California. I had a vision of a carefree teenage me taking the bends of the coast road in a convertible, hair flowing out on the wind. Rather unlike my Coldwater years. Then it was superseded by an image of Jean-Luc and some impossibly pretty girl on a beach and I wished I hadn't asked.

Too late. A light came on in his eyes and the colour came to me in a flash: *viridian*. Without realising, I'd been trying to identify it since the first time I saw him in daylight. Between green and cyan on the wheel, often known as teal. But there are no uniform hues in nature and the warm blue around the pupil gradually blended with green, bronze filaments radiating from the black. For a few seconds Jean-Luc remained still as if he knew I must not be interrupted, then we both blinked back to where we were.

'Such a great trip it's hard to know where to start,' he said.

'Bet you met some characters hitch-hiking.'

'Oh, yeah. The first bit was boring as hell. Three hours on the interstate with an insurance salesman I got talking to in a sports bar in Seattle. I mean, nice guy, but all he talked about was *an... anoo...* I can't even say it!'

'Annuities?'

'That's it. *An-ou-ité.* I still don't know what it means. Anyway, it was better when I got on the 101. Nobody travels that road in a hurry. Getting a ride was never a problem.'

'Did you seriously think it would be?'

He shrugged. 'You never know. There's something unpredictable about travelling with a stranger. It's kind of intense when you both know you'll never meet again.'

'I can imagine.' Right then I wondered what I'd tell a stranger on the road. All of this, I suppose.

'One man told me he'd been stealing from his employer for fifteen years and every day he goes to work he thinks he's going to be found out.'

'How could anyone live like that?'

'Actually, I think the thrill was keeping him going. Can't remember what he did. Some boring job.'

I didn't dare ask what oceanography students end up doing.

'Then there was this other time,' he said, blushing deeply, 'when I was picked up by two really tall Russian girls who wanted, what do you call it?'

'A threesome?' I was trying not to laugh. 'Not sure I want to know how this ended.'

'We stopped at a motel. I was going to go back to the highway and keep going but they asked me to bring their bags to the room. And then one of them grabbed me *here*,' he said, replicating the action, 'and they started making out in front of me.'

'Holy shit!' Everything about this story was taunting me and I still had no idea where it was leading. 'That sounds like most guys' idea of a very good time.'

'Not mine. I said I was going back to the car for my stuff and left in a laundry truck full of Mexicans!'

'This is making me feel I haven't lived,' I said. 'I've never done anything crazy.'

'Until now.'

'Until now.'

'But you've lived in two foreign countries. That doesn't just happen. How is that not living?'

It's all a matter of definition.

'Technically the UK isn't a foreign country, though it certainly felt like it at first. My dad's from there. He was always obsessed with California. He came to study the trees, but he loved the music too. "California Dreamin'", "California Girls", "If you go to San Francisco". It has that effect on people somehow, especially people who don't know it.'

'"Californication".'

It threw me that he'd picked something that illustrated my point so perfectly before I'd finished making it. 'Exactly! Hollywood has a lot to answer for. It's like California is this golden paradise where nothing bad ever happens and that's just not true—' A throttling sensation silenced me.

I've known this a few times now, the indelible mark places make: not just the landscape and the people, the language and the colours, but the feelings I couldn't leave behind. Of everything I'd lost. I should have told him about Christopher but that's always been the hardest thing, even now. I'm working my way up to it.

When I opened my eyes, Jean-Luc's were level with mine, bereft. Submerged. 'I know what you mean about California,' he said. Neither of us knew what the other was talking about but somehow we were entwined, without even touching. 'There's only one cure for this *mélancolie*, as I have recently discovered,' he said, wiping his face with his T-shirt as he pulled it over his head. It only took a glimpse of chest and armpit for me to start shedding my clothes like they were on fire.

It was an antidote, because there is no cure. Whatever it was, it was bliss.

35

I was sitting at my laptop at home, trying to compose a reply to Emily's long newsy email that didn't involve answering the loaded question *How are things?* Due to the school break, their family vacation in Spain and the fact I either didn't answer her calls or said I couldn't talk, *that* conversation – the one where I admitted to ignoring her advice and jeopardising my marriage – hadn't happened yet. But it was only a matter of time.

I was distracted by the sound of laughter from the stairwell, getting louder until Vanessa burst in, accompanied by two other girls.

'It's the gig tonight,' she told me. 'We're just going to hang out here first.'

'Of course,' I said, not that she was asking permission. 'Hello!'

'This is my stepmom, Alexandra,' she told her friends, 'and this is Morgane and Anaïs.'

I smiled. That was the first time Vanessa had acknowledged me as her stepmother, and not as if I was the evil kind. The two girls were looking around, sizing the place up. 'That's nice,' Morgane said, of the painting over the mantelpiece, as if it was from IKEA. They were both like pretty little dolls, about half the size of Vanessa, who looked about twenty-five next to them: Morgane pale and ethereal with long blonde hair, Anaïs dark-skinned with black ringlets. I remembered Vanessa mentioning her friend whose mother was from Martinique.

'What time will you be heading out?'

'Not for a while. We're meeting the others there. Is there anything to eat? How about some of that mac and cheese?'

Vanessa too had acquired a taste for this – I was starting to wonder if one of the ingredients was addictive. She proceeded to describe it to her friends and they screwed their noses up at the idea of powdered cheese, or it might just have been calories in general. 'There's only one box left,' I called from the kitchen.

'That'll do me,' Vanessa replied, 'these two aren't hungry.'

Obviously it fell to me to make it.

'We should text Hugo now about the spare ticket or he won't have time to get here,' said Anaïs.

'No, don't do that!' said Vanessa. 'I've found someone to take it. You'll never guess who!'

'Is it *him*? Is it, really?'

In the kitchen, I stopped stirring.

'You're not, you and him, are you?' said Morgane, lowering her voice.

Vanessa laughed loudly. 'Yeah, right, in my dreams! And you all thought Boris was out of my league.'

'Only asking.' Morgane sounded rather put out.

'To be fair, she hasn't seen the photos, remember?' Anaïs said to Vanessa.

'Ooh, show me, show me!'

I headed for the furthest corner of the kitchen even though I couldn't be seen from where I was.

'Here's one of Alexandra giving her speech,' Vanessa began. 'Come and see!' I pressed my face into my hands, breathed in deeply and went out into the living room.

'I like that dress,' said Morgane. 'My mom's got one like it.'

'You were there for the speeches?' I said. 'I thought you arrived later.'

'I was at the back,' Vanessa replied. 'That's why there are so many heads in the way.'

She was flipping through the images. 'That's me and my dad. That's this really cool thing from the exhibition,' she said, referring to the torture instrument known as *Incineration*. 'And there's Suzanne, my dad's assistant.'

'Whoa, look at her!'

'And *here we are…*'

I could so easily have returned to the kitchen but I just stood there, unable to move.

It wasn't a selfie – one of the post-grads must have taken it. Vanessa looked like she'd just won the lottery. Standing next to her, shoulders almost touching, was Jean-Luc, with the half-smile of someone who doesn't want their picture taken and doesn't care how it turns out. A dart of longing made me look away.

Morgane gave an earthy growl quite at odds with her angelic appearance. 'You weren't kidding, Vanessa. He is *so* out of your league.'

I was rescued by the smell of something burning.

36

Philippe had not only decided to leave for Nice without me, he even thought it was his idea. I encouraged him to ask Vanessa to go too. Their long estrangement meant she'd missed out on getting to know his family properly. Her teenage cousins would also be visiting the house that used to belong to Philippe's parents, now shared between their four children in a harmonious set-up that was far from guaranteed under French inheritance laws. Some would rather demolish a property or burn it to the ground than come to a civilised agreement.

The arrangements were all in place and he was due to leave next Monday. I'd be holding my breath until then, waiting for the moment when I could finally give myself over completely to the way I felt, the way I *wanted* to feel, and put an end to this bizarre swinging between ecstasy and various forms of guilt and anxiety.

Vanessa had been unexpectedly positive – she was so fed up with the oppressive heat and boredom of Paris that she would have agreed to almost anything. To my relief she didn't fancy the long drive with Philippe, so I purchased a train ticket before she could change her mind.

After the frustrations of city driving, her father liked to put his foot down on the autoroute, his southern character reasserting itself as soon as he hit the road. Having spent my entire adult life in big cities I'd never had a licence. On our trips down south I was a quiet passenger, often secretly scared, allowing Philippe to concentrate on the road. If he and Vanessa got into one of their slanging matches it could be dangerous.

I made vague noises about joining them the week after without committing myself. For all its uses, mobile technology has made a lot of situations harder to manage. The imperative to be in a certain place, for example, has been removed unless there is some physical element to it, although the need for quality time with one's lover will not do. My culinary machinations, serving dishes from the South of France such as bouillabaisse and lamb with ratatouille night after night, had successfully eased Philippe into pre-vacation mood. He didn't question my weak story about the possibility of someone connected to the monastery in Romania passing through Paris and that it would look bad if nobody from Editions Gallici was available.

Philippe probably needed a break from me and I didn't blame him. Just as the emotional distance had crept in between us, physical contact too had become infrequent and brief, making me realise I had undervalued this side of our relationship. To be technical, we hadn't had *penetrative* sex since that dire occasion at the very start of my affair. I had the audacity to feel slighted that Philippe didn't seem to be missing it despite my resolution not to sleep with two men at the same time. Contrary to the spirit of marriage, I wanted to keep myself for Jean-Luc and him alone.

There was, however, another explanation for Philippe's dark mood and the apparent decline in his sex drive: I'd found out from snooping at his phone again that he'd been dumped by Nico in the most perfunctory terms: *It's over. I can't do this anymore.* Knowing all about rejection I almost felt sorry for him, especially after everything he'd been through with Brigitte; that is, once I'd got over my irritation at the way this altered everything.

This was a sign, a deadline – as his *aventure* had ended, so too would mine, inevitably. It was getting too serious. In my mind I drew a line across a map of France, forcing myself to be dispassionate, sensible. My arrival in Nice would mark my return to Philippe and his to me. We'd had our crises and now we had to start communicating again. I hoped that we could pull ourselves together (in every sense) and decide that what we had was worth saving, that Emily was right and we would get through this. Even if I came clean with Philippe he wasn't in a position to be too tough on me, so long as I didn't identify my lover. There was always the possibility we'd come out stronger.

My lover. Although it tore at me to think of it – if I could only use one word to describe all of this, it would be *torn* – Jean-Luc was bound to be leaving Paris soon; he had his whole life ahead, as the saying goes. He was worth more, and wanted more, than I could give him. Something about him just wasn't cut out for casual.

It should have remained a one-off, but having further compromised myself since, there seemed no point in forgoing the rest of it. It was like being on a diet, when you open a packet of cookies planning to only eat two and then think, *Oh, what the hell?* The kind of logic people use to play down cheating with an ex. Sure, it was messing with my head but in other ways it was doing me good. I know I've talked about turning into someone different but it was never really that; instead, I was becoming who I would have been all along, if I hadn't been hell-bent on clutching my sorrows so close to me.

Jonathan once called me an 'emotional cripple'. He regretted it instantly. He wasn't wrong but there are more delicate ways of expressing it.

It wasn't true any more. Thirty years of numbness was enough for anyone. Jean-Luc made me feel so immensely good that it gave me hope. I was complicated and confused but there was more to me than I'd realised. It wasn't real happiness because that can never be at another's expense, but in this tornado of incompatible emotions I was hearing stronger voices than the one telling me that. I had the rest of my life to be good and I promised myself I would be.

But for now, I figured I'd earned some more fun. Excitement. Passion. There was no single word. What difference would a few more days make? For it to burn itself out, first I had to let it blaze.

37

Still Philippe didn't seem to register anything out of the ordinary and it made me start to provoke him. I left our wedding photo face down for more than a week after knocking it over accidentally – it probably could have stayed there a year without him noticing, a man who hangs pictures for a living. When I returned it to its rightful position, it grieved me to see our joyful expressions, like we couldn't believe our luck.

When I told him a friend and I were seeing the new movie from a director I hate, he didn't pass comment other than to ask if I'd be home late. I suppose I never used to ask where he was – you don't, if you don't want to know. Every time I returned from one of my fictitious activities, part of me wished Philippe would be waiting, ready to demand what the hell I was playing at. Or to say, *I know where you've been. I worked out what you were up to a long time ago.* So I wasn't hoping for much – just for the one I was betraying to save me from myself.

I wish I could stop saying *part of me*. Is anyone wholly anything?

The next time I saw Jean-Luc he'd had his hair cut. It was very short around the back and sides, longer on top, where it stood up at an angle. Now he was getting the full benefit of those cheekbones and his improbably straight Parisian nose. Whoever had done it had studied his face closely. So expressive – the way he'd brighten on seeing me made my heart falter.

'You're staring at me!' he said. Maybe if you grow up in this city you take good looks for granted.

'Right!' I said. 'Because I bet that never happens. Are you flattered?'

I thumbed his temple as my fingers caressed the back of his head, my pinkie drawn to the newly exposed strip where the hair had been shaven away. He tilted his head to kiss my palm and drew me into the studio. He took a couple of steps backward and, judging it perfectly, he threw himself on the bed, pulling me down on top of him. I kneeled forward into a kiss, my hair falling around our faces.

I sat back on my heels, adjusting myself so I was up against his hard-on, not pressing on it. He traced his hands up and down my thighs, first through, then under my skirt. Knowing what lay ahead, I found the teasing run-up exquisite, just like the moments after. Unless I was in a rush to get away, several times was the norm. I'd never been with a man who could do that, or wanted to. I was transformed by the way he made me feel, stripped of inhibitions. I shook out my hair like a *femme fatale*, my face lighting up from inside. The buttons of my blouse melted under my fingers – I was wearing one of the bras I got when I first met Philippe, black gauze with tiny polka dots and lacing in the middle, marginally more burlesque than bordello. Back then I was considerably slimmer and it was tight and uncomfortable now, my breasts spilling out the top. Jean-Luc moaned and shifted underneath me, creating some tantalising friction for both of us. 'God, I want you so bad. You can't imagine.'

I didn't have to imagine.

It was only afterward that I registered the noise from downstairs had stopped.

'The apartment can't be finished already?'

'It isn't. The Romanians stopped working a while ago because they weren't getting paid. Have you only just realised?' It used to embarrass me meeting the contractors on the stairs, their heavily accented greetings accompanied by knowing smiles. 'They don't even know where the owner's gone. They left the keys with me!' Jean-Luc gave me a look. 'Hey, that could be fun…'

'No way are we… I get all the fun I need right here,' I said, lying there with his arms around me. 'I could stay like this for ever.'

Jean-Luc turned to me, his face inches from mine. The dark rim around his irises always looked more intense after sex. I loved how he could lose himself in it but somehow still find me. 'Me too. You obsess me,' he said. *Tu m'obsèdes.*

A queasy feeling took hold of my stomach. '*I'm obsessed with you,*' I corrected, hurriedly explaining that's what an English speaker would say. 'For some reason you put it the other way round in French.' It was as if I already had an inkling that something was afoot that I didn't want to be responsible for. 'You talk about obsession as if it's a good thing.'

He laughed. 'Isn't it? A French woman would never complain to hear this. They want passion. They want to be desired.' He sighed. 'They're not easy to please.'

'Oh, is that so? I get what you're saying…' I'd thought part of my appeal was that I was more grateful than a twenty-year-old but I much preferred the idea that I was relaxed, undemanding, fun to be with. Neither of us cared that I had a few lines on my face and a body with plenty to grab hold of. With him I felt ageless now. I felt beautiful. I felt free.

'No, it's *good* you're not like that.' He looked anxious, not realising I was teasing. 'With us it feels, I don't know, natural, real. Me and my friends grew up on internet *porno*. It's all fake. A lot of girls think that's what we want – plastic dummies, all the same, going *Oh, oh, oh!*' He shook his head. 'You can feel like a freak for not wanting to fuck anyone up the ass.'

I told him about Suzanne and the man who wanted her to position her flawless, no doubt hairless, body under a glass table while he took a shit on it. When Jean-Luc said he wasn't surprised, I realised I never asked if she'd gone through with it. 'But that's it exactly,' he said. 'It wasn't *her* he wanted – she was an object, like merchandise. That kind of sex is no different to getting wasted – it doesn't feel like anything. I'd rather jerk off – it's less lonely.'

His words were confident, as if he'd really thought about it. But behind them, there was something raking at him. I wanted to comfort him so badly I didn't stop to think what I was saying.

'That will change when you meet the right person. You're intelligent and sensitive. And you hardly need me to tell you the effect you have on women.'

Now he was more miserable than ever. 'I am terrible with women. I mean, I always was before I met you.'

'*What?* You're kidding, right? I thought you said the opposite... in fact, I know you did. It stuck in my mind, if you must know.' The girls. All those pretty girls.

He grimaced. 'Yeah, well getting laid has never been the problem. When they get to know me... Do *you* think I'm intense?'

'I do, sometimes, and I think it's rather wonderful.' It was also infectious, everything paling beside it, as if there was no other way to live.

'It makes me "hard work". *Fatiguant.* It's not what anyone wants.'

'They can want what they like. You said being real is what's important. Just be yourself...'

'...because *everyone else is already taken?*'

'Oscar Wilde! Nobody could put it better. I was going to say, because you're lovely the way you are.'

His smile developed like an old-fashioned photograph. '*This* is why it's so different with you,' he said. 'We just

225

are who we are, two people, no labels. When you come, it's *your* voice I hear, it's *me* you're talking to. I was in such a bad place before you – I couldn't imagine the rest of my life. Everything was so fucking dark, like being trapped underwater.'

To think that I could be somebody's light.

Lying behind, he wrapped himself around me, stroking my feet with his. I felt his heart rate slow, the muscles relax in the arm that held me. 'I've never felt this close to anyone,' he said in my ear. 'I don't need anything else to make me feel good any more. This is all I want, every single day.' I pushed him flat on the bed and our mouths fastened together until we were dizzy. I took a breath of something sweeter than air.

I wanted to come, and cry and laugh in this new voice of mine, to silence the warning bells, because I'd never felt so good either.

38

By now I was on first-name terms with Mokhtar, the pizza delivery guy. '*Vous venez le matin aussi?*' he said, grinning, as we crossed paths in the courtyard. He was right – I didn't normally come to the studio this early. The residents who saw me regularly must have guessed at my liaison with Jean-Luc, although according to him many of them had illicit dealings of their own. The men would not be so tolerant when it came to their wives, sisters and daughters. The women, some of them wearing hijabs, didn't seem to see at me at all.

I was here now because I couldn't make time later. Without my knowledge my mother had invited the other participants from her painting course in Provence to look me up if they were ever in Paris, which not many people would do on such a tenuous connection. Having agreed to meet the woman from Alaska at the Musée d'Orsay café at four o'clock, I decided to treat myself to an afternoon at the museum, which I could justify in the name of work; several of the paintings in our next book were displayed there, including two in which Baudelaire himself appeared. And a surprise morning visit to my lover, *pourquoi pas*? We'd parted on an exceptional high.

Jean-Luc opened the door in his underwear but had already turned his back when I came into the studio, gesticulating unseen at the person at the end of the phone. Whoever it was had got him out of bed, the covers up in a heap. 'Why can't you accept it?' he spat into the handset. 'I'm not going to change my mind!'

It seemed that I'd discovered the cause of his troubles, walking in on the tail-end of the California romance I'd suspected back at the start. I didn't mean to be heartless but if it was no more than that, I was relieved. Break-ups are tough and Jean-Luc needed to be with somebody who got him. He threw the phone on the bed so hard it rebounded and landed on the wooden floor, where it separated into three pieces, the battery coming to rest inches from my foot.

'Fuck!' he said, just as he saw me standing there.

'I'm sorry to intrude. This is obviously a bad time,' I said. 'Maybe I'll see you later in the week?'

He caught me as I went to leave. 'Don't go, Alexandra.'

'Is it girl trouble?'

'What?'

'The phone call. I couldn't help hearing the last bit. You did let me in, remember?'

He laughed. 'No, for God's sake! There is no girl. That was my mother.'

'*Ah.*' Just as well I hadn't said anything. Geneviève would have been able to identify me from a single word.

'You don't normally take her calls. Is it a special occasion?' That was a cheap shot. I'd been trying to persuade him it would be less stressful just to go to dinner at his parents' place than expend so much energy avoiding it.

'I went for a drink with my dad yesterday but apparently that's not good enough.'

'Put some clothes on.' This ran against the normal pattern for us and he was about to protest. 'All in good time. Do you want to talk about it?' With the knowledge that my theory was wrong came an urgent need to get a few things straight.

'About sex?' he said, picking his jeans up off the floor and pausing before putting them on.

'*Noo*, about what's going on with your mom. The two of you seem to have issues, to put it mildly.'

'That is the last thing I want to do. I mean, no man would choose to talk about his mother when he could have you.' He snuggled up to my neck.

'Stop it, Jean-Luc, I'm serious. You will not be "having me" unless we have this conversation. I've seen how this is upsetting your mother, and it's clearly affecting you too.'

He could even sulk prettily.

'What's the problem? It's such a shame when you've only just come back. She was looking forward to spending some time with you.'

'Look, I know you're trying to help and you think you know my mother, but you have no idea what it's like to have to deal with her. You really wouldn't understand.'

'You'd be surprised.' I didn't elaborate, having nothing constructive to contribute from my own experience as a maternal combat veteran. 'Your mom loves you, I know that much. If you could only hear the way she talks about you.'

He shot me a dirty look. 'You think I haven't? I spent years listening to that shit.'

'Sure, she overdoes it but there were things any parent would be proud of. How about when you got the top score in France in that exam, what was it again?' Suddenly I could picture the Malavoines' living room, right down to where we were all sitting, the first time I heard that story. It was the day I'd met the eighteen-year-old Jean-Luc for all of ten seconds.

'The *bac de philo*. She was trying to impress you, as if you cared. There's no such thing as the best score in France. The perfect son she talks about is an *être imaginaire*, not me. Believe me, you've only heard what she wants you to know. I got the highest mark you can get, and so did other people. And it was nothing to do with her. That was down to me and László, and to luck – one of the essay questions was something we'd talked about a lot. And I didn't even write what I really thought, I just gave the answers they wanted.'

'You and László were in school together? For some reason I thought he was older.'

'He *is* older. He's thirty-two. He's in Budapest this summer but he was my philosophy teacher from when I was sixteen – it was his first job. My mother paid him to tutor me so I could get that score. He never took the money or gave me any lessons though. We used to hang out here and drink beer and smoke *shit* and talk, or play football with the kids over there.' He tipped his head toward the narrow strip of park that ran alongside the railway tracks.

I tried to manage the look on my face. 'So you're telling me you used to drink and get high with your *philosophy teacher* in this apartment? What kind of a person does that? I'm talking about him, by the way, not you.'

'He's not a paedo, if that's what you're thinking,' Jean-Luc said. '*Il aime les mecs et les meufs*. László likes men and women, but never kids. He doesn't agree with the way society puts labels on people, pressuring them to live a certain way without questioning it. He was a big influence on me.'

'I can see.' Just as well Jean-Luc and I had 'no labels' – I didn't like to think what mine would be.

'I mean, I was already thinking that way. I just had never met anyone who wanted to have that kind of conversation with me.'

'What was the essay about, just out of interest?'

'*Vivons-nous pour être heureux?*'

'Do we live to be happy? Is the purpose of life... Gosh, there's a question!'

Jean-Luc closed his eyes and I could hear the emotion in his breathing. 'László was there when I didn't have anyone else, okay? If the right person appears in your life when you need them, you don't send them away.'

I felt tears springing up as I reached for his hand, realising I'd missed the important part. 'Too bad he's not around now you're back.'

'It is. But on the other hand, if he was here we'd have nowhere to go.'

'True,' I said. 'Does he know about us?'

'Yes. I asked him, *László, my friend, do you mind if I use your apartment to make crazy love to a beautiful woman?*'

'Sure you did. And what did he say?'

'He said *avec plaisir*. So, I've answered all your questions. Are you going to make me feel better now?'

I took off my top so I could feel my skin against his bare chest. 'Oh, I can do that,' I said, sighing as he proceeded to undress me. 'What did you have in mind?'

'*Carresse-toi. C'est si beau de te voir jouir.*'

No wonder he always switched back to French for sex talk – it sounds more hot than dirty and he knew it. 'Um, thanks, but I like it better when you make me. What is it with men wanting to watch women touch themselves? Isn't it kind of a waste when we're together?'

'Who says you can't have both? You know it's not a waste.'

I stretched, my arms reaching up into the air, feeling a cascade of sensation the length of my body, starting at my fingertips. My right hand followed involuntarily, pausing on my belly, pressing hard. It's so intriguing, all these zones: touch one place and feel it in another. 'You're really making me want to.'

I didn't so much walk back across the courtyard as float. It was raining and I didn't care. Nothing could affect me in my bubble; I could feel the flush lingering on my cheeks. We could switch between states in an instant: sadness and elation, stress and excitement, post-coital satisfaction and... *sheer horror.*

As the double doors leading to the street closed behind me, a cab pulled up right outside, its passenger leaning forward to pay the driver. It was Jean-Luc's mother. If I entered the code to go back in, Geneviève would see me. If I walked off in either direction, she would see me – the car door was opening now and there was no way I could make it to the corner before she got out, even at a run. There was no guarantee she hadn't already seen me from inside, recognising the unusual blue and white skirt she once admired that reminded us both of Matisse.

I dashed into the only possible bolt-hole: the kebab place beside the apartment building. The inscrutable pairs of eyes that had seen me so many times fixed on me in pity and surprise. The man behind the counter said something urgent to one of the others, who pushed a chair in my direction. My head dropped down between my knees and for a few seconds there was a warm, fuzzy blackness at my temples. I'd forgotten to eat breakfast. '*Ma'a,*' said the older man, '*sokkar.*' They gave me water and a sticky chunk of baklava and we stayed like that for a long time, watching the rain pelt down. There was an almighty crack of thunder directly overhead. Refusing more food and trying to block out the sight and smell of greasy meat on a spit, I drank a glass of sweet mint tea in small sips before the downpour came to an end. One of the men went outside and looking up at the sky he said, '*Inshallah*, it is over now.'

39

Vanessa was with me in the kitchen, leaning on the door-frame and feasting on her nails as she explained her theories about race relations, a burning issue not just for France but for her too following Asradi's exhibition. There wasn't room for both of us and I was the one making dinner but since she was sounding rational and articulate I was trying to listen, thinking of those men in the café, so steeped in their culture yet so at home in Paris. They had been so kind to me. Although her father was in the living room, as usual Vanessa seemed to prefer my company. I hoped that would change when they went to Nice.

'But there hasn't been any trouble recently, has there?' I said. 'I haven't heard anything on the news.' I hadn't been following the news all that closely, I'll admit.

'True,' she said. 'But it might be about to kick off again.'

Just as I was about to enquire how she would know, the doorbell rang. There was no entry phone system in the building, which meant the caller was right outside in the hallway. For that reason, it didn't happen often. 'Are you expecting anyone, Philippe?'

Philippe was so busy emailing his brother to set up fishing trips that he didn't even look up from his laptop. The buzzer sounded again, for longer, and I pushed past Vanessa with a sigh.

'Geneviève! *Quelle surprise!*' And it really was, the worst kind. Had she seen me leaving the studio? I threw the towel I'd dried my hands on behind the door as I invited her in, glad the apartment was looking presentable. Philippe got up to greet her and made Vanessa do the same, pushing her in Geneviève's direction. Neither of them looked very happy about it.

'We were about to have an apéritif,' I lied. 'Vanessa, could you fetch the rosé in the fridge – and some glasses, please?' Without this level of micro-management she would be capable of delivering the bottle alone as if we were supposed to pass it around and swig from it like *ados*.

'I won't be staying long,' Geneviève said. 'I was visiting a friend in rue Servandoni and we decided to go to Mass at Saint-Sulpice.' I breathed again. There was no sign of Geneviève abandoning her habitual decorum to cause a scene. Between my ability to relive every past *chagrin* in technicolour and to conjure up new ones, I wished I had a less active imagination.

'Very good,' nodded Philippe, who went through the motions of Catholicism, albeit not to the point of attending Mass unless there was a party involved. He was good at concealing this from Geneviève.

'Henri tells me you're too busy to go to Nice, Alexandra.' Before I could get a word in edgewise, she continued. 'So I had an idea the two of you might like. Or the three of you, perhaps,' she said, looking at Vanessa with distaste. At that, Vanessa slammed the tray down on the table with a grunt and made herself scarce.

As Philippe made no effort to play host, I set to work opening the wine, a Bandol we'd been looking forward to. There was to be no let-up on the Côte d'Azur theme until he'd packed his bags and left. I went to the kitchen in search of some olives or crackers to accompany the drinks. Needless to say, we had neither. The awkward silence in the living room told me they were waiting for my return.

'So,' Geneviève said, as I sat down, 'Henri and I thought you could join us this weekend at my sister's near Honfleur. That way you'll get a little break from Paris.'

When I caught Philippe's eye he was trying to stop himself grinning and I pieced it all together in an instant: Henri had orchestrated this. They couldn't seem to get enough of each other.

'That's so kind,' I said, not trusting myself to look at my husband again. There was no point – he wasn't going to help me out.

I handed her a small measure of wine. She was looking at me expectantly but on her face my memory super-imposed her expression the day we ran into each other in the Bon Marché grocery store. That excruciating moment was still lingering and now there was another – had she seen me or not? I'd never been comfortable in her presence but that was nothing compared to the crawling unease she produced in me since Jean-Luc had come back. They talk about 'fight or flight' – I didn't have either option. The Malavoines were so tightly woven into the fabric of our lives that there was no escaping them without ripping it end to end.

'Thank you,' I said. 'That would be lovely, won't it, Philippe?' As Geneviève turned toward him I grabbed a second's respite from my false smile. It must have used different facial muscles from usual and they were smarting with the strain.

'Véronique's place?' Philippe asked. Like him, Geneviève had an entourage of siblings.

'Yes, do you remember, Alexandra? The one right on the coast.'

'Oh yes, I remember,' I said. 'I liked it very much.' Philippe and I had spent a weekend there, not long after we married. It was a typical Norman country house, half-timbered, with a steep tiled roof. I was already formulating survival strategies: long walks, taking charge of the kitchen (Geneviève didn't really cook), studying the news so I could talk with the men and not find myself marooned with her as so often happened. But there were limits: if I asked to go out in a boat with them, Philippe would know for sure something was wrong.

'That's settled then,' Geneviève said, with the satisfaction of someone whose will is rarely disputed. 'Come for dinner on Saturday and stay the rest of the weekend. The traffic going back shouldn't be too bad at this time of year.'

I listened for the elevator to be sure she'd gone. 'You knew about this,' I said to Philippe. 'Is this the real reason you're not leaving for Nice until Monday?'

'Not at all. I told you, there won't be space for me and Vanessa in the house until then. We can hardly share a room!' He motioned to me to sit back down. 'I don't see what you're so upset about. Geneviève means well, you know. Henri says she finds you distant – did you realise that? She didn't have to make an effort with you when we got married but she always has. You could try being a bit more gracious.'

'I said we'd go, didn't I?' It wasn't exactly true and I certainly couldn't claim to have been especially gracious. Geneviève hadn't phrased it as an invitation, more of a *fait accompli*. 'This dinner's not going to cook itself,' I said, retreating because I couldn't stand to be in the same room as Philippe. I was in danger of throwing a fit and forcing him to choose between me and the Malavoines – in fact, that could be a neat way to resolve all of our problems because as things stood I doubted any such gamble would go my way. *Always made an effort!* As if I'd have cared if she didn't. I should never have played along with this charade; Philippe had other friends whose wives I didn't know. Geneviève was more than twenty years older than me, for God's sake!

That had always felt like the issue, that and the fact that she and Henri knew my husband so much better than I did, making me feel like an interloper. But now the issue was much bigger. When I was with Jean-Luc I bought into an absurd illusion that the people close to me didn't exist; the rest of the time I was tormented by thoughts of them even when I was alone. I may have avoided coming face to face with Geneviève at the studio but something about the penetrating looks she was giving me convinced me she knew things she shouldn't.

I'd taken my drink into the kitchen along with the conviction that I was slipping my mental moorings. Was it possible to develop a personality disorder out of nowhere? I did once take a strong blow to the head. I was horrified to find myself thinking that a brain tumour might explain everything. Even benign masses could make people become violent, disinhibited, change beyond recognition. The summery strawberry bouquet of the wine reminded me so much of happier times that I had to gnaw at my knuckles to keep myself from howling. In our five years together there had never been a problem I couldn't share with Philippe. I imagined pulling him into the hallway and telling him, *I've gotten myself into a terrible situation.* He'd say, *What is it, Alexandra? Don't get so upset, just tell me.*

But that was an obsolete version of us. The reality was me, on my own, trying to cut myself in two. Wanting to have it both ways.

Vanessa had chosen some huge glasses we rarely used and in my desperation to make contact with the contents I tilted mine back too far, slicing the top of my nose with the rim. That made me bite my tongue as I yelped in pain. A ribbon of blood unfurled against the pretty pink.

I was going to be made to suffer for what I'd done. Somehow I knew that all along.

40

The night before we were due to head to Honfleur, Philippe slumbered away oblivious to my endless sighing and fidgeting. I had moved through 360 degrees in quarter turns so many times that when I lay still the room seemed to be spinning. Finally I sat up, noting the contrast between my body heat and the coolness of the dark air. The numerals of Philippe's alarm clock cast a greenish glow over our bedroom. Peering over his back I saw it was 02:20.

The hour of nothing, or at best, a good night drawing to a close. I had never embarked on anything at 02:20. Worries are often worse at night but crazy ruses can seem like good decisions at any time of day. No, more than that: they can feel inevitable. It was like something was propelling me to leave the apartment. I was certain Jean-Luc would hear from his parents that Philippe and I were going to Normandy. I had to make him promise to stay away and I had to do it in person.

With another glance to check that I hadn't disturbed Philippe, I pulled a skirt over the satin slip I was wearing in bed and slid my feet into the nearest pair of ballet pumps lined up with other shoes against the wall, resulting in a mismatched getup of polka dots, florals and zebra print. Grabbing my bag and keys, I paused outside Vanessa's bedroom door. The weight of my tread on the old floorboards must have made the lock shift in the frame, for it swung open to reveal an empty bed. After the initial fright I continued on my way, vague stirrings of concern over her whereabouts easily dismissed.

At the nearest taxi stand I asked a weary driver if he was familiar with a tiny 24-hour gas station near the Porte de la Villette (if Jean-Luc had told me more than this, the details escaped me now). My pretext of having left something of value there was compromised almost immediately when the man asked me what the place looked like. Was it kind of triangular, next to a Lebanese restaurant? And why didn't I drive back there myself? I replied that I'd been drinking and didn't remember – did he want the fare or not? He shut up when I said I would pay him to drive me around until we found it.

As it happened, his original guess was spot on. The smell of gasoline mingled with the spicy tang of food as I crossed the deserted forecourt toward Jean-Luc. His head was propped up on his hand behind the glass of the night-service window, earphones in, eyes tight shut, looking dreamy. If he was listening to *The Earth Is Not a Cold Dead Place* he'd be out for a long time. I tapped gently on the glass and he did a double take: of surprise first off, followed by delight. I pushed my hand into the shallow drawer where customers put their payment and his fingertips reached out to mine before he got up to unlock the main door. He couldn't wait that long to touch me.

'What are you doing here?'

I couldn't think.

He rushed me through to a small back room, answering my puzzled looks with a nod at the CCTV camera pointing at the cashier's desk.

'But won't you get in trouble if they *don't* see you?'

He laughed at me. 'It's weird enough that you turned up. It would be a coincidence if there was a robbery the same night. Besides, look. It's dead out there.'

We were kissing hard before we fully made it into the dark and narrow space. I pushed the door to because he didn't seem to care.

'The next few days are going to be tricky—' I began.

He shook his head. 'When are you going to realise there *is* no other day, Alexandra? Stop worrying about yesterdays and tomorrows. When we're together, there is only now.'

Living in the moment wouldn't be a problem if there were more moments like these.

There was something so romantic about his brand of naïveté, if that's what it was. Maybe he was the one who was right, with his total lack of concern for anything but the present. He stroked my face and even in the dingy surroundings those eyes scintillated with eagerness when he looked at me. His philosophy had such strong appeal: ignore the complications. Disregard the consequences.

Forget everyone else and give yourself over unconditionally to doing whatever the fuck you want.

I was more of a convert than he knew. If anyone had told me I'd find myself taking a taxi across Paris to an unknown gas station to visit my lover in the dead of night, I would have thought them deranged. Doing it was more exhilarating than I could have imagined.

I shrugged off my cardigan and Jean-Luc's eyebrows shot up. 'I like this look,' he said, his hands roving over my chest, searching for the edge of the shiny fabric so they could slide up underneath. He reached around me to unzip my skirt, which pooled at my feet. 'What if you get a customer?' I asked feebly, but he wasn't listening.

My body arched involuntarily against some coats hanging on the wall as his hand gravitated to the wetness below. His words about being comfortable in my skin returned to me, both of us relishing my arousal. It's a *secretion* so secret it doesn't even have its own word. Women aren't supposed to want sex like men do, but I'm no longer convinced men and women are so very different in the force of our desires.

And the epitome of that desire is wanting the other badly enough to do it in the back of a car, in a closet (which this effectively was) or against a wall, another popular fantasy I had never had. Based on our current fumblings it wasn't surprising; everything about our bodies that was normally a perfect fit was suddenly in the wrong place. There was a lot of panting and giggling going on – we were like two clueless teenagers who'd finally made it to third base.

'Is anyone there?' thundered a man's voice, accompanied by banging on the window. 'If not, you can't blame me for not paying!'

I groaned. I was so, so close. Jean-Luc fastened his jeans the best he could and tugged his shirt down as low as it would reach. *'Deux secondes,'* he said. 'Don't go anywhere.'

For all that I was in a state of acute frustration, in a corridor that smelled of dirty mop, there was no place I'd rather be. When he returned, it worked. We needed it – this had to see us through the whole weekend until Philippe left on Monday. That reminded me why I'd come here in the middle of the night, half dressed and unkempt.

'There's something I have to say to you,' I whispered, when we were decent and back out in the shop, me purchasing overpriced Coke and cookies for the sake of the CCTV film no one would ever watch unless there *were* to be a hold-up tonight, which there wouldn't, of course. Dramatic events are rarely anticipated.

'There's no sound recording – you can say it,' he said. And I did, though I had a strong feeling I was wasting my breath. I was asking more of him than I could manage myself: to stay away from what I most desired. When we were together it no longer seemed possible that what we were doing was bad. I pitied anyone who would think so, or wouldn't have done the same if they felt this way. I was very late to it but would not now die without having experienced a hidden seam of emotion I cannot put a name to even now. The world is full of violence, injustice and tragedy; it was hard to see what could be so wrong about two people loving each other.

The truth hit me like a collision with an invisible obstacle. We weren't just fucking for the heaven of it. I'd fallen in love with Jean-Luc. The thrill turned to panic as I sped home in another taxi, tearing across the city down boulevards slick with rain most Parisians wouldn't know had fallen, empty and silent but for the occasional police car. The sound of sirens. I hated it even then.

41

With morning came the payback for being up half the night. I ached all over, plus I had a lump on my head from bashing it repeatedly on the coat hooks, not that I had cared at the time. I had slept in and unusually it was Philippe bringing me coffee in bed.

'No run today?' he said. 'You've been working too hard.'

He slid under the covers and buried his face in the gap between my shoulder blades as I lifted the cup to my mouth, sending scalding rivulets down my chin. I grabbed a wad of tissues from my nightstand and pressed them to my mouth to keep from snapping at him.

'I'm going to miss you in Nice,' he said. 'I remember going there on my own just after Brigitte and I separated. It was a bad time.'

Poor man. Thank God he didn't know what was happening to his second marriage. My mind cast around for a soothing response that wasn't falsely reassuring, but 'We're together now' was the best I could do, a statement of fact.

I turned in time to see Philippe's expression transform from doleful to glad and felt the nauseating wrench I first came to know as a ten-year-old watching my mother mourn. I wasn't sure how much of this I could blame on him anymore and there was a masochistic comfort in heaping it at my door. Guilt was never something I wanted to share. I used to cut myself no slack, even when it wasn't all my fault.

When I'd checked Philippe's phone again before returning to bed I saw what a lousy spy I made. There were no new texts between Nico and him but in my previous haste, I'd got his speech bubbles and hers mixed up. She didn't call a halt to their affair – he did. And perhaps it was just a detail but it felt significant that it wasn't my husband who'd sent a text saying *I want you*. His was a wrong which he'd addressed (*righted* would be too strong – he'd still cheated) whereas mine was ongoing, gathering pace, leading me further and further out of control.

I willed Philippe to plead that I change my mind and go to Nice with him. He didn't. But he was after something that was part of the deal between couples. 'You're my wife,' he said, before I'd even attempted to wriggle out of it. There was something odd about the emphasis but I couldn't play it back accurately and I could hardly ask him to repeat it.

Did he say:

You're my wife.

You're *my* wife.

You're my *wife*?

I guess it all comes down to the same. He liked the idea that I belonged to him, when I'd been busy discovering the kick of being my own person, the distinction between existing and living. There are days I wish I'd never found out that passion is lived in sparks, billed in gouges.

'How long is it since we made love?' Philippe nuzzled up against me, all needy. 'It feels like a long time. Like I'm losing you.'

It *was* a long time. And I realised with a pang that he *had* been missing it.

'We should make the most of this morning,' he went on in his best seductive tones. 'You know you won't be in the mood at the coast and you can't seem to say when you're coming to Nice.'

People often say, *looking back, that was the turning point*, but I knew it even then. It had that decisive feel. There'd been others, but this was the very last moment we could have turned the whole thing around. Jean-Luc didn't know I loved him – or at least I hadn't told him – I'd been extremely slow to admit it to myself. This was the time to confess everything to my husband, unselectively, to face his hurt and anger and disgust. It would be the second of my secrets he'd have to keep from his best friend, far worse this time, since my brother's death had no bearing on the Malavoines. Philippe's instinct would be to avoid the shame of revealing what I had done and the pain it would cause them. Nothing would be said between them but it would be corrosive all the same. Their friendship and our marriage were at stake and this time it would be me playing rough with others' hearts.

I couldn't do it.

I hadn't bathed or changed my underwear when I came home but I had washed my face and cleaned my teeth. I lowered my head and scooted down the bed, letting saliva collect in my mouth. If I couldn't give my husband what he really wanted, he'd have to be content with second best. For him, that is, not for me.

A taste of bitter medicine was what I deserved.

42

'But Véro won't expect a gift,' Philippe told me, as we approached Honfleur in the car. 'They're not going to be there.'

My face stiffened as he failed to slow down for the *Centre Ville* exit and we carried right past it, heading for the house on the coast. 'What do you mean?'

'They're away. In the States, actually, Geneviève will tell you where. She has the use of the place while it's empty.'

Geneviève's younger sister Véronique was the only person who'd made the prospect of this weekend bearable. I'd met her several times and never failed to be amazed at how different they were; Véro had a great sense of humour and not a trace of snobbery. She and her husband had three teenage kids. And none of them was going to be around to dilute the tension. My confusion was pierced with intermittent moments of clarity which revealed my behaviour as anyone else would see it, stripped of all emotion. A mature woman with a much younger man was unusual but it wasn't unheard of; nobody would bat an eyelash the other way around. The fact that I was married tipped the balance against me, without doubt, especially where I come from. That I was *having sex with the son of my husband's dearest friend*, a good man I respected and who loved Philippe like a brother, was a fact I was unwilling to reveal to a living soul. A fairly reliable sign of knowing you're in the wrong.

'Take the next exit and double back to the town,' I said, more sharply than intended. 'If Geneviève is hosting us, we need a gift for her.'

Philippe's knuckles flexed on the steering wheel. 'Jesus, Alexandra! Couldn't you have thought of this before we left? You Americans and your obsession with *things*,' he muttered. He'd been pleased with his nice surprise in bed that morning and I was spoiling the atmosphere. He only resorted to Anglo-Saxon type gibes when he was extremely irritated. 'Okay, if you insist,' he said, braking so hard my seatbelt engaged. 'It'll be worth it if you lighten up.' On the roundabout just off the highway we passed the road marked PARIS. That's what would have made me lighten up.

We drove around the town for at least twenty minutes looking for a parking space. I would happily have spent the rest of the day wandering the narrow streets of Honfleur or sitting by the picturesque port so familiar from Impressionist paintings, with its tall historic buildings and boats reflected in the water. Some of the movement's most celebrated artists were born in the area or enticed here by the landscape, light and camaraderie, and the souvenir vendors were not about to let anyone forget it. Philippe was less enamoured of the north coast and could never resist making unfair comparisons with the Côte d'Azur. 'It's chilly,' he said, rubbing his arms when he could easily have put on a sweater, and then, apparently without irony, 'and it's heaving with bloody Parisians!' When I looked around the harbour bathed in weak sunshine, if anything there was a higher ratio of people wearing immaculate linen, Prada sunglasses and long faces than you'd get in the capital.

I bought some beautifully wrapped soap for Geneviève that was sold in an expensive boutique two streets from our apartment – a fact I chose not to mention – and Philippe got a bottle of brandy for Henri. They would sit up talking half the night, as they did whenever they were staying under the same roof. As Philippe's mood brightened at the prospect of spending time with his friend, mine took a downward trajectory. He put his arm around me and suggested we get ice-cream before going back to the car, with a smile that undid me when I didn't think there was much left to be undone. Maybe he felt bad for snapping at me or felt some sympathy with my lack of enthusiasm. He had to know I was doing this for him. Do all couples veer between feeling intensely bonded and questioning what the hell they are doing together?

We were both making compromises: I didn't get to live in my own country and speak my own language but that was my choice, made before we met. Philippe's compromise was being married to a foreigner who didn't quite get France. Plus the fact it happened to be me – I could

254

be *insupportable* – un-put-uppable-with – but he was fine with that.

'It's my brother's anniversary today,' I announced flatly. 'Thirty years. It doesn't seem possible.' It touched me to see Philippe swallow hard as he turned to look at me, pulling me closer then releasing me as we joined the long line.

'I wish you'd said earlier. You know what I'm like with dates.'

'That's okay.' I didn't normally leave it until the day to mention it, given everything the anniversary entailed. Philippe knew the hardest part was dealing with my mom and with a nine-hour time difference I was accustomed to having it hang over me like a dark cloth.

The ice-cream parlour had more flavours than I'd seen even in Nice or Italy. I chose strawberry and marsh-mallow, in need of the sickly sugar high Christopher and I used to love, the whole family toasting marshmallows on long skewers around the fire pit dad used to build. Mom used to smile when he said he'd found paradise in giant redwood country, and he said it all the time.

For once I didn't try to push the memories away – some of them *were* happy. But as I was about to discover, the ice-cream was flavoured with the marshmallow herb, not the candy, and was so strange and unpleasant that once the strawberry was gone I had to throw the cone away.

By the time we were back on the road it was almost six – about as late as we could decently arrive and call it late afternoon. Philippe and Henri were back-slapping and talking about beer within seconds, disappearing inside with the wheels of our weekend bags making furrows behind them.

Geneviève and I were left giving each other stiff, awkward smiles and talking about the traffic when neither of us gave a damn. I was babbling away without thinking, a risk I could ill afford, but an overwhelming fatigue was afflicting my brain as much as my body – a regular and unwelcome counterweight to the euphoric rushes I shouldn't have been getting.

We went into the old-fashioned kitchen with the stone floor and the local woman cooking for us looked up only briefly from the stove. Geneviève and I stood side by side at the large window, silently looking out to sea. The sky was overcast until the sun edged one cloud with a blinding mercury border, causing us both to shield our eyes. It felt like someone up there was playing games with me, the last person on earth who believed in silver linings, but it was something that I could stand here at all. There was hope for me the day I discovered I could look at the sea and be more affected by its beauty than its savagery.

'We always spent summers in Normandy when I was a child,' Geneviève said. 'I would have preferred to grow up here.' She stole a glance at me as if she knew that I'd grown up too fast by the sea, my childhood ending in the space of a day. I'd missed out on the luxury of figuring things out over time and having some fun doing it, getting my heart broken the way it's meant to be done.

Even before she said it, I realised she *did* know about Christopher. 'This must be a very painful day for you and your parents, Alexandra.' Inside my head I could hear myself repeating the same two words:

How? in a blend of outrage and disbelief.

Don't! in a small wounded voice.

But Geneviève couldn't hear what I didn't say. She placed her hand on my arm, that sterile gesture of hers that was the best she could manage. I had to restrain myself from shaking it off. And *I* was supposed to be the cold one?

'When your *maman* spoke to me of your brother's accident she assumed I already knew. I was so sorry to hear it. Such a tragic story.'

'It's not a story,' I said bitterly. *It's our life. It's all we are to each other, all we'll ever be.* I cursed my mother and her opposite approach to our family tragedy, her compulsion to share it with anyone who'd listen. Her need of a new confidante was so great that even one five and a half thousand miles away would do. On *my* territory. I cursed the day my mom's endless fascination with the Malavoines had driven me to point out that she could call Geneviève herself.

The strongest urge to turn and walk out of the house rose up inside me but that would be pure histrionics. I wouldn't do that to my husband, who, along with Emily, had always respected my wish not to tell other people about my past. That was how I wanted it after two whole years of being *that girl* and having to explain to other kids that it wasn't *drowned to death*.

In the nick of time I acknowledged that my anger was misdirected. It wasn't Geneviève's fault she knew or that she didn't do displays of emotion. She was trying to be nice. 'Thank you,' I said, touching her hand fleetingly to bring the exchange to an end.

The gift that Philippe and I had gone to so much trouble for was well received. Geneviève closed her eyes as she inhaled the orange blossom aroma of the soap, giving out a ragged sigh which took me aback. I had never seen a sensual side to her. To think that at my age she'd given birth to Jean-Luc, the defining event of her life.

She showed me to the room Philippe and I had stayed in some four years ago. As soon as I saw the carved wooden headboard I knew Philippe was mistaken: I remembered making love in this bed, and that it was good. Geneviève left me to freshen up and before I could get roped into anything, I slipped out of the house with my phone and down the steep path to the side of the garden which led to a sandy beach.

My mom is a great one for anniversaries. For a long time I didn't understand it but I do now. Her grief for Christopher was so overwhelming that she never acknowledged mine or my father's, driving him to seek comfort elsewhere and when that wasn't enough, to leave the country. But for me it had been there all along, some days more than others. Sometimes a handsome dark-haired stranger on the Metro made me think of the man my brother might have become. Sometimes I thought of the wife and family he may have had and the joy that would have brought my mother, of all the happiness that could have occupied the space taken by sadness in our lives.

I used to believe that because there can be no solution to grief there was no point talking about it. It's a shame I couldn't do this before. But here we are, and I think the time has come.

43

For Mom, the anniversary of Christopher's death was the one day she could legitimately air her loss and have it acknowledged. She'd have brought it up with her hairdresser, the mailman, our neighbour Lenny, as if he could ever forget. They'd heard it all a thousand times so no wonder she was always on the lookout for fresh sympathy, the inevitable change in demeanour when you land that on someone. But the two of us still had to go over it every year, without any prospect of comfort. Since my dad left, first for the woman in the next town, then to pursue his career in the Amazon rainforest, I was the only one bound by her grief. It followed me everywhere I went.

She'd wanted me to be with her where it happened today so I could say it again to her face: *I'm sorry.* The round decade anniversaries are the worst. I'd accepted by the first of them that I'd never hear her say *It wasn't your fault, Alexandra.*

Mom would be waiting for the call, likely pacing up and down near the point where Christopher was swept away. I pictured a beautiful California morning, as far removed from that day as could be imagined, the kind of calm that makes such horrors seem impossible.

We knew a storm was closing in but after several days of being cooped up with us, Mom sent me and Christopher out with our dog Gershwin in a break between downpours. It wasn't a large house and we were driving her nuts with noisy games I'd dreamed up. I was forever giggling and acting the fool and Christopher, much quieter by nature, was my audience. He adored me.

I was ten years old, so innocent I'd only found out about sex the week before, from a friend who'd got most of the facts right. That morning on the beach I passed my new knowledge on to my little brother, only eight – it was an irresistible chance to show off once we were on our own. I can still recall Christopher's expression as the wind whipped our hair so hard against our faces that it stung. The beach was deserted, the sky so dark it felt closer to late afternoon than lunchtime. At first he didn't believe me, then he was so frightened and appalled (as I secretly was too) that he burst into tears and was inconsolable, even when I pretended I'd made it all up.

If we went home with him like this it would all come out and I'd be in big trouble with Mom. I let Gershwin off the leash despite her strict instructions because Christopher loved to chase him along the beach. But Gershwin did something he'd never done before, bounding up onto the rocks and leaping at the waves as if daring them to wash him away.

My brother would have done anything for that dog. I'll never know if Christopher heard me screaming not to go after him. So I was forced to go after both of them, my useless Keds slipping on the slimy boulders, taking me down almost immediately. I bashed the side of my head so damn hard when I fell, just out of the water's reach, registering overwhelming pain in the seconds before everything went black. It could easily have been both of us.

As little chinks of daylight reappeared I fought my way back to consciousness. I was no use to Christopher knocked out. I was no use to him at all. The wretched mutt survived.

So you see, I have prior knowledge of situations like this. Enough understanding not to judge those whose instinct is to judge me. When terrible things happen it helps to have someone to blame.

The beach was almost deserted at the hour when vacationers leave the shore in search of hot showers, apéritifs and dinner. In the distance a big family group was traipsing toward the car park, laden with the equipment of a day's fun. Despite myself, the traces of these strangers' enjoyment made me smile: a fairy-tale *château*

de sable with a moat, names scored in the sand waiting to be washed away by the tide (Jérôme, Clarisse, Ludovic, Marie-Jeanne), a swirl of shells.

Since I had left for Coldwater my mom and I had spent just two of Christopher's anniversaries together (doubling the misery, it seemed to me) and I had never had this ritual conversation whilst actually on a beach.

The clarity of the ringtone told me it was going to be a good line.

'So you did call in the end,' my mother said, without saying hello. 'I was starting to think you'd forgotten.'

I knew it would be best to keep moving, to step out of my flip-flops and douse my feet in the spray, but the lurch of anger in my chest made me sit down, pulling my knees in tight to contain it.

'There was nothing to stop you calling me.' That idea had never occurred to me but now it was like something I'd picked up and couldn't shake free from my hand. 'You never have called me on Christopher's anniversary, which is odd, really, when you think about it.'

'What exactly is your point, Alexandra?'

'It's like you're the only one who lost someone that day. Do you ever think about me and Dad? Do you ever think about the fact that I was *there*? Don't answer that,' I said, although my mother had not attempted to. 'You do, but only so you can pin it all on me. You've never thought what it was like for me to see it happen. Christopher was my brother. I tried to save him!'

'He was my little boy,' my mother said, playing the trump card. There was something theatrical about the tremor in her voice. A stoking rage lifted me to my feet and my finger hovered over the end call button but I was powerless to press it.

'I don't care that you loved him more than me, I honestly never did. But only one of your kids died and you could never seem to see that. I was only *ten years old* and I used to wish I'd died too because that would have been easier on both of us. You wouldn't even *look* at me.' She was crying now. Again. I used to think she'd never stop. 'You told me not to call you Mom anymore.'

'I never did such a thing! I don't know what you're talking about.'

'You think I'd make that up? Or imagine it?' Maybe she never meant it and just blurted it out in the agony of those early days, not realising the words would remain for ever carved into me, growing as I did, never healing over. 'I was there that time Dad came back from Brazil, I know you didn't fight for me. Do you remember what I said when he told me I had to go to school in England?'

'No,' she said. Of course she didn't.

'I said, *I can't leave Mom all alone.*'

'Your father made the right decision. He was holding up better than me. Christopher's death didn't affect him the same way.'

'It *broke* him!' I was shouting now. 'And it broke me. Other people cared' – I thought of Emily and her mother and big sisters, all the different-shaped hugs I got used to, and I was grateful for them – 'but it was you I wanted, and you were never there.'

'So I was a terrible mother. Are you done? Anything to add before we say goodbye?'

'Nothing.' I said. 'Nothing at all.'

44

At dinner we were served *poulet Vallée d'Auge*, a sublime chicken dish with mushrooms and apple slices in a heavy cream sauce laced with Calvados liqueur. I was about to comment on it being a traditional Normandy recipe when I stopped myself. There was making an effort, and there was trying too hard.

It's been a dilemma ever since I married Philippe. Should I be trying to act French? That's not something you can consciously decide, it would just happen. France may have been my home for a long time, but I still don't belong here. And if home is where you feel whole, it'll never happen now.

Making a virtue of my otherness hasn't been an option either. As Americans go I'm aware that I'm a disappointment. Not having lived there in years I'm not in tune with life in the States and I don't possess the qualities everyone expects: I'm not *super friendly* or effusive. It's too boring to explain about my British half and the French don't make much distinction anyway, but I do have some supposedly British traits: reserve, sarcasm, hang-ups about sex... (I can cross that off now).

Philippe and Henri had been laying into the booze ever since we arrived and Geneviève's expression told me this had not passed her by. She may have delivered the invitation but there was an indefinably strange atmosphere that made me wonder how she felt about us being here, whose idea it had really been. I don't think she wanted it any more than I did.

The men were speaking loudly, occasionally using words of *Niçard* dialect not even Geneviève would understand; hotly debating one controversial topic after another although they mostly agreed, thumping the table for emphasis.

'This country's going to shit,' Henri said. 'Record unemployment, *l'islamisation*, our inability to think globally. We're basically ruined. What do you think, Alexandra?'

Why was he asking *me*?

Geneviève looked so pained that I felt sorry for her. The longer I had known them, the more I suspected that Henri had married her for the advantages her wealth and connections would bring to his career. He had probably only ever done one thing right in her eyes – giving her Jean-Luc. Yet instead of turning her attention to her husband or to me in anticipation of my reply, Geneviève was staring at Philippe, or in his direction. In her mind she was probably somewhere else entirely. It was tempting.

'Well,' I said; it was easier for me to neutralise the discussion with platitudes than it would be for someone with a firmer grasp of the issues. 'It's true you like the good life in France. You take more time for family and friends.' *Lovers*, I added silently, certain that Philippe and Henri would be thinking the same. 'That's not such a bad thing. There has to be more to life than work and money.'

After agreeing with me, the men immediately returned to their theory that socialism was damaging the art market. 'Everyone's so depressed in Paris,' Henri said. 'Successful people, happy people, they all want to move to London. That's where they're buying art...'

'*Exactement!*' Philippe said. 'Depressed people make art, they don't buy it.'

When Geneviève went to clear the table for cheese and dessert, I got up to help whether it was the done thing or not. She set the stack of dirty plates down on the counter and it fell to me to scrape the remains into the garbage. The sight of curling chicken skin was making my stomach churn. As usual I'd eaten too much, leaving no morsel untouched. When Philippe and I were first together Geneviève once complimented me on my appetite and I'd felt self-conscious about it in her company ever since. But I was so tormented by the cruel and heartless tirade I'd unleashed on my mother that I accepted whatever sustenance I could to make it to the end of this miserable day, all the while counting the hours until we returned to Paris and Philippe and Vanessa left for the south. I'd get Jean-Luc out of my system for both our sakes, before we got in any deeper. And then I'd finally get my head together. It's good to have a plan.

My mouth began to water as Geneviève arranged tiny raspberries on the *tarte au citron* with architectural precision but I expressed my admiration as if for an object of beauty, not one I was desperate to devour. It was time to start taming my hunger.

Henri made a lewd remark about Valérie Trierweiler, which was followed by a particularly raucous burst of laughter from the dining room, and one of the men, I couldn't tell which, shushed the other almost as loudly. I was embarrassed for them, behaving like a pair of overexcited frat boys at their age; mostly for Philippe, of course – we were guests here – but also Henri. He was a cultured and intelligent man but right now his son seemed far more mature.

'Like little children, aren't they?' I said, though there was nothing endearing about their antics.

Geneviève arched her immaculate eyebrows and my ridiculous observation merited no further response. 'How is your charming friend from Montréal? Didier, was it?'

That threw me. Was she just trying to change the subject or did she actually think there was something going on between me and him? Surely not. She would never be so indiscreet as to raise it.

'Daniel,' I corrected, deciding not to take issue with 'charming', since he'd been so smooth with her. 'Oh, we say "Hello" when we pass each other running but we haven't really spoken since that day at Bon Marché.' Which we hadn't, despite Daniel's many attempts to waylay me. It would be so much easier if I were sleeping with him, a player, someone I could cut loose when I wanted out, especially as he planned to leave Paris soon. If I'd set out to have an affair, Daniel would have been ideal. With his sense of humour he'd probably be good in bed. A bit of harmless fun. Trust me to go for the other kind.

Geneviève had made it to the dining-room door with the cheese board when she span round to look at me. 'Alexandra—' she said. The suddenness of her movement combined with the trepidation in her voice made me turn cold. She retraced her steps to the table. Just when I thought it couldn't get worse, Henri had started singing.

'I would have preferred not to mention this today but I need to speak to you about Jean-Luc,' she said. If I could hear the alarm in my short, rasped inhalation, it's a fair bet she could too. I sounded like I'd had a gun pulled on me. This was it; she was biding her time the day she came to our apartment. Everything was about to go sky high. 'Oh?' I said, fear making a passable impression of surprise.

'Something is wrong with him.' I was acutely aware that she was monitoring my reactions. 'He is only halfway through the masters programme but he says he's not going back to America.'

I decided against a banal comment about the pressures of overseas study.

'He seemed to be enjoying it so much,' she continued. 'When he took that trip in the spring he was sending Henri photos almost every day. Something's happened but he won't tell us anything.' She pressed her hand to her brow like someone in the grip of a splintering migraine. 'He won't come home, not even for dinner. Henri hoped he might open up if they went sailing together but Jean-Luc refuses to go and he has always loved the sea. He has friends and cousins in Marseille and Nice who want him to visit but he won't hear of it. Even that has changed.'

At least my troubled and confused response was not an act.

'I thought maybe... it's just that you and Jean-Luc got on so well at the launch, chatting about California. That was by far the most relaxed I've seen him since he came back.' Either Geneviève was more worldly than I thought or vastly more naïve: what she was referring to was chemistry, not conversation. I could see how much she hated revealing disharmony in her perfect little family. She glanced away and then, in an unfamiliar tone, heart-felt and despairing, she asked, 'Did he mention anything upsetting that night?'

'No, not at all,' I said.

'Oh,' she said. 'Or since, maybe?' Geneviève didn't release me from her grey scrutiny. I knew better than to look away, the subtext as clear as if she'd said it out loud. 'I was really hoping you might know something about it.'

'I'm sorry, Geneviève, I don't,' I replied, but of course it wasn't enough. If I had not seen her son since the launch it would have been natural to say so. Sometimes failure to issue a denial is a confession by default.

Geneviève busied herself rearranging the cheese on the wooden board. We'd taken so long by now that the

Camembert was starting to ooze and release a strong ripe smell. I went over to the kitchen door and opened it into the darkness, filling my lungs with cold sea air in an attempt to keep my dinner down. This is what it took for me to feel a connection with Geneviève, finally: Jean-Luc was an adult but, first and always, her beloved only child. Today of all days I was moved by that. Just when I thought I'd waited long enough for her to return to the dining room I heard her voice close behind me, so soft I could barely hear it. 'If you find out, please tell us.'

45

It was nothing short of a miracle that I slept soundly that night, my body at the stage of depletion where it simply had to recharge. Having lost the art of balance, my brain retained only two functions: overdrive and shutdown.

I had no idea what time Philippe finally made it to bed but he was going to be in for an almighty hangover, that much was certain. The bedroom reeked of stale alcohol fumes but all this was to my advantage. He wouldn't feel up to sex and the morning would be half over before he got up. When I went to let in some fresh air I was thankful to see Geneviève leaving to attend Mass in Honfleur, as she had planned. Since I woke I'd been picking our conversation apart in an attempt to piece together what it meant. Was she so desperate that she *wanted* me to talk to Jean-Luc? Did she *know* we were doing more than that or just strongly suspect? It would be devastating for Jean-Luc if he had developed an aversion to the sea. I had never seen him by the ocean but I didn't have to. I had heard him talk about it. I could tell when he was thinking about it. I could see it in his eyes.

I was hungry again and went downstairs while it was safe, with nobody around. I pulled on some jogging pants and decided my tank top was decent enough if I encountered Henri. Geneviève had already been out to the bakery. Next to a couple of grease-flecked paper bags containing croissants were three baguettes, one of them missing the tiny length she must have eaten for breakfast, no more than you'd give a small child to nibble on. I set a pot of coffee to brew and crossed the room to gaze out at the ocean. It was a pretty day, yesterday's clouds gone, the pale grey-green waves spuming on the shore. It would have been a waste to close my eyes but I was in a sort of trance all the same.

After a minute or two the sound of a vehicle intruded and at first I tried to push it away. Geneviève couldn't be back already; she'd only been gone twenty minutes. When I opened the front door Jean-Luc was standing right there, inches from me, and behind him there was an old motorbike – not vintage old, decrepit old. I gawped at him, not sure whether to step outside or drag him in. When he smiled at me I felt such a heart-dance that I very nearly forgot where we were and that I was not alone in the house.

'Are you insane?' I said to him in undertones. 'You promised not to come here.' He had that raffish look that normally had me tugging at his fly or the buttons on his shirt but for once I resolved not to be such a pushover.

He shrugged. 'You were the one who said *promise*, not me. This is my aunt's house – it's not so strange for me to be here, is it?'

I grabbed hold of him and led him toward the outbuildings, out of earshot of the bedrooms. 'It's *strange* because of what's going on with us,' I said. 'Are you seriously telling me that's not why you're here?'

Jean-Luc reached behind me for the handle on the shed door and gently pushed me inside. I shook my head so hard it hurt. 'No, Jean-Luc,' I said. 'No way. Absolutely not.'

'Come on, please, one kiss at least,' he said, blocking the doorway and cupping my face in his hands. 'I've never rode so far on a motorbike.'

'*Ridden*. Did you get it from a scrap yard? You could have been killed.'

But everyone knows young men feel immortal. He wasn't wearing leathers and the helmet hanging from the handlebars looked older than he was. The thought of him coming to harm made me feel physically ill.

'Look what you're doing to me,' he said. 'You're very sexy when you tell me off.'

It always made me laugh when he was like this, on a high. I got my share of admiring glances in Paris but few men had ever bothered flirting with me. Something probably told them it wouldn't work, although bizarrely it was happening more as I got older, not less.

'That's all well and good,' I said, 'but if you think I'm going to have sex in your aunt's woodshed when your mother is at Sunday Mass...' I shuddered. 'I mean, thank *God* she is.'

'My mother never misses Mass, you should know that. I've been waiting up the road for her to leave. I had to see you. You know how it is...'

I certainly did. He kissed the side of my neck, working up from the collarbone, just like the first time. At my ear, he switched to licking and my body began to respond as if he were much lower down.

'Don't do that,' I told him in entirely the wrong tone of voice. Arousal and extreme stress were playing havoc with my ability to think but the danger of us being found out had never been greater.

I stepped back. 'I'm sorry, you have to leave *right now*. This is getting completely out of hand – you don't seem to understand what's at stake, but I do.'

Knowing the delight Jean-Luc took in thwarting his mother at every opportunity, I figured it would only encourage him to mention her insinuations or her concern for him. That weird shadow crossed his face, the one I thought I'd imagined the day we lay on the floor of my office. But since then I'd seen it often; the light went out in his eyes, only to come back brighter.

'I'm not leaving without you,' he said loudly and I feared whatever came next would be louder still. What if he burst out of the shed into the driveway that ran across the front of the house? I'd left the bedroom window wide open. One of the things I found so irresistible about Jean-

Luc was never knowing what he was going to do next. At the same time, it scared me witless.

How do you contain something that has no definition, no limits? It was bad enough confronting my feelings for him but his for me worried me more. I'd survived four decades without this kind of drama and delirium. But Jean-Luc went after what he wanted and assumed it would always be that way, everything there for the taking. He couldn't settle for life at less than full blast. And when it was me he wanted, I went for it just the same. As he said, it wasn't for me to question what he saw in me.

But he saw something that could easily – far less painfully – have remained buried forever. He'd brought out an undetected side that repelled and terrified me as much as it thrilled and turned me on. No more, no less.

'Hey, don't look so sad,' he said. 'Let's go for a ride.'

If I'd been keeping any kind of a list it would have been called *All the wrong and stupid things I've done*. Not only had I never ridden pillion, I had no crash helmet, nothing covering my arms and only flip-flops on my feet. But he couldn't stay, and I couldn't bear to see him leave so soon. His hold on me was so strong that I was willing to risk a horrible death, simple as that. 'Okay, but I can't be long,' I said, surprising him. There's something to be said for remaining a mystery.

There was no sign of activity from the house as I negotiated the path in cautious steps, which was point-less considering Jean-Luc crunched over to the bike in Caterpillar boots. 'So where *did* you get this wreck?'

'From a scrap yard,' he said. 'Or my boss at the gas station did. You could say it belongs to him.'

'Have you been at work all night?'

'No,' he said. 'I went to a party in Sarcelles with Mokhtar the pizza guy and some others. It was boring.'

'Did you meet anyone nice?' The words half died on their way out. I wanted him to say *yes*. I wanted him to say *no*.

The question seemed to vex him as much as it did me. 'You must be joking! The girls who weren't completely wasted just wanted to whine about their problems. Vanessa was there – she's not like that.'

'*Philippe's daughter* Vanessa? Did you go together?' I asked, thinking back to the day of the concert.

Jean-Luc sighed, understandably. 'No, she was with some friends from Neuilly and had her tongue down some guy's throat half the night. It made no difference to me who was there. Being around other people only makes me want to be with you.'

I flapped my hands as he started the engine – it was even more deafening close up and juddered like it was about to fall to pieces or explode. Which is precisely what would happen to my marriage if Philippe or Henri were to look out the window.

Jean-Luc had just kicked back the stand when I said, 'You need to tell me what to do. I've never done this before.'

I wasn't sure he'd heard me over the roar of the engine. He turned in the seat, handing me the helmet. 'You say that about everything!' He kissed me and the rush of adrenaline and desire nixed all guilt and fear and danger – we could have done it right there on the spot for all I cared. There seemed to be no turning back on this road we'd taken.

I held on to him for all I was worth. And with every bend and turn and lean, wherever he led, I followed. Easy.

46

'I'm too old to stay up drinking til three in the morning.' Along with his self-induced suffering Philippe conveyed a hint of pride, as if he'd made it through a white-water rafting expedition. We all like to think we've still got it.

'You had fun, that's the main thing.' I wasn't going to give him a hard time – I wouldn't have enjoyed myself half as much if it weren't for his hangover.

'But I'm shattered. If I don't get a decent night's sleep I might have to wait and go to Nice on Tuesday.'

'I'm sure you'll be absolutely fine in the morning,' I said, stopping short of offering to help him pack.

The traffic was bad coming into Paris due to an accident on the *Périph*. I went up to start making dinner while Philippe parked the car. Vanessa appeared the moment I opened the door having apparently just got up after sleeping in last night's make-up. 'Where's Dad? I need money.'

'Charming welcome! *Hello* to you too. *Did you have a nice weekend?*'

She mumbled something incomprehensible before saying, 'I know who you were with so there wasn't much point in asking.' She flapped her hand in front of my face. '*Geneviève?* Your friend?'

'Geneviève, yes, of course. It was okay. Go easy on your father – he's feeling a little delicate.'

I was in the bathroom when the row erupted. With her usual regard for my advice, Vanessa had accosted Philippe the second he walked in the door. By the time I materialised they were talking, or rather shouting, numbers.

'You cannot just demand a hundred euros and think I'm going to hand it over! What am I, an ATM? Maybe when you find out how long it takes to earn that much, you'll understand.'

'But I owe Anaïs for two concert tickets – she asked me for it again last night.'

Philippe shook his head, and then he clutched it and groaned. 'You should think about whether you can afford something *before* you commit yourself, not after. I don't care if your mother would be okay with this. I'm not!'

'Well if you think you could have done better, maybe you shouldn't have fucked off for years. You've never given me anything!'

'Why don't you both take a step back,' I said. 'All this yelling gets you nowhere.'

Vanessa spun round, her face wild with fury and black smudges. 'Why don't *you* shut up and stay out of it?'

Philippe and I looked at each other open-mouthed. 'Bet you can't wait for us to leave. Then you'll get some peace.'

'You must be joking if you think I'm going anywhere with you,' she told him.

For a moment I forgot to breathe or swallow. 'Put some shoes on,' I said. 'You're coming with me, right now, and don't even think about arguing.'

I frogmarched her down the street to the Jardin du Luxembourg. We walked half my running circuit before I could trust myself to speak. 'Let's sit for a while.' I handed her a tissue and she dabbed at her face. To my horror Daniel sprinted into view. Seeing that he was slowing down as he drew closer, I shook my head and mouthed *no* at him. He carried on past with a smirk that said, *fine, if you want to be like that.*

Of course Vanessa had to see it. '*C'est ton amant?* Oh my God, it is! You're *cheating* on my dad – I can't believe it!'

'How dare you, Vanessa? You're the one who's beyond belief. You've crossed so many lines I don't know where to start. If you think Philippe didn't want you in his life for all those years, you're completely wrong. Did your mother tell you that?'

'Not exactly, but what was I supposed to think? She never mentioned him, I never saw him – I thought he'd forgotten I existed.'

'Well, that's not true. It's also not true that he wasn't willing to support you.' Philippe had saved the money in an account but having seen the fight they got into over one hundred euros I wasn't going to tell her that. 'You're practically an adult – I'm sure he'd rather discuss it than have you hurling accusations. And I don't know your mother, but maybe you should try to get her side too. It can't be easy raising a kid alone.'

'She never wanted me – I just got in the way of her career. You know what she said the day I got my period? *I don't have time for this.* And she didn't speak to me for days after I first met you.'

'But isn't that the whole reason you came to us, that you weren't getting along?'

'Not then! I mean that wedding where I saw you with my dad.'

'I still don't understand. We didn't even talk to you that day. We would have *liked* to, but—'

'She wouldn't let me. So I told her I wished you were my mom.'

'Oh gosh.' I squeezed her hand, not sure if I was trying not to laugh or not to cry. 'Poor you, and poor your mom. *Any*ways,' I said, standing up, 'now you know it wouldn't have been so great with me either.'

'Oh, I don't know. Sometimes you can be a judge-mental bitch but…'

'Hang on a minute, I thought you said I wasn't a bitch?'

'That was before I knew you.'

On the way home it felt like there had been a change in the weather. When we reached the bottom of the steps I said, 'You know that making up with me was the easy bit. Philippe's probably taking a nap now but you're going to apologise, right?'

'Yeah.' She went up to the first half-landing and looked back. 'And you know I was only joking about you having a lover. Obviously.'

'*Obviously.*'

47

Vanessa had apologised, if saying the words without a trace of regret or sincerity counts. It counted for Philippe. He'd slept well and was packing for Nice when my excuse for not going was vindicated by a call out of the blue. His movements slowed as he placed clothes in his suitcase with great care rather than tossing them in any which way. I wandered over to our bedroom window to look down at the street, turning my back as the caller explained that he was in Paris and free tomorrow or at the end of the week. He'd been trying to reach me for days.

'Friday is perfect,' I said.

'So the Romanians *are* in town?' Philippe said. I couldn't even recall who I'd said might need to call on us at Editions Gallici. But whatever I'd told him, it wasn't what had just happened.

'It's way better than that, Philippe! That was someone from an art foundation in the US who's interested in the English translation rights,' I said. 'He's in France on vacation. Of course he was hoping to meet with Bernard too but he seems happy enough to make do with me for now.'

None of our titles had ever been translated.

Philippe came over and wrapped his arms around me, his body leaning into mine as he breathed the scent of my hair. It felt good – clearly not just to me – and I saw there could be more to this dimension of us, more than there'd ever been. It may have taken a man to unleash my sexuality but it was mine to keep. Philippe would be surprised now I knew what I wanted. He'd like it a lot.

'That's fantastic! That firm would have sunk by now without you – I don't think Alain has a clue. Your instinct about this book was spot on: it has meaning for believers and a spiritual feel for art lovers who want that without religion. There's something very "of the moment" about icons.' I sensed that Philippe was getting one of his ideas. 'I wonder if Nasim Asradi has ever considered...'

I moved away so he couldn't feel me bristle – this was *my* turf. Another positive development for *Icons* that I hadn't been able to savour properly. But I was counting down the minutes until he left now and steeled myself to keep everything on the level. He was waiting for the morning rush to die down before doing battle with the *Autoroute du Soleil*.

'Thank you for saying that but please don't go putting ideas in Asradi's head. It wouldn't work anyway. His pieces aren't representational.'

Philippe loved controversy – contemporary art thrived on it. But what worked in his world could be lethal to mine. I dreaded to think what a creator of blasphemous sado-masochistic wall hangings might be moved to produce on the theme of icons. But the whole notion was ridiculous – from what I'd heard of Nasim Asradi he didn't tolerate interference from anyone, not even his gallerist.

Philippe pulled his *Bof!* face as if the loss were all mine.

'So you'll be able to join us by the weekend, if you're seeing this guy on Friday?' he said, closing his suitcase and pressing hard on the lid. He probably meant nothing by it but I felt myself redden as if this business meeting with a random male was the forbidden pleasure I had planned. Philippe looked at me expectantly when I failed to reply and it hit me then, that this genuine appointment had superseded the fictitious one that I could have postponed to suit my purposes. I'd squandered my only excuse.

I nodded and attempted a smile although I'm sure it didn't look like one. Questions would be asked if I didn't show my face at the Darrousier residence by Sunday at the latest. Philippe knew the Baudelaire manuscript had been delivered in relatively good shape and anyway, I could just as easily work on that in Nice as in Paris. Knowing how depressing he'd found it returning to his family alone after his first marriage ended, I didn't want to put him through that again. The feeling or the fact.

On the surface, Philippe and I would be the ideal candidates for a clean break: no kids together, both economically independent in our own way. In theory there was no reason I couldn't go back to blowing a large proportion of my take-home on a rented shoebox. I never wanted it to be over between us but I had the sudden feeling we might not make it through.

I wished there really could be two of me so I didn't have to choose: one a loyal friend and good wife to Philippe – the woman he thought he'd married; one who was content with her lot, which was a lot better than it had been before he showed up.

The other was a very different me: mercurial, spontaneous, uninhibited. Free to savour every last drop of my *aventure* with Jean-Luc and our selfish pursuit of gratification with never a thought for how I'd go back to the outrageous ordinariness of life before him.

As I said, we never worry about the right things.

'We'll talk every day,' Philippe said, when he was finally ready to head out, but there was a lack of conviction in his goodbye kiss, our lips barely making contact. I remembered the night we met, how sweet it was that he'd asked if he could kiss me and how long and hungry and wonderful it was when he did. When I asked him later why he waited to take it further he'd told me he was desperate to make love to me, *fou d'envie*, but wasn't sure I was the kind of woman who would do it so soon. He laughed when I told him I would have with him.

But that was then. I wondered what would fill his head on the long drive south, stopping at a friend's in Lyon overnight, and hoped he'd be looking forward to the sea and the company of his noisy demonstrative family, not wasting his energy missing me. The distance had already opened up between us even as we stood only inches apart.

I pressed the button to call the elevator, impatient for him to be gone before I could open my mouth and tell him I was coming with him after all. His face would break into a genuine smile, the first in days, if not weeks. There'd be that fracture in his reply that he can't help when emotion gets the better of him. And despite the leisurely weeks ahead, we'd rewind to where we were five minutes ago and the kind of kiss that really can't stop there, rushing back to the bedroom though I'd already pulled the sheets off the bed and left them in a heap in the corner. It would be passionate and intense, as if we were brand new people, bringing us both to the brink of tears.

But only if I said I was going with him and didn't come out with something else, like the truth. Since the confrontation with Geneviève and the things I'd said to my mother I didn't trust myself any more. Some people are banned from driving, some are barred from owning pets or practising law. By rights, somebody should have taken a long red thread and sewn my mouth shut. For the longest time it felt as though they had. Talking only caused pain to others or trouble for myself.

It's just occurred to me why you sit behind me during our sessions. It's not just to give me this unbroken view of the sea that gives me the strength to keep going. It's so I can't see the look on your face. And I've completely changed my mind about talking, you know that. It has saved me. You've helped me pull out the stitches so I can scream.

Philippe's good linen jacket was slung over his shoulder, the hanging loop cutting off the circulation to the tip of his finger, which was turning white. We didn't touch again before he stepped into the elevator and the mood that washed over me was a diluted form of grief.

'I'll make sure Vanessa gets the train okay,' I told him. Nothing more was said about me joining them in Nice. It was as if we both knew I never would. I never even bought a ticket.

48

That afternoon is a time I return to often. Sometimes it is solace, sometimes torture, but it contained every element of what there was between Jean-Luc and me. The windows in the studio were wide open, heat and sunlight streaming in around us, bedcovers long since kicked to the floor. The exertions of sex seemed to invigorate him. He barely took his eyes off mine, the mutations in his gaze like the changing patterns of a kaleidoscope: desire, release, tenderness. In the languor that followed I liked to close my eyes for a while, knowing that he didn't. It exhausted me, in the best possible way. My heart sprinted on under his trailing hand.

'How is it you never fall asleep afterward?' I said, spiking his hair up, pushing it back and then onto his forehead.

'You've given me a new reason not to,' he said, and when he kissed me, I could taste us both. It was effortless, no need to give directions. He had a map of me; I'd learned to lose myself in him. And those lost moments held the most astounding discoveries. In French, sexual climax is sometimes referred to as *la petite mort*, the little death, an instant of almost spiritual revelation. With Jean-Luc it was a revelation every time, an ecstatic sensation of being *alive*. I think, I *know* it was the same for him, being with me. I've stood on bridges telling myself that, fixing my eyes on some cloud or building, an airplane light, anything but the river or the railroad below.

A train was pulling into the Gare de l'Est, the wheels screeching the same four notes over and over. 'Sounds like a bird call, doesn't it?' I said.

Jean-Luc got up and looked out of the small high window, standing there perfectly naked. 'I recognise some of the trains by the sounds they make.' Seeing me smile as he turned back, he added, 'Only since staying here! It's not a hobby of mine. I always preferred boats. When I was a kid both sets of cousins taught me to sail, in Normandy and in Nice. That's where it all began.'

He spoke so sadly of the beginning that it sounded like an ending. He talked of the sea less and less, and since Honfleur I couldn't stop wondering why. Fearing to know. He'd taken me inland to a wood that morning we went out on the bike, picking leaves from each other's hair before he dropped me back at the end of the road to the beach so I could say I'd been for a walk. It was my first (my only) experience of open-air sex and I loved it. Even if I live to be old, the sight of ferns will always take me back there. I hope I'll remember that always.

'We should go out,' he said. 'It's a beautiful day.'

We'd never risked being seen together but I raised no objections, recalling my intention to abandon myself for a few short days. Philippe would be halfway to Lyon by now and Paris was half empty, its citizens colonising the Var, the Ile de Ré and every other inch of French coastline.

I reached under the bed for my clothes and my hand made contact with a book. 'What's this you're reading?' I pulled it out. 'Baudelaire! I guess that's not a coincidence?'

'No. When you were telling me about your next project it reminded me of reading *Les Fleurs du Mal* in high school, and well, László has a good library...'

He did indeed. And it said everything about Jean-Luc that I had never once taken the time to examine the shelves.

'I only discovered *Mon cœur mis à nu* working on this book,' I said, seeing that the *journaux intimes* were in the same volume. *My Heart Laid Bare*, such a perfect description of what had happened to mine. 'You see another side to Baudelaire in each type of writing. He can be quite funny.'

Jean-Luc nodded. 'Like when he says that love's a crime you can't commit without an accomplice. You're the perfect accomplice, Alexandra.'

I returned his smile, not wanting to tell him that it really wasn't as cute as he made it sound. What Baudelaire actually said was, *the trouble with love...* By *love* he likely meant sex, like a lot of people. But it was *crime* that jumped out at me.

'One of my all-time favourite poems is from *Les Fleurs du Mal*,' I said, dismissing it immediately because it was so wrong for an idyllic summer day, with its talk of anguish and *ennui*. But then Jean-Luc began to recite it: '*Quand le ciel bas et lourd pèse comme un couvercle...*' (When the sky bears down low and heavy as a lid.) 'Not today, true, but there are many days like that.'

'And he wrote so many poems! How on earth did you guess which one I meant?'

'The same things speak to us,' he said, and then, seriously, 'That one stayed with me. I read it again yesterday. Interesting man, Baudelaire.'

'Wasn't he? Such a sad life, losing his father so young and hating the man his mother married. But fascinating – I love the story of him being packed off on an ocean voyage for squandering his inheritance and jumping ship before the final destination. He got so much inspiration on that journey. Just think, he would never have written *L'albatros*. The casual cruelty in that poem makes me want to cry.'

I could see that Jean-Luc knew that one too. I felt the dread on his face. The truth was gaining on us like a tidal wave and it wasn't about broken hearts.

'Look at the page I turned down,' he said, choked. 'Read it to me.'

My skin turned to goose flesh and not because it felt like I was about to be sent out on stage completely unprepared. I looked at him, my mouth buckling on one side. It seemed a small thing to ask; I knew it wasn't.

Homme libre, toujours tu chériras la mer!
La mer est ton miroir; tu contemples ton âme

(Free man, you'll always love the ocean

The mirror where you see your soul)

That's as far as I got before the panic took hold of him. Even when I held him as tight as I could, my arms bound across his back, I felt his shaking through my body.

'Breathe! Copy me,' I said, grabbing his face, trying to make him look at me as I took exaggerated breaths in and out, though his eyes were blind with terror. It took a long time for him to fall into my rhythm and for the gulping and spluttering to end. It was like witnessing someone drown all over again.

Someone who knew how that felt.

So fucking dark, he'd said that time, *like being trapped underwater*.

No, hindsight is not a wonderful thing – it's a curse. I know I'm not a mind-reader. Perhaps I *am* being unreasonably hard on myself but isn't that what everyone does, scrolling back, saying if this, if that, if everything had been different? I don't know if I can keep doing this.

I tried, but I didn't push him that afternoon because I know you have to want to talk. To be able to find the words. 'Something terrible happened to you in California, didn't it? Something that's made you afraid of the ocean?' I said. 'You have to let somebody help you. It's not going to go away.'

'I can't,' he said. 'Everything makes it worse except being with you. As long as I have you, I'll be all right.'

I felt a searing in my chest. We were two boats tied together, heading not into harbour but out into treacherous waters. Whatever the problem, I was not the answer and I couldn't let him believe that I was. 'You wanted to go out,' I said. 'So let's go. You'll feel better in the sunshine.'

And he did. We both did. In the light of that perfect afternoon, we strolled along the *quais* of the canal. We sat on a bench and were one of those couples who kissed without caring who saw. It was the only time.

49

Vanessa had gone home to fetch some things for the beach.

I stuffed the bed sheets into the washing machine and sank to the kitchen floor watching them go round. I was churning with no chance of coming out clean. My reflection in the curved glass door was distorted past recognition against a backdrop of suds. I was not that woman with the shiny hair and the nice tits and the lovely clothes. With my eyes closed I could see myself more clearly, a fuck-up in an agnès b. cardigan. With my foot extended I could probably kick the door and shatter it, along with all my toes. With my back against a kitchen unit and the angular metal handle level with the base of my skull, I could obliterate myself in one slam. Anything to get out of my mind.

Almost. I settled for slapping myself in the face, hard. I don't suppose many people have tried it – I never had and even without the element of surprise, it worked. This was about damage limitation, which ruled out presenting my stepdaughter with a bloodbath. I needed to be able to think. The countdown was on to extricate myself before anyone got seriously hurt. For a situation that so intrinsically involved two people (not counting Philippe in his ignorance), it felt like I was in it on my own. Even if I could have shared my dilemma there was nothing anyone could have said or done. I wasn't ready to tell Emily she was right in all her predictions about me and Jean-Luc because the moment I did, it would feel real. It *was* real, obviously, and already none of the outcomes I could contemplate involved the key figures walking away unscathed. It was never supposed to be a love affair.

I just didn't know how I was going to do this. First I had to get out in the open. Jean-Luc and I normally texted but with Philippe gone and no one else to overhear there was no reason not to call.

'*Allô?*' I could tell from that one word that he'd snatched up the phone without seeing who it was.

'Did I wake you?'

I heard Jean-Luc yawn and could picture him stretching, naked under the sheets, and rubbing his eyes. 'Oh, it's you!' he said, perking up instantly. 'I was working until six but it's okay,' he said. 'You know me, I never sleep much.'

Did I know him? In some ways, deeply; in others, hardly at all.

I stepped off the kerb without looking and a scooter narrowly avoided me, its rider leaning on the horn and veering into the middle of the side street where he almost collided with someone else. 'I'm on my way to the office,' I told him. It was utter nonsense – in my mind I was en route to his studio. I would end this in the same place it got started, to the sound of railroad tracks, and I would beg him to get the help I couldn't give him.

'I've got a better idea,' said Jean-Luc. 'Come join me in bed. First thing in the morning is always extra good.'

I could have taken issue on both points – for a start it was just past midday and as far as I was concerned when we were together it had never been less than stupendous. This was the wrong time to be thinking about sex. As I walked along with the lunchtime crowds swirling around, how many of those people were physically longing for someone in this precise moment as I now was? The sight of a young couple pawing at each other in a doorway clinched it. I didn't just want what they had (and the stares of other passers-by told me I wasn't the only one) – I could have it. A soft breeze on my bare limbs and along the neckline of my dress carried the promise of Jean-Luc's touch on my skin, my temperature rising at the thought of him in me.

'I'll be there as soon as I can,' I said.

'Hang on,' he said. 'I'm not at the studio. László turned up last night – he's brought his new girlfriend to visit Paris, so he needs it back for a few days. I'm in the Seventh.'

He could refer to it as obliquely as he liked but it changed nothing – it was the Malavoines' place. I stopped abruptly near the entrance to the Odéon Metro station, forcing the people around me to change course. *Putain*, muttered a man with a dog, glaring. Having heard me speaking English on the phone, he graciously translated.

I moved to the edge of the steps. 'You cannot be serious,' I said to Jean-Luc.

'I'm completely serious. What's the big deal? You know my parents are not here.'

'Where are they?'

'Are *you* joking now? They're in Normandy all week!'

What an idiot I was – of course they were still in Honfleur. I should have told Jean-Luc to shut up for a minute – I couldn't hear myself think with his voice at my ear, murmuring at me in French how he longed for me, how he missed me, what he wanted tó do to me. He wasn't going to take no for an answer – not that I had any real intention of saying it.

'Okay!' I snapped. 'I'll be right there.'

This was far too urgent to waste time taking Line 10, laying my *Navigo* card on the reader to open the gates, having to change lines at La Motte-Piquet – Grenelle. I ran to the nearest taxi stand and as a cab drew up, like a true Parisian, I barged in front of another person to take it. As we turned into the rue Saint-Dominique I tried to marshal my thoughts but it was useless.

I needed to end the affair but I was wet with antic-ipation of another outstanding fuck. And I was on my way to the last place on earth I would actually consider sleeping with him. My inability to control myself was making me fear for my own mental state as well as his. The balance of my mind was disturbed. A phrase normally used in defence. But when it came to Jean-Luc, I had no defences.

50

Memory has many components: places, sounds, smells. The texture of something at the fingertips; a flow of emotion, painful either because it always was or because that particular joy is no longer possible. The things I most wish to hold onto are sometimes hazy to recall. Not so the unwanted memories. They are everywhere.

The last time I was at Geneviève and Henri's apartment was to deliver the bouquet just after my mother's intervention; it was her doing to convert Philippe's infidelity from an unpleasant suspicion to the catalyst for me to outdo him by a factor not quantifiable on the same scale.

Geneviève's keypad code hadn't changed in the five years we'd known one another. Giving it to me was a minor act of faith but even this troubled me. As I approached the building I smelled lilies that weren't there, reminding me of a time I was still worthy of anyone's trust or good opinion.

Jean-Luc answered the door barefoot, wearing cargo shorts he'd just pulled on, I guessed, from the misaligned buttons and the fact he clearly wasn't wearing anything underneath. He greeted me with the same radiant smile as the day I'd decided I couldn't make one afternoon with him last the rest of my life.

Not much had changed. Despite the good weather in Paris a combination of his nocturnal hours and those he spent in bed with me meant that his tan had faded since LA. I still did a double take at the new haircut, currently adorably mussed up from sleep. Behind horn-rimmed glasses I hadn't seen him in before, his eyes looked bigger than ever. I'd lost my head and more besides over this young man who was convinced I could fulfil his every need. His tongue hunted for a gap in my teeth but I turned my head away. 'I'm very uncomfortable being in your parents' apartment.'

'Oh, come on, Alexandra. Don't make me wait any longer. If we lock the door like this,' he drew the safety bolts that could only be operated from the inside, 'you can be sure nobody will disturb us.'

He saw that this didn't reassure me at all. Prising his hands off my body, I went into the living room and over to that awe-inspiring view, which, depending on my mood, either made me feel I belonged in this city or that I absolutely didn't. Today I could only think on a smaller scale. Paris wouldn't raise an eyebrow at my amorous indiscretions. Philippe would be appalled. Geneviève would fucking kill me.

Jean-Luc pulled at my arm, saying, 'Come with me. You said you'd be able to relax this week, remember?'

How could I ever have believed it?

He led me to into his childhood bedroom, which I had never seen, at the far end of the hallway. Like all the rooms in the apartment it was generously proportioned, the bed a double. I tried to filter out the guitar on a stand, Explosions in the Sky posters, games consoles which even I could tell had become obsolete in the few short years since he'd left home. At the end of a row of books, *Le Petit Prince* had fallen flat on the shelf.

'Let's get comfortable,' he said, patting the bed. 'My God, it's such a huge turn-on getting to do it here.' He grinned. 'All those times I dreamed of having a gorgeous woman in my bed when I was growing up...'

I waved my hands in protest. 'Stop right there!' I said. 'Let's be very clear – you didn't know me then. I don't want to think about you being a kid.' He shrugged. 'Which kind of brings me to what I wanted to tell you. Your mother suspects something between us, even if she doesn't know for certain. She said something in Honfleur the night before you showed up.' It was cowardly, but I was grateful to Geneviève for giving me an excuse and glad that I'd kept it in reserve until I really needed it – as a get-out.

Jean-Luc gave a derisive snort. 'Make up your mind! One minute I'm a proper grown-up and the next you think my mother cares who I'm fucking?'

I felt faint with shame. 'You really don't get it. Do you seriously think she *wouldn't* care, if she knew it was me? And so would your father and Philippe. I'd be surprised if anyone was okay with this situation. You may not like the

303

idea of boundaries laid down by society and all that, but they exist, and what we've been doing crosses a line. You were right that we're just two people, but we're not *any* two people. Your father is Philippe's best friend. You're not the one who's ever going to get the blame for this, Jean-Luc, *I* am. Things could get extremely ugly. Unless I show up in Nice by Sunday, Philippe's going to smell a rat...'

Jean-Luc frowned. 'It means *get suspicious*,' I explained. 'Start to suspect something's not right.'

'I know what it means,' he said. 'I can't stand the thought of you being with him.'

'He's my husband,' I said, as gently as I could.

Jean-Luc strode over to the window. 'Does he want you like I do?' I tried to interrupt but he wouldn't let me. 'Do you fantasise about me when you're doing it with him?'

My head dropped into my hands and my feet drummed on the floor. The only possible escape was total honesty. The kind that was yet another violation of marital intimacy. I looked up at Jean-Luc.

'What Philippe and I have is very different. And if you must know, he and I haven't been *doing it* as such.' Admitting Philippe and I hadn't been having sex was as excruciating as if we'd been caught doing it in public. 'Our marriage hit a bad patch this summer. Just before you and I hooked up I found out Philippe was having an affair and I took it badly. I hate to say it, but I doubt you and I would have happened otherwise.'

304

He shook his head, a look of pure disgust spreading over his face. 'So sleeping with me was a way to get back at him *and* my mother?'

Confused, I laughed.

'Are you saying what I *think* you're saying? Philippe wasn't having an affair with *Geneviève*! It was some Italian woman called Nico. What on earth gave you that idea?'

'Oh, I didn't think they actually *were*. Can you imagine my mother confessing that to the priest on a Friday? But if you haven't worked out how she feels about Philippe, you must be blind. I've never seen her look at my dad that way.'

The taste of vomit filled my throat. I clamped a hand over my mouth so tightly that I had to swallow to keep breathing. 'How long have you thought this?'

'I don't know, probably ten years. An only child spends a lot of time watching adults, overhearing their conversations. I know she made a deal with her cousin so Philippe got that nice apartment after his divorce. And it was her idea for Dad and Philippe to go into business together. She put up the money for the gallery.'

To create an obligation. To keep him from drifting away.

'And when Philippe and I got married—'

'—she had a new way to keep him close. You.'

All this time I had participated in a charade of friendship with her thinking it was for the sake of a friendship between two men. As if they needed any help from us.

'Do you think your father knows?'

'Oh, he knows. I'm not sure Philippe does though. But in a way that makes no difference. My dad trusts Philippe above anybody – that's probably what makes it bearable. He's his closest friend. Nothing will ever change that.'

A lot of things made sense that never had. I'd been right about Geneviève all along. She didn't like me. Her frostiness wasn't upper-class reserve, it was envy. No wonder she only showed any genuine interest in me when something was wrong. She liked to see me suffer.

Jean-Luc put his arms around me. 'God, I'm sorry,' he said. 'I thought you knew.'

I drew away. 'So it's a coincidence then, that of all the women in Paris you chose to make a move on *me*? If there's one thing I know about you, it's how much you love to piss your mother off.'

Voicing my theory, I realised it would only have its full effect if Geneviève found out. He didn't care if she knew about us or not.

Now it was the hurt in his eyes that was magnified. 'Why can't you believe it's you I want? I told you, I've never felt this way about anyone.'

I got up and started wandering aimlessly around the room. 'I'm sorry, that was a horrible thing to say. I'm really worried about you – getting dragged into this was the last thing you needed on top of everything else. I'm not trying to tell you how you feel but this can't be good for you, no matter what you say. You should be with someone your own age, who's free to love you the way I'm not.'

'Are you saying you love me?'

I took a deep breath. Neither confirm nor deny. He could read me so much better than I could read him.

'What you just told me changes nothing as far and you and I are concerned.' I was lying, of course – the need to end it had never felt more urgent. 'I care about you very much, but it was wrong of me to get involved in the first place. My judgement was clouded. I don't suppose either one of us was expecting things to get so intense. There are so many reasons I'm not right for you, more than you know. Whichever way you look at it, this has no future.'

He was staring at me in complete stillness, as if he'd stopped breathing.

By now I could barely get the words out, my mouth speaking out against my heart. 'This really hurts now, for both of us, but hopefully one day we'll look back on it as something beautiful that had to come to an end.'

Jean-Luc let out an inhuman roar of anguish, more like a large animal that's sustained a fatal wound, and delivered a series of random kicks to whatever objects were nearest, the side of the desk and my bag, which shot along the polished floor, the contents pushing the flap open to fly everywhere.

'Please, don't!' I said. 'You're frightening me.' I watched in horror as he swung his arm back to punch a fist-size hole in the plasterboard wall. When he pulled his hand out, blood was streaming down the valleys between his knuckles. In London I once saw a brutal fight in the street but I'd never witnessed self-inflicted violence, right in front of me where there was no option to look away.

I grabbed him by both wrists so he couldn't throw another punch. The hand must have hurt like hell but I'm not sure he even felt it. I led him to the bathroom to wash the blood off and searched the cabinet for a first aid kit. There were some bandages in amongst the arsenal of prescription medicines common to French homes: for indigestion, erectile dysfunction… In case of depression… In case of anxiety.

Jean-Luc seemed to snatch a pack of pills at random, and pressed one directly into his mouth through the foil, shovelling water into his mouth with his good hand. He kept wincing as I tried to patch up the other one. We had to keep starting over. Tears sting like sea water.

51

Hours evaporated between me leaving the Malavoines' apartment and arriving home. Too shaken to walk and unable to face the crowds on the Metro in my dishevelled state, I went to sit in the Champ de Mars.

After a while I saw a woman walking in my direction: alone, around my age, not dissimilar in appearance, both of us with long dark hair. She was wearing a deep green fifties style dress with a wide black belt that I would happily have worn. The way she was sauntering along, the tilt of her face to the sun with the hint of a smile, everything about her seemed to say, *Isn't this wonderful?* When she passed me it was all I could do not to grab her and demand to swap lives before she disappeared at the corner near the restaurant where I'd eaten lunch with Emily. I realise now what a mistake it is to think of anyone else's life as ordered and harmonious and contented just because it looks that way. If it really is, that's called luck.

Surveying the scene again like a visitor sad that it was their last day, I took in the Eiffel Tower and the group of noisy Germans with their maps and cameras and I had a premonition that I'd blown it for Paris. Right here was where it all began for me but my time was coming to an end. I'd tried to play this city at its own game and lost.

Back in the empty apartment, I couldn't process the afternoon's events or reframe our relationship with the Malavoines whilst in my usual surroundings. Geneviève had sat here drinking rosé only last week. There had been that awkward silence between her and Philippe when I left the room – did she not trust herself to look at him, to talk to him with nobody else around? I think it was safe to say that Philippe had never picked up on her feelings, still less reciprocated them.

He'd texted to say he'd arrived safely in Nice and would call later but I deliberately left my phone downstairs when I went up to the attic. I was seriously considering packing a bag and leaving Paris immediately, but where would I go? The options were: to Philippe, to Emily in England or to my mother in California and none of those was the answer. An atoll where I would have no contact with other human beings would be perfect. I'd have to sacrifice love and companionship but with it, the risk of pain and betrayal and deception, to me and by me. There would be no more sex – and I'd miss it in a way I never would have thought possible – but no more being screwed over.

When I first heard the noise, I thought it must be crows on the roof. But as it got louder, there was only one person it could be. I'd completely forgotten about her. It was my stepdaughter and all I wanted was to be left in peace.

'Thought you might be here,' she said, invading the maid's room just like any other without a by-your-leave. She glanced around, nodding with approval. 'It's kind of weird, isn't it? But I like it.' She sank down next to me against the wall, the baseboards digging into our backs. 'So,' she said. 'What's wrong? You look terrible.'

Since I couldn't begin to answer that, I asked how she knew where to find me.

'I've been up here myself a few times.' She made a toking gesture and pointed to the mansard window. 'What you said about not disrespecting your home and all.'

I managed a feeble smile.

She reached in her pocket. 'You left the door to the courtyard open and when I saw your house keys in the kitchen,' she twirled them from a finger, 'I thought you might want to know you'd locked yourself out.'

Vanessa wasn't expecting the hug I gave her. She laughed, looking pleased. 'What's brought this on? Going to miss me now you're finally getting rid of me?'

'Yes, Vanessa, I'll miss you. We've had our moments but you're a good girl. I feel sorry for you landing on us – you couldn't have picked a worse time. I'm sorry if I made you feel any of it was your fault – it wasn't. There's been a lot of difficult stuff going on.'

'Don't worry, I knew it wasn't just me. I'm used to all this shit – first my parents, then my mom and her boyfriends.'

God, what must she make of it all? I'd spent my teenage years without adults to study at close quarters. But I trusted Vanessa not to see any of us as role models. She had more sense. 'It's Dad making you unhappy, isn't it?' Evidently I was too pitiful to play any active part in my misery. '*All* men are bastards, if you ask me.'

'Men are *not* all bastards,' I said. 'Believe me, women can be just as bad.'

'They're the only ones interested in me. I met someone at the weekend. He said he was going to call but I know he won't. I really liked him. He said I was beautiful.' She couldn't stop a pair of tears escaping.

'Oh, sweetheart, of course you are! It's only Monday. Give him a chance.'

'He knows I'm going to Nice tomorrow. Why would he wait if he wanted to see me again? Aargh! What's wrong with me? Why do I keep doing this?'

'You slept with him?'

She nodded, then said, 'Not exactly. He wanted to but I wouldn't because he didn't have a *capote*.'

'Well, that was a smart decision. Once you're on vacation, you'll probably forget all about him. Your cousins have been going there for years, they have friends in the town. You'll meet a lot of people and you know how persuasive men can be. Just remember it's not all about what *they* want. Look after yourself, okay?'

'Okay,' she said, but her smile was quick to fade. And then it was the kid in her looking at me. 'I wish you were coming to Nice with us,' she said. 'What if the

Darrousiers hate me? The only one I can remember is my grandma and she's dead. She died when I was twelve and guess when I found out?'

'Tell me.'

'Yesterday. Dad says he told my mom but she didn't think it was important enough to pass it on.'

'I'm so sorry,' I said. 'But your dad's from a lovely family and of course they're not going to hate you. You're one of them. You *are* a Darrousier.'

'But you're not.'

'No,' I said, 'I'm not.'

'Are you and Dad going to split up now? I don't get why anyone bothers getting married.' The way her lip wobbled made me crumple.

'I have no idea what's going to happen,' I told her. 'You mustn't tell him we've talked about any of this. Please?'

Vanessa cocked her head and raised a single eyebrow. 'Oh come on! When have you ever seen us have a cosy chat? He's always yelling at me.'

'Yeah,' I said, 'and you're always yelling back. Give it time. In his mind you're still a child. I know for a fact it made him very sad not to see you grow up.'

'Dad's so lucky to have you. I don't have anyone.'

'Yes, you do. He wants to be a father to you now, if you'll let him.' I paused as she stood up to leave. 'And whatever happens, you have me.'

After she'd gone I rubbed my back and stretched my arms out. My whole body had been folded in on itself for so long I felt pain in every atom. On the inside, on the outside. It was twice my size. On the underside of my wrist was a stripe of blood I'd missed.

52

When the time came, it was hard to let Vanessa go. I was sad that we hadn't done a great job of looking after her but I also felt I was finally getting the hang of it. After we'd hugged and said goodbye I hung around the Gare de Lyon waiting to watch the TGV leave. In six hours she'd be in Nice and Philippe would get another chance at fatherhood – maybe they'd do better without me.

The receptionist from my doctor's office had called me at 08.00 to inform me that I'd missed an appointment my insurance would not cover as well as ignoring letters and phone calls. Doctor Lafarge was back in Paris for a few days between trips and had asked her to try me on the off chance.

I was alone in the normally busy waiting room and the doctor came to fetch me herself. 'Alexandra,' she said. 'I was starting to think you'd left the country.'

I found Melissa Lafarge a year ago on the recommendation of a friend. I was so pleased to find an American gynaecologist in Paris and not have to endure the humiliation of French doctors having to speak English to me (the facts were bad enough, who needed the extra stress of foreign jargon?). Dr Lafarge managed the expat experience much better than me. She has a French husband too and sounded like a native even when we were speaking English. Having bilingual kids and raising them here must have played a part in that. Naturally there were no family photos on her desk – that would be insensitive in her line of work – but she'd mentioned her children when we were chatting one time. Now she'd just returned from the States and was about to go to her in-laws' in Brittany. If it wasn't her job to worry about my private parts, we could easily have been friends.

'I'm sorry I missed my check-up,' I said. 'It's been a strange summer.'

She chased away her frown with a tense smile. Women waited months for an appointment with her. 'You're here now. So how've you been since your surgery?'

I had never felt so good. The procedure performed by Dr Lafarge had been far more successful than previous attempts by other surgeons. She'd been confident she could significantly reduce my symptoms and she was right.

'How's the pain?'

'Hardly any after the first couple of weeks. It's a transformation.'

'And the bleeding?'

'Again, since things settled down, very little. This new IUD seems to be working better.'

I thought she'd be pleased for me. Instead, she pressed her lips together and studied the computer screen, before turning back to me. 'Have you been seeing someone else?'

'Excuse me?' I said, in the same vaguely snippy tone.

'Are you being treated by another doctor? Is that why you've stayed away?'

I laughed. 'No, absolutely not. Why would you ask such a thing?'

Dr Lafarge brought her hands together and looked at me gravely. 'Clearly there's been a misunderstanding. I didn't fit the IUD during the surgery. That was supposed to happen at the appointment you missed.'

'*Oh.*'

'It's excellent news that the surgery alone has produced such good results,' she said. 'But if you agree, I think we should go ahead and sort this out. The device will help to maintain the improvements for longer. What do you say?'

I felt unbelievably foolish at my mistake, like a child dressed up as an adult. 'Okay, let's do that.'

'Have you had unprotected sex since the procedure?'

I nodded.

'In that case, you need to do one of these.' She fetched a blood test kit from a cabinet. 'The lab is very quiet at this time of year so we'll have the results first thing in the morning. I can see you at midday if that works for you.'

The following day at 12.02, I was back in her office, heading for the couch.

'Take a seat first, if you wouldn't mind,' she said. I watched the necklace rise on her collarbone as she breathed in. 'Alexandra, the blood test results came back. You are pregnant.'

I stared at her, waiting for her to take it back, to say she was looking at someone else's results, that it was a mistake. 'That's not possible,' I said. My head was pounding.

'You'll need time to process,' she said. 'I'm as surprised as you are, but I never said *never.*'

'I know you didn't.' By the time she began treating me, motherhood wasn't even up for discussion. I'd moved on, to the extent that's possible. I know it destroys some women but for all my sorrow it wasn't this that nearly destroyed me.

'I have here that you tried to become pregnant a long time ago,' she said, looking at my records.

'Yes, in my late twenties. I couldn't conceive. We couldn't afford IVF and they said the chances were poor anyway. Once we had the full picture, we gave up. I was thirty when my fiancé left me and it was years before I was in another stable relationship, when I met my husband.'

On the doctor's instructions, I undressed below the waist and got up on the couch to have yet another probe. She was studying a screen. 'See that?' she said, indicating a tiny flicker, where the image repeatedly deepened and paled. 'There's a heartbeat. It's very early, no more than six weeks, seven max.'

'What are the odds…?' I couldn't say it.

'Well, the odds were against you ever conceiving naturally, especially at forty. All pregnancies are vulnerable in the early weeks, of course, but now it's implanted and following your recent surgery, the chances are comparable to those of any other woman of your age.'

My entire body felt rigid, melded with the couch. I couldn't grasp that what I was seeing, what the doctor was telling me, had anything to do with me. It was such a relief when the tears spilled down my cheeks. Those I recognised.

Dr Lafarge took my hand. It touched me to see that she was blinking. 'We won't discuss this further right now. Go home and talk it over with your husband. This is bound to be a shock for him too.'

It was a paralysing shot. The doctor fended off the receptionist as she escorted me to the door. Outside, I leaned against the wall of the building, immobile, and for a while all reality was suspended: the crowd, the noise and motion of the city, my life up to that moment. I braced myself for the battering rush of emotions. All but the one I'd imagined.

53

Sometimes when I look back on last summer, it's like the woman who had the affair isn't me. Well, she is and she isn't. There's so much that I couldn't see when I was in the middle of it. I suppose that must mean we're getting somewhere. I'd hate to be putting myself through this for nothing.

Up to this point we'd all behaved dishonourably to varying degrees, as people do. I'm not saying that to make myself feel better, because it doesn't. We couldn't undo what had happened but we could have worked around it, forgiving each other or not, our lives remaining entangled or not. I'm saying it to distinguish those events from the final act. I know now that I wasn't the only factor, but without me it wouldn't have ended the way it did.

It wasn't my fault I'd fallen pregnant. I was a sterile woman who had never had any cause to think it could happen. Abstract hope, sure, but not *signs* of hope. They told me my best chances were when I was young and that had come to nothing.

Of all the things I ever thought I was and turned out not to be: prudish, incapable of love and being loved, a decent person, the discovery that I was not infertile after all rocked me the deepest. There's a kind of logic there. It was cellular; I carried the evidence of this revelation like the longing for a child, which was such an intrinsic part of me I barely noticed it any more, just as I only registered now and again that my nails had grown.

And now there was a fragile chance that I could have what I'd longed for. That I would get to scream with the joy and agony of delivering a new person to the world, to hold a tiny warm body against mine, to love someone I'd created with someone I loved. It was the only chance I was ever going to get.

My original plan had been to go straight into work after leaving the doctor's to start preparing for the meeting with the American publisher later in the week. Since the others had left for the mountains and the beach my visits to the deserted offices at Editions Gallici had been infrequent and unfocused, mostly spent staring into the middle distance in anticipation of my next hook-up with Jean-Luc, and now there would be no more of those.

But that was before I knew I was carrying his child. I went home.

Every day dealt another blow to my ability to focus. My head was a vat of anxiety and it was as if someone had set an electric mixer on it. Some of this must be down to my condition. I'd heard a lot about Emily's three pregnancies but when I tried to recall the symptoms I wondered if I'd ever been paying attention: crushing fatigue, nausea, vomiting. Emotional volatility, increased libido, crazed bursts of energy. I had only some of these and even less idea at what stage they belonged. Ten minutes on the internet would have given me the facts but I couldn't do it. Nothing about my situation felt like a fact, more like something dangling in front of me that would vaporise the moment I started to invest in it.

I decided I would go to the office after all, to get out of the four walls of the apartment. Back on the street, crowds jostled me on the narrow sidewalk of the rue de Seine. As I reached the river the sight of a Ville de Paris trash can – just a metal cage with a transparent sack hanging from it – brought back a recent news story that had made me furious. It was Vanessa who originally told me about the fifteen-year-old girl tracked down somewhere south of Paris after abandoning her newborn baby in a dumpster. The baby had survived but there was talk of the mother – this *child* – facing criminal charges. It was mooted that she may have been acting out of fear and desperation – as if there could be any doubt. And there was something else: she was reported to be *from a good family*, which made me want to shake these clueless unfeeling people and demand what difference that was supposed to make? That girl must have felt so frightened and alone – maybe even more so now. Did she have anyone to say *I understand*? What would her life be like in ten years, twenty, thirty?

I could no more foresee where my own would lead, if the clutch of cells I'd tried to decipher on that screen would ever be a child, a student, a grown man or woman. It could just as easily dissolve into red emptiness at any moment. If I wanted certainty or to limit the damage to us all, at my next appointment with Dr Lafarge I'd have to tell her this had come too late for me.

In pitch darkness even the faintest beam is worth grasping and with my mom there wasn't anything left to lose. She probably wouldn't take the call but I had to try. I moved the furniture so I'd be sitting in front of the seascape over the mantelpiece, to give her something pretty to look at if she didn't want to look at me. Hours after I could have tried to reach her I was still making excuses: she'd be walking Bernstein (she's had two more dogs since Gershwin), eating lunch, in her studio painting. For the first time in over a week I put on make-up but it looked sinister against the pallor of my skin, so I took it off. I changed my top from blue to white.

If my mom had ever been tempted to break with me, my outburst would surely be all the provocation she needed. But I decided way back not to give up on her, no matter how bad things got. It was the one aspect of my life where I was determined not to fail outright. It seemed to me that for a mother the only thing sadder than losing a child to death was losing one in life.

When my mother pressed the button that proved me wrong there were the usual issues with poor connection, the image buffering. She was rotating the screen, talking when there was no sound. Suddenly her voice filled the room like she was there with me, 'Can you hear me? I can't hear you.'

'It's okay. I didn't say anything yet.'

The router was near the front door back home. She walked onto the porch and it sorted itself out. The sun was shining, and I could hear the sound of the Pacific half a block away. No other ocean sounds the same. 'Well, well,' she said. 'This *is* a surprise.' I was stunned to realise she thought I was cutting *her* off when we spoke on Christopher's anniversary. There must be so many rifts caused by one side believing the other doesn't want to talk any more.

Despite my procrastinating, I wasn't prepared. There's no rehearsing a script where you don't even know your own lines. I decided to let her speak first.

'I thought maybe you could use a break from me,' she said. 'After what you said.'

'And I thought you probably didn't want to talk to me.'

My mother's face was swooping back and forth with a disorienting effect – she was on the swing seat and any other day I would have asked her to sit still.

'For goodness' sake, you do say the silliest things, Alexandra,' she said. 'You're my only daughter and for all my shortcomings, I'm still your mother.'

'I didn't mean those awful things I said. I feel so bad about it.'

She must have anchored her feet on the decking and was studying me as if she'd never seen me before. 'You meant every word,' she said. 'Whether you meant to say it is another matter.'

'Okay then. But I went about it all wrong. I never meant to be so hurtful. I was trying to explain that I miss Christopher too but I know that's not how it came out.'

In the beat of silence that followed I had the feeling of something giving way. Rupturing, for all I knew.

Finally my mother answered. 'What you said hurt because it was true. I did the same to you over Philippe when it wasn't any of my business. I've been thinking about you a lot since we spoke. I wish I'd done that more over the years.' She narrowed her eyes. 'It's actually kind of a relief that you decided to lash out – people tiptoe around me. Although why you couldn't have told me you felt abandoned when I could still do something about it…'

'You can still do something about it,' I told her. 'You're doing it already.'

For once, and it felt like the first time, our words weren't laced with unspoken resentment. And if we could now speak openly about the past I figured there was no point holding back on the present.

'*Mom*,' I said, without even thinking, 'I've got something to tell you. Hear me out before you say anything, okay?'

'Okay.'

'I'm pregnant—'

She squealed like a little girl with the gift she's always wanted. 'Oh my, that's wonderful! Well, things can't be all that bad between you and Philippe.'

I looked away from the screen, knowing I had to go through with it now. 'After I found out he *was* cheating on me I started seeing Henri and Geneviève's son.'

'Their *son*? Seeing as in…?'

'Yes, it's been going on all summer.' My mother is obviously aware of the facts of life but the facts of mine would be hard for anyone to absorb. 'It's Jean-Luc's baby.'

'Do any of them know? Does Philippe?'

'Nobody knows except you. I'm in terrible trouble here.'

It was understandable that my mother didn't know what to say; I don't think anyone would. But I felt her heart go out to me across a continent and an ocean. In her face was everything I'd been missing for thirty years.

54

I never told him not to call me. You can't say that to a man who's punched a hole in a wall for you. 'Jean-Luc…' I answered.

'Alexandra…'

There was a pause as we both struggled to compose ourselves.

'*Je n'arrête pas de penser à toi.*' He was never going to stop thinking about me. We'd never spoken much French together – not proper conversations – and his voice sounded deeper, more knowing. Like someone really down on his luck. He wasn't doing this to put me at a disadvantage. Some things are so hard you just have to spit them out whichever way you can. 'If this meant anything—'

'Don't,' I said, and then, because it would be a lie of omission not to, 'I've been thinking about you too.' There was no point asking if he was okay.

'Meet me, please,' he said. 'You're right, I can't go on like this. It can be anywhere you want. Outside, if you prefer. I promise not to touch you.' This week was supposed to be our time for that.

It brought back the cool marble of the Malavoines' bathroom floor beneath my body, the dress I was barely wearing, buttons at the front unfastened, the skirt pushed up, my legs damp with blood and come and water. The dropped bandage had unwound itself around us in implausibly long loops, like someone was trying to write us a message. That first text Jean-Luc ever sent me said: *just to talk*. Look where that had led us.

'Parc des Buttes-Chaumont,' I said, off the top of my head. It was between the studio and Belleville, where Philippe sometimes talked of moving the gallery because it was an up-and-coming neighbourhood, cheaper and more receptive to the kind of work he wanted to show. I hadn't been there in years.

'See you at the belvedere in an hour?'

I should have changed my mind at the familiar lightening of Jean-Luc's voice as soon as I agreed to see him. If all we'd done was screw each other senseless it would have come to a natural end. Sooner or later one of us would have lost interest and it probably wouldn't have been me. But having allowed him to get hooked on me, I had to make him see what a disastrous idea that really was.

I was genuinely more concerned about him. He may have been a thinker, an *intello*, an amazing lover, but underneath he had a kind of innocence that went with his refusal to compromise. I remember thinking that our history would mark him for ever. We were the same in that respect.

But I was tougher, and it's not very often I get to say that. I'd get through this somehow because of the other shit I'd gotten through. I gashed my head open on a boulder and willed myself out of unconsciousness and my brother still died because of me. My mom and dad's marriage had foundered on those same rocks. Leaving the wreckage, I'd spent my adolescence as an orphan with two living parents, the three of us on different continents.

I always had the feeling I'd never *get over* any of the traumas in my life and that's not what this has been about. It's about figuring out a way to *live with it* – there's a difference – and to understand there's more to that than just continuing to draw breath. Who was it who said you can search for happiness or you can search for meaning? Having to choose between two options usually makes you want both. I'd stopped believing in either one.

I turned to you when the pain was too great to live with but not so bad that I wanted to die. Nearly, but not quite. I couldn't do that to my mother, or Philippe, or to a life that depended on me for the opportunity to be lived – so I suppose that was a win for meaning. Happiness isn't 24/7 – sometimes it's ephemeral, in the very smallest things: the baby kicking, the sunlight glittering on the ocean, a crunchy apple. Some days it's *really* hard but I owe it to all of us, even myself, to give it a shot. I can't claim any of this comes naturally, but I'm getting there.

I'm also getting ahead of myself.

It was a fittingly ominous afternoon for my meeting with Jean-Luc, humid and grey with a menacing sky. I hadn't done anything with my hair after showering the night before and scraped it into a lank ponytail without checking the sides. I put on dark jeans that were uncomfortably hot and a T-shirt I hadn't worn in years. I'd long since adopted the standards of the well-groomed Parisienne: no casual gear unless actually doing sport and even then it should look good. I had no need of a mirror to know I looked anything but.

The Parc des Buttes-Chaumont was too far to walk. I took a counterintuitive route, heading for Line 10 on autopilot at the start of my journey – I didn't care if it didn't go where I wanted. My ability to think was so limited that I could only plan one segment ahead. Change at Gare d'Austerlitz. Change at République. To avoid a third change I got out at Pyrénées and set off down Avenue Simon-Bolivar.

Despite my convoluted journey, I was early. Outside the entrance to the park a group of street vendors from Côte d'Ivoire were shoving their displays of knock-off sunglasses and perfumes into sports bags at the sight of two gendarmes approaching. An undernourished busker was murdering 'Yesterday' – the poor guy was off-key but he'd captured the depressed mood. I couldn't recall the last time my troubles seemed far away. I tossed a two euro coin into his guitar case without a glance, to spare him having to manage a smile.

I walked through the park in the full leaf of summer. As I crossed the bridge leading to the island with the belvedere up on the butte, the sight of Jean-Luc leaning heavily against the black railings reminded me of Philippe and the low iron balcony at the living room window. It was a sheer drop to the lake. I feared for the men who fell for me.

55

The afternoon was fading and the park emptied as a stiff breeze set the trees in motion. As I walked up the steps to the belvedere, the clouds arranged themselves into a doom-laden backdrop to the Paris skyline – this place was known for its dramatic views with the Sacré-Cœur on the horizon. The last visitors to the lookout passed me on their way down, leaving Jean-Luc alone. I'd seen them kissing, which would have been more than either of us could bear. I couldn't believe I'd picked such a romantic spot for something like this. I may have told him yesterday that it was over but of course that would be hard to accept after what happened next. And now he'd decided to confide in me after all. I couldn't turn around and say I didn't want to know.

He heard my footsteps. Unusually, he was clean shaven, probably since we'd spoken, his skin so smooth and perfect that my fingertips tingled. It was like there was an electric fence separating us. I leaned on the railings at some distance so we couldn't see each other face on. Even so his eyes glowed like a gas flame. He edged a little closer.

'You did clean up the bathroom, didn't you?' I blurted.

He looked at me in utter disbelief and we both laughed. I edged a little closer.

'*Yes*, I cleaned up the bathroom,' he said, in a tone that was falsely jokey, genuinely despondent. He held up his injured hand, a suppurating mass of scabs, flakes of dried skin and lurid raw patches.

'That looks horrific,' I said. 'It should be covered up, you know.'

He shook his head and his mouth stretched into a bitter line. 'You think *this* is what hurts? Because let me tell you, this is nothing. I can't even feel it.'

How I envied the next one who made him feel this strongly. The right woman would feel euphoric when she realised how relentlessly he was capable of loving her back. That was never going to be me.

When his other arm stirred I flew over and grabbed it, thinking he was about to take a swipe at one of the stone pillars and break something. Turned out he was only reaching for his pocket. Realising my mistake, I let go. On the second attempt he took the cigarettes out of his jacket and offered them to me. We both smoked only when nervous or stressed and I was about to take one when I remembered I couldn't.

'What is it?' he asked me, frowning. 'For God's sake, one a week's not going to kill you.'

'I have to sit down.' I positioned myself on the cold stone base against a pillar as there was nowhere else, knees bent, my feet on the raised structure in the middle. Jean-

Luc put the cigarettes away and took up the same position at the next pillar along, our backs to Paris, his newish Converses next to my battered ones. Nobody wants to be a grown-up any more. He offered me his leather jacket when he saw me shivering but I refused, hugging myself tight against the chill, against an unbearable longing for him to hold me. It would smell like him, be warm like him. My nipples hardened against my forearms.

He gave me a puzzled look and I thought of everything he didn't know.

He might be – *was* – looking at the future mother of his child, but I couldn't lay that on him in his volatile state when it might still come to nothing. Even in the animal frenzy of that first afternoon I'd told him there was no need to be careful. Keeping it to myself was my only option; it would be a lonely few weeks before I knew if I'd have to own up to everything, derailing several other lives. I'd always wanted a baby, but not like this.

'I can't remember not knowing you,' he said.

'It's not been all that long.' I reproached myself for trying to talk it down. My entire life could have ticked away without me experiencing what we'd had for this one short summer. I didn't mean the fantastic sex or the thrill of the forbidden. There are rarer things.

'And now you're dropping me just like that—'

'*Just like what?*' The wind amplified my words and it sounded like I was shouting. 'You think this is easy for me? We've been having the same conversation practically from the start! We can't do this, okay? We have to stop whether we want to or not.'

'So you admit you don't want to stop. But who *says* we have to?'

'I do. Nobody else knows. At least not for certain,' I added, mindful of Geneviève, who had more reasons to be incensed than I'd originally thought. 'Believe me, if they find out they'll have plenty to say.'

'Why can't we just do what we want? What's the point of anything otherwise? You don't even know what you want. You turn up at my parents' place saying it's over and we end up making love like *that*? That wouldn't be possible if we didn't feel the same way. It just wouldn't…' His voice trailed off and it was torment knowing we were both reliving moments almost violent in their passion, knowing it was the last time. I faced him straight on, the thudding in my chest echoing at my temple like the second heartbeat.

'Don't you think it's possible I was disturbed by you putting your hand through a wall? That's not normal behaviour.' There it was, the difference in his approach to living and mine: I thought about harming myself and backed out; he went ahead with absolute commitment. 'You've had a charmed existence if it's taken you nearly twenty-four years to realise you can't always have what you want.'

Witnessing his anguish was like pressing hard on a bruise. Two people began climbing the steps to the lookout and soon changed their minds, turning around and heading in another direction, whispering.

'You don't realise what you are to me,' Jean-Luc said. 'You make me forget all the bad shit that's happened.' I watched his Adam's apple dip as he swallowed hard. '*Tout est foutu*.' Everything's fucked.

It really felt like it.

'This is all my mother's fault,' he said. 'I will never forgive her for ruining things between us.'

For an instant I questioned whether Geneviève, or anyone, really had any right to object to me and Jean-Luc. It wasn't the done thing, that was a given. She was entitled to be angry, to feel that I'd betrayed her trust and our husbands' friendship. I could understand her resenting me for cheating on the man she'd secretly loved for years – with anyone, let alone her *own son*. It was hard to argue with any of it.

'Don't blame your mother,' I said. 'It's not her fault or yours. What you feel for me is very strong and very real – I don't doubt that. But you said yourself it's an obsession, a way to block other things out. I'm just a fix, Jean-Luc, and even that's not working. Think about it – you've had some of these episodes when we're together. I wish I could, but I can't make this right. You've got to get to what's causing it.'

'But who can I talk to, if I can't talk to you?'

I had long sensed a kind of exclusion zone around him which I had breached somehow. 'You can tell me anything,' I said, hoping I'd be better than no one.

I recall that conversation not in words but in sensation, movement, contagious emotion. A diving accident in which Jean-Luc and another man had narrowly escaped death because of what happened to him. There was a name for it, though I didn't discover that until later: Blue Orb Syndrome. When divers panic, become disoriented, behave irrationally. He talked of feeling claustrophobic, trapped. Tearing off equipment, pulling the other man down, all logic abandoned, all survival instincts suppressed. He gripped me so hard the colour drained from his hand to leave five tiny marks on my arm. Behind my back, my other hand clung to the railings of the belvedere: it was activating my own walls of water, black rocks, helpless terror. For him that day was followed by nightmares he could only avoid by sleeping in daylight, panic attacks that struck without warning, that same conviction he was about to die.

But the worst part was coming to fear what he had always loved. *'Je n'ai plus rien sans toi.'* Without me he had nothing. He was looking for a replacement passion when he found me but I'd already proven that I was no match for the ocean.

'You're not going to die, Jean-Luc. You're going to get through this and get on with your life,' I said, stroking his head, my T-shirt soaked through.

'You won't tell my parents?'

Geneviève's words at Honfleur came back to me. *If you find out…* But he wasn't a kid and I wasn't a snitch.

'Not if you promise that you will,' I said. 'It's nothing to be ashamed of. If you don't deal with things like this, they can mess you up.'

56

My teenage dreams used to stay with me in every detail, often leaving me in a state of agitation for hours, not helped by being surrounded by those who featured in them. Both asleep and awake under the covers my imagination ran wild with Emily's assurance that it was even better when someone else made you come. In my imagination there was no shortage of candidates for the job, although when I finally enlisted male help I found she wasn't always right. Not only that, but I wasn't too keen on what the boys wanted in return.

As an adult, I don't often remember my dreams, but those I do have one thing in common. They could never happen.

There's one that I've had repeatedly, sometimes years apart. My brother Christopher and I are in our late twenties. It is fall and we are walking in Prospect Park in Brooklyn, close to where I used to live, albeit not at that time (I was in London with Jonathan then). I am wearing a beautiful red coat I've never owned, Christopher, who's much taller than me, a pea coat with the collar turned up and a green wool scarf. He's smart and funny, still earnest like he always used to be. We pay little attention to our surroundings, covering large distances as we talk something out, I never know what; perhaps some problem I'm trying to help with. Suddenly he grabs hold of me and pretends to push me into a huge pile of leaves. We both start kicking them up into the air, shrieking with laughter like we're eight and ten again.

And then there was the new dream, of a very different future to my now.

I'm on the Côte d'Azur with the others in this story, having lunch at a beachfront restaurant. It's not hot or crowded so it must only be late spring or very early summer – the sky Yves Klein blue, that caressing warmth in the air. Everyone's on good form, drinking rosé and eating grilled fish, talking across each other, waving our hands about. It seems we're all still friends.

Some Italians at the next table are making a huge fuss of a little boy who has his mother's dark hair and his father's eyes. It's my son, maybe three years old. It's true, he is adorable. Everybody says so.

Philippe looks at his watch and gets up to leave the gathering, circling the table to embrace us all in turn. He slaps Henri Malavoine on the back, as usual. He kisses the boy's head, ruffles his hair, and last of all, he kisses me. Not quite on the mouth, not quite far enough away.

'Time for a siesta,' I say. Jean-Luc catches my eye and tries not to smile. He and I leave with the little boy swinging between us.

Wrong. Wrong. All wrong.

I still have that dream often, there's no predicting when. Sometimes I'm just not strong enough. Those nights I can't sleep for fear of its blissful torture, right up there with the happiest I've ever been. It's so vivid, so close, I want so much for it to be real that when I wake I have to remind myself he's gone. I would be okay with the woman not being me – I didn't try to keep him for myself. The sadness hollows me and for a second or two it's all I can do to exist, let alone live.

And then I remember Jean-Luc left me someone to fill that space, when I could have been left with nothing. And the biggest lesson I have learned from everything I've told you is this: love comes in many kinds.

57

Just as I decided there could be no more calls, texts or meetings, Jean-Luc broke off contact completely. I felt as empty as it's possible to feel when you're pregnant and ravenous, and indescribably lonely. Eating packet mac and cheese made it better and worse with its new associations of Vanessa. The way I missed her was very straightforward compared to the way I missed her father. That's right, I missed Philippe. We all spoke often on the phone, both of them keen to keep me up to date with their latest disagreements. Vanessa was getting on well with her cousins and had learned to ride a Vespa – against Philippe's wishes, but he was overruled by his family, who teased him for becoming an uptight Parisian. Hearing about her escapades made me smile just when I needed to remember how.

That Friday I had lunch as planned with Robert Levitsky from San Francisco, who unexpectedly brought along his partner, a Japanese-American dancer who was prettier and more feminine than most women. 'It's okay,' said Robert, 'nobody can stop staring at him.' The object of our attention pouted fetchingly at us with one eye on the very handsome and not-at-all-gay waiter, who missed no opportunity to look down the front of my dress. I placed my hand over the top of my wine glass hoping nobody would notice I didn't touch it as my companions laid in with enthusiasm.

We mostly talked about *Icons* and secular iconology, Robert's area. He was writing a book that sounded a million times more marketable than ours (Che Guevara, Lady Gaga, David Beckham) but as his foundation had recently secured a large donation from a patron of East European descent, he wanted to make ours available in English. For the sake of both Editions Gallici and Baudelaire, whose volume we could otherwise barely afford to produce, I jumped to accept a figure more generous than I'd dared to hope for.

Negotiations concluded, we agreed to wait until September to proceed. I began to unwind, relieved I'd managed to carry off the meeting and summon some trace of the competent professional woman I was before I lost my grip on everything. Over dessert we switched to chit-chat about Paris and I realised how little I'd seen or done that summer, disregarding all the lies I'd told Philippe. I'd just launched into an anecdote about the Impressionist exhibition I dragged him to at the Musée Marmottan when instead of those luminous paintings, I saw our Metro ride that day like a couple of frames from a movie: Philippe looking at the little kid with the toy horses and how upset he'd been with the father. How sad he was about Vanessa. Him saying I would be a good mother.

I dried up mid-sentence, staring straight ahead although I couldn't see a thing. The Japanese boyfriend touched my shoulder gently and Robert asked me if I was okay. I had to excuse myself for a moment. Nothing was okay. I couldn't see how it ever would be.

Meeting over, I crossed the Pont d'Austerlitz, relieved to have swapped my heels for sandals. I mentally sketched a route home through the Jardin des Plantes, a place I used to love. I walked the full length of one of the avenues lined with plane trees, taking in the riotous display of nature in full bloom. What would happen to me come fall, come bare branches, by the next time these plants came into bud? Past, present, future: there was no sanctuary. There was no ending in which I got to keep Philippe, Jean-Luc and my child. I walked through the Fifth and finally took a short cut through the familiar territory of the Jardin du Luxembourg, the one patch of grass where the Keep Off signs were ignored barely visible for all the tourists lounging around. For once I would have welcomed bumping into Daniel – he wouldn't be able to make me laugh but I wouldn't have shooed him away this time. I'd become quite attached to him, albeit not in the way he wanted. He would know when to drop all that. He would have listened.

Eventually I could put it off no longer. I'd been avoiding computers and tablets as though they might spontaneously bombard me with unwanted information:

the size of a seven-week embryo, French divorce law, details of therapists specialising in whatever was wrong with me. (Sorry, I know you don't like that phrase.)

The times of TGV trains from Paris to Nice.

At two days' notice it was going to cost a fortune but my decision was made. It didn't even feel like a decision. When I came face to face with Philippe I would tell him about Jean-Luc's accident, so he could tell the Malavoines, and in doing so I would have to reveal everything. I had no choice – for once I would do the right thing, no matter how disastrous the consequences.

I entered my date of travel but before I hit search, I heard the soft clunk of the elevator coming to a halt on our floor, which was strange as our neighbours on both sides were away. Someone must have pressed the button for the wrong floor. They looked very similar: three doors, three mats, three minuscule labels below the bells. Whoever it was would realise their mistake soon enough. It wouldn't be the DARROUSIER-FOLGATE residence they wanted.

I'd turned back to the screen when I heard the sound of a key in the lock. My eyes swept over to the front door without the rest of me moving, like one of those living statues you see everywhere. 'Vanessa?' I called out, anxiety plucking at my vocal cords. She'd had a bust-up with her father and come back early. That had to be it.

The first key was snatched away, another inserted with force and finally the door swung open. It was my husband standing at the threshold of our home and something told me he wasn't thinking anything good about me now.

58

Until Vanessa moved in with us I had never once seen Philippe really angry. Irritated, pissed off, of course, just as anyone is from time to time. We'd lived here in this respectable apartment building in the chic 6th arrondissement our entire marriage – five years already – before the neighbours started shouting at us to stop shouting. It was a quiet life, but now I wanted Philippe to lose his temper because his silence was intolerable. My doubts about whether my husband still felt passion for me disappeared before he said a word. If only I could have found out some other way.

He shoved his suitcase into a corner, rocking it from side to side without using the wheels; on top he dumped his nice jacket, now bunched up in his left hand like a rag. He suspended the car keys above the ceramic bowl where we kept them and, opening his fingers, dropped them from a height. I wish it would have shattered.

'Have you driven all the way from Nice?' I guessed as much from his pleated brow and hunched shoulders, the way he held his head like a dead weight. When Philippe came into the living room I instinctively took a step backwards and he gave one of those exhalations that is virtually a word. 'What, you think I'd hit you?'

My gut response was that I didn't think either of us had a clue what the other was capable of but I immediately revised this. I knew where I stood with him. I tracked his gaze to the train website still open on my laptop, now displaying the search results. He couldn't conceal his surprise. 'I've spared you a trip,' he said.

We were both still standing, awkward and ill at ease in our apartment that felt like an empty shell. I waited to find out how much he knew, how serious it was on a scale of basic, bad and dreadful. It was curiously empowering that he couldn't know everything, although the part he couldn't know would only make matters infinitely worse. Whatever accusations he made, I was guilty. It was reassuring to know I could put up no defence. I didn't have the energy.

When Philippe could finally bring himself to look at me, his eyes were about to spill over. '*Toi, qui es si bonne,*' he said, in sheer desolation. He thought I was a *good person* and for reasons I couldn't fathom he was still using the present tense. I leaned across to him, tears of my own building up. 'Don't, please,' I said. 'I'm not worth it.'

He wiped his face on the back of his hand. Even before I was unfaithful I'd never given my husband any reason to think so highly of me. But maybe that's what love is, a willingness to accept the other person for all that they are, to consider their flaws outweighed by the good.

I'm ashamed to say I pitied Philippe. It had to be anger and jealousy that had driven him home – nine hours on the road – and now he was here, he was too beat to yell at me. 'If I had heard about this from anyone but Geneviève I would have thought it was a lie,' he said, perhaps still hoping it was.

'How long has she known?' I asked, my voice not rising because there was a significant element of me that didn't care.

'Maybe this is news, but you're not very good at this, Alexandra. And you don't know a warning when you hear one. Geneviève told me she spoke to you in Normandy, thinking you'd back off. If you had, I would never have needed to know. She never wanted it to come to this.'

'So you *didn't* know?'

'*Me?* Good God, no! But she's been onto the two of you a long time, after calling on you at the office.' I held my breath – she knew my entry codes too. 'Says she got no answer but her son only went and left his *skateboard* in the courtyard.'

How could Jean-Luc have been so stupid? Philippe's eyebrows did an uphill/downhill in response to my expression. 'Well, you're no better. Geneviève found all sorts of things of yours in his bedroom when they got home yesterday. She got particularly worked up about a lipstick for some reason.'

After Jean-Luc flipped out and injured himself, I didn't check the floor carefully for the contents of my bag.

Before I left I registered having the three important items: wallet, keys and phone, and gathered up anything else I could see.

'I mean, doing it in their *home*! That was what made Geneviève crack. Have you *no* shame? I used to read Jean-Luc stories in that room when he was a little boy and he ends up...'

I held up my hands. 'Stop it!' It was pointless to explain how reluctant I'd been to go to the Malavoines'. The problem was what we'd done, not which room we'd done it in. 'I've never done anything like this before, I promise you.'

Philippe snorted bitterly, and it was a ridiculous claim, now I thought about it. *I've never had an affair with your best friend's son before, I swear.*

'I mean, not even remotely.'

'You clearly have no idea how it works.'

'Too bad I didn't ask for your advice then, since you're such an expert.' There was a flicker of uncertainty in his expression. 'That's right,' I said. 'I know about you and Nico.'

I don't know what I expected but it wasn't this disdain. 'You want to talk about that now? *Really?* So I'm not perfect either. That's been over for a while, and it was nothing to me—'

Oh, here we go, I thought.

'But more to the point, she was nothing to you. You will never have to look Nico in the eye. You will never find yourself struggling to account to anyone for what I did. Whereas I have had to apologise for your behaviour. I'm ashamed of you.'

That made two of us. But even so, what Philippe did wasn't nothing. 'I found out about your affair before anything happened with Jean-Luc,' I said, for the record.

Now Philippe's mouth fell open. 'You're unbelievable, Alexandra! Are you suggesting *I'm* somehow responsible for this?' He looked away, shaking his head over and over. 'I hold my hand up to my own actions but yours are down to you. No one else.' He extended the fingers of one hand and stirred the air with them, inhaling deeply, as if about to explain something to an exceptionally difficult person or a very dense one. '*You don't shit on your own doorstep,*' he said, in English. It's funny how the French have no equivalent of that delightful expression but maybe they don't need one. They just know. 'So you were upset, you wanted to get your own back – fair enough. But did you have to do it like this? Of all the young men in Paris, why pick our friends' son?' He paused as an unwelcome thought occurred to him. 'Why are we even together if that's what you want?'

'I would never have *picked* Jean-Luc. You have to believe I didn't go looking for a younger man or *any* man, Philippe. It wasn't about revenge.'

His shoulders dropped and he gave a sigh. 'There's no end to what Henri and Geneviève have been through with that boy.'

'What do you mean?'

'He was a nightmare as a teenager: angry, depressed. Going missing. Bunking off school.'

'Why have you never told me this?'

Philippe threw me a furious look as if I'd suggested it was his job to vet my lovers.

'Have I ever told anyone about your brother? You know how Geneviève likes everything perfect, she wanted to hush it up. Well, from now on you can keep your secrets, all of you! I am sick of it!' After a moment he was off again. 'Did it start after the launch? I saw you talking, and you took a long time to show up for dinner.' He turned away, as if looking at me and thinking whatever he was thinking was too much to stomach. 'You didn't do it in my gallery?'

'Philippe, for goodness' sake, nothing happened in your gallery! It started before that when he came to the office.'

'Oh, that's classy!'

'All this when and where is irrelevant. It is already over. He is very clear about that now. And it was me who ended it,' I added, recalling that this had been a consolation when I found out Philippe had broken it off with Nico. A slim one.

It was completely dark now and over Philippe's shoulder I could see the shapes of people moving around in the apartments opposite and our reflections in the living room windows. 'Of course it's over *now*,' he said, ignoring the order of events, which irritated me unreasonably. 'I still cannot imagine how this began.'

'We are not having this conversation,' I said, aware I had very little dignity left to preserve. 'If something is over it makes no difference how it started.'

'*It does to me!* It was you who made the first move, wasn't it? You should have told me if I didn't satisfy you. Not that I can compete with a pretty little bastard less than half my age, of course.'

'Don't call him that.'

'The least you can do is answer me.'

'It won't make you feel better.' As if anything could. 'If you insist, he made the first move, on the spur of the moment, I'm sure. I should have ignored it. It was a mistake, it was wrong. I don't know what else to say.'

'Well, you could tell me why, if you regretted it, you kept going back for more?'

He made the assumption most people would. Mistakes and regrets usually belong together. I couldn't tell Philippe that I'd wrestled with my conscience but been overpowered by desire for Jean-Luc. Or that it had turned out to be so much more than sexual.

I deeply regret the way it ended but to this day I cannot say I regret it entirely. I know it's shocking, but it's not as if I choose to feel that way. And I'm grateful I can remember that it wasn't all horror and pain and deceit. If I can hold on to that, one day I'll have a chance of explaining to our daughter how she came to be. She's the proof that it *was* something beautiful. It wasn't only about what we could destroy.

'Now I understand why you've been so distant. Why you didn't want me anywhere near you.' I went to protest – I'd provided intermittent sexual favours with all the warmth and affection of someone doing it under a railway bridge for twenty euros a pop. But we both knew that wasn't all he meant. 'I was trying to be sensitive, after that time it was obviously so distressing for you.' My hand went to my mouth. That time. He *had* sensed something was wrong, he just didn't know what.

'I can honestly say it was just sex with Nico – she was often here from Rome on business. It was a casual arrangement for both of us. It began in the winter, when you were feeling bad and you and I weren't sleeping together much. I was flattered. Nothing was going well and it made me feel better. That's all it was.'

A whoosh of indignation powered me up. We could argue all night about who did what but there were no innocents here.

'*That's all it was?* You put our marriage at risk over someone you didn't even care about and it's no big deal? I realise I wasn't supposed to find out, but if you thought this was okay… At least I have the decency to feel bad about what I've done.'

Philippe held a balled fist to his mouth and it was a while before he spoke again. 'I can see now that it was pretty despicable, especially given the circumstances. But I would never have done it if I thought it would harm our marriage – you mean too much to me. I'm such an idiot!' he said, turning his anger inward. 'I don't know if you can forgive me.'

It was amazing how little comfort it gave me, infecting him with my guilt.

'The issue isn't going to be whether I can forgive *you*, Philippe.' There was only one option left that felt anywhere near right, one I'd considered several times back when it could have done some good. It was too late, but I would do it anyway. I would tell my husband the whole story. Except that I didn't start at the beginning. I never do. First I heard the words in my head and then they were out in the open, a knife pulled from a wound. *Now* he sat down.

59

Philippe and I were still under the same roof but that was as far as it went. We weren't in any sense together. I'd spent most of the four days sleeping, finally surrendering to a hormonal fatigue I'd been living with for weeks, which was no longer offset by endorphins or adrenaline. I ate and drank because it wasn't just about me – I never wanted to harm another living being.

Philippe spent most of the time out – I didn't know where – but when I heard him moving around the apartment I made sure to stay in the guest room, where I'd been sleeping since that night. I was like a mother trying to shield her child from some traumatic sight that could leave lasting mental scars. But I was Philippe's wife, pregnant by another man, and the sight I wanted to protect him from was me. And it pained me to look at him in turn. For a tall man, he seemed diminished in every way. Haggard, caught between shock and devastation. I know that place and I wouldn't wish it on anyone. 'Did you have to fall in love with him?' he'd said.

I ended up saying the same to both of them, word for word. *I'm sorry. I never meant to hurt you.*

Those strange, vacant days brought back one of my few clear memories of childhood that predate Christopher's death. I was six years old when a major earthquake took place off the coast of Humboldt County. My parents were glued to the TV as we waited for aftershocks. Men in suits pointed at weather maps with sticks, predicting further tremors, of which there were many. But now, as with everything, I'd completely lost my bearings. This was nothing of the kind – so far all we'd had was the foreshock.

When I ventured outside for the first time since Philippe's return, craving sunlight, I found a small padded envelope in the mailbox addressed to *Alexandra Darrousier*. The pointed courtesy of this gesture made me want to throw the contents around the courtyard – its message as clear as if it were daubed all over the wall in the Chanel Coromandel lipstick inside: Geneviève might refuse to get my name right but her behaviour, unlike mine, would remain beyond reproach.

I tried to tell myself it had found its way into the envelope by accident when she was retrieving my lost belongings; the greatest indictment wasn't the lipstick, the cheap mirror compact or the BHV special edition of *Paris Pratique* that screamed *you will always be a tourist*. It was a chip of plasterboard from the wall of Jean-Luc's room, two or three centimetres wide with jagged edges, one of them softly tinged with red. I put all of it in the trash.

On that walk I made it as far as the tip of the Ile de la Cité, near the Pont Neuf. For over an hour I sat listening to a man play Spanish guitar. When he left, he came over and asked if his takings would be any help to me. 'Why would you do that?' I said, realising I had left home with nothing but the keys in my pocket. 'People normally say this to me,' he said, 'but you made me feel so sad.'

The receptionist at the doctor's office handed me some forms and a sample pot before turning quickly to the next woman in line, whose belly was so huge that her maternity dress hitched up at the hemline. The *future maman* gave me a sisterly smile and I clutched at the edge of the desk as fear lashed at me. I dreaded thinking what kind of mother I would make. Loving the right people was something I found difficult – what if I didn't love my baby? Cold sweat beaded at the roots of my hair.

When I was summoned, I handed my sample to Dr Lafarge who set it down on the desk. 'How have you been?'

The answer couldn't be hard to guess. The last few days had leached the colour from my skin, the area around my eyes looked frail, the capillaries visible underneath. When she suggested an examination, there was a tentative quality to the question. I forgot my stoic act when she inserted the scanner. Almost immediately there was that winking again on the screen, darker, lighter. I felt the doctor lingered on it. She concluded with, 'All normal for eight weeks.'

My sigh expressed something I had not been capable of articulating but it was a lot more complicated than relief. Dr Lafarge ventured a smile as she handed me tissues to clean myself up. The weird hollowness that always follows an internal felt different now I wasn't sick any more.

'It's not my husband's baby,' I told her when we were back at her desk, my voice devoid of emotion. I don't know why I told her, or what I expected by way of a reply.

For a split second I could see the whites all the way around her irises. 'Ah,' she said, turning away to a drawer. She spent a long time flicking through papers before handing me a brochure for a counselling service. 'In case you need to talk to someone,' she said. Unwanted pregnancy, genetic abnormalities, testing for hereditary conditions; numerous scenarios were listed, none of them mine.

'Otherwise I'll see you in four weeks, and by then...' Her voice trailed off but I got what she meant. The end of the first trimester would be approaching. As I was leaving, she said something to me in an off-the-record tone. 'I feel for you, Alexandra.'

Her office was near the Gare Saint-Lazare, a short walk from the big department stores on Haussmann. The contrast between the gravity of the medical consultation and a shopping trip had a certain appeal; I craved a moment of lightness and frivolity. It was my mother's birthday in two weeks' time but given the unreliability of the French and US postal services, it was not too soon to send a gift. Something special was called for to mark the big thaw between the two of us. Since everything blew up with Philippe she was checking in on me almost daily and we were already talking about her next visit. *If the worst comes to the worst, you can always come home*, she said. I tried to imagine myself back where everything went wrong the first time, a single mom working some deadbeat job, dependent on my mother to watch my kid. Back amongst people who knew my story (it's not the kind anyone forgets), good honest people who might shake their heads sadly and say to each other, *The odds were always going to be against her, after what happened here.*

I was casting around for gift ideas as I walked when I became aware of a fracas on the opposite side of the street. A police officer was raising her voice to someone on the edge of the square in front of the church of Sainte-Trinité, and you don't see cops on the streets that much in Paris. People were walking by, shaking their heads and covering their noses. *Dégueulasse!*

Suppressing my instinct to steer clear, I crossed over and the scene began to take shape. The offender was a woman of maybe sixty years old sitting on the ground, her skin nut brown and wizened by the sun, wild grey hair all over the place, layer upon layer of ragged skirts fanned out around her. And from underneath them copious streams of urine were tracing a delta across the asphalt. She was cackling, oblivious to it all.

'*Laissez-la tranquille!*'

The police officer rounded on me with a look of pure aggression, which transformed into amusement when she took stock of me, a nondescript member of the public, scared stiff. She was an intimidating presence, at least six feet tall, her uniform tight around ample curves, hair in tight cornrows under her cap. On her belt were the standard issue gun and baton. Her authority and confidence gave off a charge as powerful as any man's.

'You think this is the way to live, madame?' she asked me, pointing at the woman with her reinforced boot. 'There are services available for these people. And public toilets, over there.'

'I just… It's just so sad,' I said, like an imbecile.

The police officer crossed her arms over her chest, tilting her head in mock anticipation of my miracle solution to all the city's problems. What a job like hers would do to anyone's view of human nature, day upon day. How randomly life deals the breaks. Take the three of us women, who couldn't be more different. A few opposite strokes of fate and it could be that officer on the wrong side of the law. The woman on the ground could be a respectable grandmother. It could be me sitting there in my own filth, raving. It could yet happen.

60

Philippe was watching the news. He looked over his shoulder and greeted me but it was just a reflex. I hung around in the hall before taking the groceries into the kitchen. It was about time we ate a square meal, and if he decided to walk out that was his call.

In the event we managed eight or ten minutes at the dining table together, at right angles rather than facing each other as we used to, eyes locked on our plates. Philippe poured red wine for himself and stared at the contents of his glass. I pleated and smoothed my linen napkin so often that it remembered its folds like a Roman blind. 'Arrête!' he said in the end. I stopped.

After cleaning up I went to what was now my room, the previous haven of guests who were neither entirely welcome nor entirely unwanted. Which about summed it up, really.

It was very late when I was woken by the unmistakable noise from the street. There was something very wrong with that motorbike. My phone rang while I was still at the bedroom window. For once I had to stick to my guns. 'You can't be here, Jean-Luc. Philippe knows everything.'

More than *he* did. It was wrong, and I knew it.

'You have to let me in,' Jean-Luc insisted. 'Tell me the code.' I recognised the odd note in his voice from that day at the Malavoines' and other times I'd made him mad and it made my windpipe constrict, as always.

'I'll come down.'

'No, let me in, I said. If you don't, I'm going to bash this door down. Watch if you don't believe me.'

As I surveyed the scene from the fourth floor, he angled the motorbike towards the wooden doors to the courtyard, looked up to check I was there and revved the engine. I had no doubt he would do it.

'Stop, please, before you wake the whole street. I'll tell you the code.'

He killed the engine and my courage ebbed away with it. Now what? Did I stay inside the apartment or try to head him off at the stairs? If we had any kind of conversation in the courtyard people would hear. It was almost two in the morning.

I guessed before he even reached our floor that he was drunk, high, or both. I hadn't seen the crash helmet a minute ago, and he wasn't carrying it. As he clomped up the stairs I stood in the doorway, trying to occupy the entire width.

'You said you'd let me in.'

'I didn't mean into the apartment! You know Philippe's here – he drove all the way back from Nice after your mother said her piece.'

It was some twisted comfort knowing Philippe was home, fast asleep only metres away. In what kind of a sick situation does a woman need her husband as protection against her lover?

'Actually, it's him I want to see,' Jean-Luc said, staggering. 'Philippe! Are you there?' he hollered, his cries echoing up and down the stairwell. As he was so close to the top of the steps I had no option but to grab him like I had in the restaurant the night he returned to Paris, only harder. As I pulled him toward me he tried to kiss me, tasting of whisky. My stomach heaved with an urge to be violently sick but I didn't have that luxury. I was behaving like the hostage negotiator in the crappy film Vanessa and I had watched, with artificial calmness, manufactured reassurance. The *humouring you until you do what I want* approach.

'Philippe!' he roared again.

From downstairs a neighbour threatened us with the police.

'Don't do this, Jean-Luc, you're not thinking straight. Let me get you a cab.' He was in no condition to be riding around Paris on that heap of junk. 'Or I'll call your father to come pick you up.'

Nobody else knew the state Jean-Luc was in, I was sure. It was the one thing I hadn't told Philippe – it seemed like an insult too far expecting him to care.

'What the hell is going on?' He appeared behind me in his robe. It was only then that I registered I was standing there in a sleeveless nightdress that was only mid-thigh length. I pulled my raincoat off the rack inside the door and Philippe pushed past me out onto the corridor, where Jean-Luc was now leaning against the elevator.

'*Philippe*,' I said. He ignored me.

'You've got a nerve, showing your face here,' he said to Jean-Luc. 'What do you think you're playing at?'

'There's something I want to tell you.' Jean-Luc sounded drunker than ever but that wasn't it. For all his bravado, he was scared of Philippe and I was scared for all of us.

'I don't want to hear it. Go home!'

I stepped forward but Philippe blocked my way with his arm.

'I didn't just fuck your wife. I love her.'

Philippe flew at him, landing a punch in the face before gripping his shoulders, giving him a vigorous shake. 'You little bastard! Alexandra is *my wife*, you said it.'

I said nothing as I slipped past Philippe to form a physical barrier between them.

To hit Jean-Luc again, my husband would have to manhandle me first, although from the aggression flooding off of him I would no longer rule anything out.

'Go, Jean-Luc, please! I've told you it's over. Philippe knows everything.'

Jean-Luc gave a manic laugh. 'You think?' he said, with an unsettling look aimed at both of us. 'Did you know I fucked your daughter last night?'

I heard Philippe take a huge breath in and took advantage to manoeuvre him back into the apartment.

'If your father wasn't a good friend I would kill you this minute, you piece of shit!' he yelled across me. 'If you've laid a finger on my daughter… You'd better be lying.'

I turned to Jean-Luc, recalling the photos on Vanessa's phone, her saying *in my dreams*. The way she'd been used by Boris and the boy at the party who didn't call. 'Oh, please tell me that's not true. Vanessa's a kid – I can't believe you'd do that.'

Philippe was watching closely. I didn't know if it was true or not; my doubt became his certainty. His fury turned to anguish in front of us.

'What have I ever done to you? What has Vanessa got to do with this?' he asked Jean-Luc. 'Wasn't it enough for you, knocking up my wife?'

'*No!*' I warned Philippe under my breath. He stared at me, realisation breaking over his face. 'God almighty,' he groaned. 'When did my life turn into such a disaster?'

Jean-Luc had sobered up in an instant, his eyes piercing me. 'You're pregnant? Is it mine?' I didn't have to answer. He knew. We all knew. 'If that's true how can you stand there and let him send me away?'

I didn't know how I could be so heartless when I felt the way I did inside.

'Nothing here is yours,' Philippe said, with scant regard for the facts, giving him another shove. 'And if you don't get out right now I'll call the police myself.'

Jean-Luc stumbled down the half flight of steps and steadied himself against the wall.

'I love you, Alexandra,' he said, looking up at me beseechingly. 'I can't live without you.'

I was embarrassed for him, resorting to the language of cliché and cheesy ballads. Of course I didn't think he meant it, not the second part.

'You're going to have to try,' said Philippe, slamming the door to the apartment. From inside we could hear Jean-Luc ranting all the way out into the street.

'I want to be with you, Alexandra,' he shouted. 'I know you love me.'

I lay my cheek against the cool glass of the bedroom window. Lit by the streetlamp, his expression as his eyes searched for me was as clear as if he'd been lying right beside me. My sadness had always been serene, gentle. Now it flayed me to the core.

61

Philippe found me about twenty minutes later still in darkness, still in that same spot. Even in the dim light from the hallway I could see his face was drained of colour. 'I said terrible things,' Philippe said, his voice cracking.

'We've all said terrible things. He's not just in a bad way over this – there was a diving accident in California. I only found out a couple of days ago. I made him promise to talk to his parents but I don't think they know.'

'Go to him,' Philippe said. I went to protest, but he wouldn't hear it. 'Go on,' he insisted, snatching clothes off the chair and pushing them at me. '*Please*. You have to. He's not going to want to talk to me. I'll go and see Henri first thing in the morning.' I left him sitting on the bed, head in hands.

After the taxi dropped me at the studio I tore up the stairs that always made me so nervous two at a time, never making it to the top floor. As soon as I saw the open door to the unfinished apartment with its exposed rafters, I knew. I took Jean-Luc's weight against one shoulder and with a sharp tug of the electrical cable he went crashing to the floor, almost taking me down with him, still involuntarily committed to breathing, if not to being.

A single minute earlier or later and the outcome would have been different. I couldn't stay away from him in the depths of his despair. Even then he couldn't have what he wanted. I couldn't save him from anything in the end, only cause more suffering. Months of it.

He looked so young when the paramedics arrived that they assumed I was his mother and I didn't correct them, afraid they wouldn't take me if I told the truth. I couldn't bear for him to make that journey alone. As I ran across the courtyard after them, I saw Mokhtar arrive home at the end of his shift. He stood with his mouth open and the moped clattered to the asphalt. It was only then I took the full impact, buckling like cheap metal as one of the men bundled me into the ambulance and we sped away on the siren's first note.

Since I'd fled the hospital after handing the doctors Henri's phone number, he and Geneviève had practically taken up residence in the intensive care unit. Nobody, nothing could help Jean-Luc now, trapped between life and death. I was beside myself to think of what he'd done and to know exactly where he was and not be able to see him. Every day was a battle to stop myself from going there; from turning up to be turned away, even though all that awaited there was another scene of recrimination and impossible desire, like the night he came to our home.

We would never be together again. Sometimes I indulged in vengeful fantasies in which I screamed at

Geneviève for interfering. I railed at humanity in general for having rules about who you can fall in love with and at myself for caring what anyone thought. I reproached Philippe for his callous behaviour that night and for never sharing what he knew about Jean-Luc. Poor Philippe, the secret keeper.

Jean-Luc had told his parents he wasn't going back to California. They worked out for themselves that he'd developed a fear of the sea, but not why. When Henri had the sombre task of contacting the institute, he discovered Jean-Luc had been asked to leave after causing the accident in which he and the marine biologist he'd been diving with had almost drowned. The man had threatened to bring charges unless Jean-Luc left the programme. He later wrote the Malavoines a letter saying he regretted his extreme reaction.

Jean-Luc's problems began when he was fifteen years old. He saw the best doctors but resented their diagnoses, being 'labelled'. He took his medication reluctantly. A charge on his credit card led to a psychiatrist he consulted in Los Angeles after the accident, who'd prescribed a new medication that made the panic symptoms worse. He'd gone back to the original drug before deciding he didn't need it when he met me. Love is its own kind of mania and we'd both been high on it.

But I judged nobody and blamed only myself. As I said at the start, I was the one who should have known better. Jean-Luc was only twenty-three, an occupant of another sort of in-between, the suspended reality between adolescence and full-blown adulthood, where you think you get it precisely because you don't yet know what there is to get. He knew far more than most and, I sometimes think, far more than me.

He was my awakener, the father of a child I never thought I'd have. He was Geneviève's son, her only child, and she lost him. There really are no measures, and there could only ever be one small consolation.

62

'Everyone thinks it would be best for us to leave Paris,' Philippe said with his back to me.

We were at home, where we'd been circling each other for weeks since that terrible night, barely talking, never touching. He made me get out of bed and wash and eat and I followed his orders just because the default position is to stay alive. The only communication of note was when he told me Vanessa hadn't seen Jean-Luc since returning from Nice. Hearing the relief in his voice, I felt it in my chest, a reminder that in the world beyond us, fear and guilt and grief were not all there was.

I had not been to work since it happened; it hadn't even occurred to me, even though my involvement was normally essential in the run-up to sending a new title to print. Maybe the new book had been put on hold. Nobody had questioned my absence, not Alain, not Lisette, and I knew she had a soft spot for me. Suzanne hadn't called.

Bad news travels fastest, as I well knew. Alain had become friends with Geneviève through me and I guessed it was a relief to my colleagues that I stayed away. I wasn't who they thought I was. For a while Emily wasn't just my best friend – she was my only friend. Some may never speak to me again.

It took a moment to sink in, what Philippe had said about us leaving Paris.

'What difference would it make?' I said. 'I can't see...Our life is here, Philippe, our work. I don't want to leave.'

He turned to me with a look of contempt fused with pity. 'It's not about what you want, Alexandra.' He held my gaze for the precise length of time it would have taken to complete the sentence, although of course he didn't have to. *It's about what you've done.*

'Where would we go?' I asked quietly.

He told me Henri wanted him to look into opening a gallery in Nice, said they'd been considering it for a while, which was odd because I would have expected Philippe to mention that. He missed the south.

I wasn't fooled in the slightest. This had to be the last thing on Henri's mind as his son lay comatose in the hospital. The very thought of my presence in the city was more than they could endure; that I understood. Henri simply wanted me gone and could only achieve that by pushing both of us away. He probably felt for his dearest friend, who had done nothing out of the ordinary.

Philippe went out without any effort to persuade me. It was late enough to call my mother in California. I told her what he'd said about Nice. 'It would do you good to be back by the water,' she said, her distant voice somehow underlining our new coexistence in a delicate ecosystem. 'You've always loved the ocean.'

It wasn't true at all but that didn't matter right now; I was touched that she was trying to remind me who I was, or more precisely, who I was before this happened. We had only recently come to an understanding and her wish to align herself with me in any way was something I could scarcely comprehend. 'What's going to happen about the baby?' She could hardly bear to ask. I couldn't answer, but one thing – the *only* thing – I knew was that I could no more still that heartbeat than my own.

When Philippe returned, I couldn't contain it any longer. 'I don't know what you want me to say about Nice. There are other ways I can leave Paris. Don't feel you have to stand by me. Nobody will blame you if you don't. *I* wouldn't blame you.'

He hesitated, and I willed myself to be strong enough to hear it. To bear it.

'I want us to go back to how we were,' he said. 'But that's never going to happen, is it? I have to live with knowing you would have chosen Jean-Luc over me – I've never made you feel the way he did. But you're going to need someone.'

'I'm going to need *you*, Philippe, if you think we still have something. I'll carry on loving you because I never stopped. I would do it even if you gave up on us completely.'

'Never,' he said, with a smile, and for the first time in a long time, our fingers touched. It was the kind of kiss that doesn't stop there. I nodded at the question in his eyes before he reached for a different body to the one he knew, still the same at heart.

63

I saw Jean-Luc one last time.

Philippe was standing at an angle to me when he said it, no preamble, nothing to warn me. 'Henri says you can go to the hospital this afternoon, if you want.'

I thought I must have misheard but Philippe told me Geneviève had a doctor's appointment at four o'clock. I couldn't imagine what it had cost him to ask this extraordinary favour or Henri to grant it without his wife's knowledge. For Philippe's sake, I knew, not for mine. 'I don't have the right.'

Philippe was not about to debate that point with me. 'It may be the only opportunity you get,' he said. 'But if you do go you'll need to be prepared.' His jaw flinched and I knew without doubt that he had been there, perhaps often. Them, us, four people milling around in different districts of hell. Philippe knew there was no reply to wait for. 'I'll go with you. You won't have very long.'

The staff recognised him and took no notice of me, a nurse leaving the private room as we entered. 'The doctors' rounds are at five,' Philippe said. 'I'll be back to fetch you in twenty minutes.'

The first glimpse of Jean-Luc had me seizing Philippe's hand, begging him not to leave. 'It's still him,' he said, breaking up. 'Talk to him. Tell him how you feel.'

I sat down by the bed. 'Jean-Luc, it's me, Alexandra,' I said. 'There's so much I wish you'd told me, things I would have asked if I wasn't so scared of talking. But I'm going to try and hold onto the good times and how happy we made each other. Every time I look at the ocean I will think of you. Somehow we always found our way back to the sea, though I never once saw you there. But I always loved the way you talked about it – it sounded like poetry, but I couldn't say so in case you clammed up.

'One time you explained the zones of the ocean to me. The one I remember is the abyssal zone, *bottomless*, which accounts for three-quarters of the ocean floor and where there is perpetual darkness, no light at all. And that's how it feels to be without you.'

I had to stop. Without the smile and laugh and the spark in his eyes – or even the shadow – this wasn't Jean-Luc. It was shocking to see his hair growing back and a day's stubble on his face. This body that was once so full of life, that had loved me with no limits, didn't know that he was gone. But I knew he was never coming back.

His skin was bluish, his forehead clammy when I bent to kiss him. But his hand was warmer than I expected. Underneath the gown I could see his muscles were already wasting away. And then I remembered who had made my presence in this room possible, and that time was running out. I told Jean-Luc that Philippe forgave us. He hadn't told me so, but I don't see how else he could have found it in himself. Sometimes I feel I didn't know him at all before last summer.

I told Jean-Luc the baby was doing fine and that we were going to be okay. I said what I should have had the courage to say the night he came to the apartment. I'd never actually told him, but he knew. He'd said so.

And then I said goodbye.

After and Before

The rest you know. We moved to Nice, just as everyone thought best, and for a while I couldn't even see the point of blue sky. Jean-Luc once told me he couldn't imagine the rest of his life before he and I met. And I couldn't imagine mine afterward, not until I found you and began to make my way back from the depths. When I started to take walks by the sea, strangers would smile at me, the woman with the ballooning silhouette that spoke of the future, not the past.

Four months later in Paris, Philippe attended the funeral of Jean-Luc Malavoine, twenty-four years old: son of his dearest friend, my lover, father of a child my husband would raise as his own. That day I watched the gulls swoop across the sky to the lilac mountains on the far side of the bay, mesmerised by the light on the waves like scattered chunks of glass. In the midst of such immense sorrow, there could still be beauty.

My mom and Emily were with me when Léa was born soon after, tearing at my body, reluctant to leave me. When the Malavoines arrived, their granddaughter was the only one not crying. Jean-Luc was right about Henri and Philippe. The torn threads that once bound us all would gradually darn together in the colours of a new life and another we would always remember: viridian with bronze filaments, often known as teal.

My mom has done much to console Geneviève where I can do so little. She refused to let the door slam shut when we couldn't talk. There were always others around when Geneviève came: Henri, Philippe, Vanessa, who dotes on her 'sister' and plans to move here next year. The first time Geneviève and I found ourselves alone we went for a walk along the *Promenade*. 'I see both of you in her,' she said, as we watched Léa shaking a toy, laughing. 'And then he doesn't seem so far away.'

On my way home from our session last time, an old lady had a fall on the bus, close to me. We got off at the same stop and I walked her safely back to her apartment, hardly going out of my way. She was dressed in widow's black and I wanted so badly to ask how many years she had mourned him, if there was ever an end to it. I didn't, because there isn't, and I know that now. As I went to leave, she said something I'll never forget, something for which I have never been more grateful. 'You are a good person.'

If she knew me she may not have said it. But I'm better than I was. I think we all are.

We'll live.

Author's note

Readers who know Paris may notice that I have taken the occasional liberty for the sake of the story. The bell-ringing schedule at Saint-Sulpice in summer 2014 is one example.

Acknowledgements

I am grateful to so many people for their support on my well-documented road to publication that this is quite a challenge. However, it's not difficult to know who to thank first. My husband JC has supported me in every possible way, taught me a great deal about perseverance and never doubted I would get there. Our sons Rowan and Stefan made me laugh every day and kept me in touch with the real world, albeit one where school letters often went unread and dinner was rarely served at a reasonable hour.

By sharing her love of books, languages and France with me when I was growing up, my mum Mary influenced and enriched my life beyond measure. My dad Bob, long gone and much missed, gave me unconditional love and was the first good man I knew.

My brilliant and lovely agent Diana Beaumont has shown unwavering loyalty and belief in me and my writing, forever raising the bar, and I am grateful.

From far away in Minnesota, wonderful friend and critique partner Kristin Celms has been a constant source of wisdom and guardian of sanity.

Seven years ago my book group friends Delyth, Joanna, Ellika, Judith, Claire and Janet encouraged me to stop talking about writing and do it and have been with me every step of the way. Thanks to Christina Dunhill and writer friends from City Lit – Clare Brailsford, Vijayadipa, Lindsay Gould, Chloe Cookson – I enjoyed it from Day One.

Merci mille fois to a French team which includes some of my oldest and closest friends: Armelle and Sébastien Haëntjens, Niels Haëntjens, Gaëlle de Quelen, Wallis and Lisa Sauvée, Nadine Chadier, Roselyne and Jean-Marie Morello. A special mention to Jean Guellec for his hospitality, Paris expertise and some of the best nights out and worst mornings-after ever!

A brief but unforgettable stay with Linda LaMarr and Bill Guevarra in Crescent City, California, inspired Alexandra's west coast origins. There's nothing like toasting marshmallows over a fire-pit to the sound of the Pacific Ocean.

I could not have reached this point without the supremely generous friends I made on a writing-related trip to Brooklyn in 2011, who along with everything else have given me the perfect excuse to keep going back: Donna Zaengle, Clyde and Irene Turner, Nancy Rosenthal.

Thanks to poet Isabel Rogers and psychologist Voula Grand for specialist input on the first draft, Van Demal for proof-reading the submission draft and Heulwen Reading for expert medical advice. Over the past few years editors

Debi Alper and Gillian Stern have provided invaluable guidance on and off the page.

This novel seems to make people – even British people – want to discuss the kind of things we don't often talk about. I am thankful to those who, without being asked, confided deeply private experiences which indirectly added to the story in many ways.

There are countless individuals I would have liked to mention by name; friends from every stage of my life, from childhood to the many writers and book people I have met in recent years, those who read and support the Literary Sofa blog, my Twitter followers and everyone who greeted *Paris Mon Amour* with such enthusiasm on its first release in digital and audio. I hope you will take this as a personal thank you.

Thank you to Henna Silvennoinen at Audible for enabling Alexandra's voice to be heard.

Heartfelt thanks to Iain Millar and everyone at Canelo for your passionate belief in *Paris Mon Amour* and insightful finessing of the manuscript. Your ongoing support is of the 'above and beyond' variety and it's a great pleasure to work with you.

The paperback edition brings yet more wonderful people to thank: the readers who asked (and kept on asking!) for it; Simon Collinson and Rebecca Souster for their technical expertise and unfailing helpfulness; Dan Mogford for the stunning cover design and Matt Bates, for more than I can say.